RESIST

M. VAN

42Links
Publishing

Cover design by
Jolua Specialized Design & Graphics Studio

Edited by
Book Helpline

ISBN: 978-90-827447-2-9

ONE
MAECE

THICK BLACK CLOUDS of smoke billowed up until they clashed with the ceiling overhead. The ventilators used to recycle the air couldn't keep up as the fire spread throughout the power plant. The place didn't even have a proper name, just a designation—Two.

The underground facility was the size of a small city, although this place could be called anything but a city. The designers of the plant hadn't had any interest in the people who had to live there. Every structure or piece of machinery had only one purpose, and that was to provide power for the shields protecting the few remaining cities above ground.

Thousands of people had to survive under the harshest conditions, and they worked hard to provide for strangers, but all of that was about to change.

A loud explosion made me flinch. Without ear protection, the noise echoing down from the dome-shaped rock ceiling above my head would have been enough to have my ears ringing for a week, but fortunately, the heads-up display strapped to my head, one of the few remnants of my enforcer days, protected me from the sound invasion.

Moments after the impact, the blasts of magnetic weapon fire took over again as smoke rose from one of the structures up ahead. I couldn't tell which of the buildings had been struck because of the throng of panicked people running around and the heavy machinery blocking the road.

Green letters scrolled across the lenses of my heads-up display as I scanned the area. The device provided me with all the communication feeds essential to this operation, but I tended to ignore most and focused on the ones I knew to be of consequence to me. One of the things that I had picked up from the chatter in my ear was that all of this was taking too long. Somehow our lines weren't advancing fast enough, and the delay cost lives.

I pushed through the crowd and made my way to a metal structure used as a crane. The machine towered over the area, and with the help of the support beams, I climbed up to see if I could get a better grasp of the situation.

From thirty feet off the ground, I had a better overview of the plant. This place didn't have anything like the multilayered structures that we used for housing back in Subterra nor the high-rise buildings blocking the skyline like I had seen in the City of Umbras.

All I could see were the machines that generated

power. Metal constructions no higher than single-story buildings stretched out over the ground. Pipes and wires led in and out of different sorts of devices, and lights blinked on and off all over the place. Only weapons fire from the battle raging around me and the occasional explosion drowned out the constant roar of the engines and machinery.

The people living here had—and it seemed prudent to use the term *living* loosely—taken up residence deep underground. But even at the lowest sublevel, one couldn't escape the everlasting hum of machines and the tremors they created as they reverberated through the ground.

In the middle of all these structures stood the distribution hub. The sight reminded me of the platform inside the rebel base hidden underneath the City of Umbras, although this platform was a lot bigger. Four-feet-wide conduits that jutted out from several places in the walls and ceiling all converged upon this one piece of machinery that towered over the rest. Scaffolds used for maintenance surrounded the device, but no plant workers would be working there anytime soon. I just hoped no one would be foolish enough to take a shot at that thing. The chain reaction from a direct hit could cause this entire plant to blow up.

"Maece!" a voice called up. "Are you trying to get yourself killed?" I glanced down and saw Saera staring up at me. Saera Lux, my best friend and sister by choice, looked fierce in the Subterran version of an exoskeleton suit, and seeing her staring up at me threw me off.

It wasn't the suit or the array of weapons that came with the intimidating-looking armor that had me waver. The stone-cold glare Saera shot me with those blue eyes of hers and the way her sharp jawline flexed in annoyance made me feel like a kid again. Saera was a few years older than me, and after our parents had died, she had taken on a role that surpassed a big sister's. She'd always taken care of me, and that fact made me wish I could step back in time and undo some of the things that had happened. Unfortunately, the battle raging around us didn't make this the right time to address personal issues.

We all wore the body-fitting suit made of armor reduced to an atomic-scale honeycomb lattice that would protect us from a lot of the assault weapons available these days and the built-in exoskeleton could absorb most forces exposed to our limbs. Well, at least the suit would protect me from most of those things. My armor was different and had been developed by the ArtRep corporation. The suit I wore was more advanced than the Subterran version. My suit was another reminder that I had once served the Combined Districts of Tenebrae as an enforcer. Both types of suit did a hell of a job of protecting our people, and even though rebel engineers had been able to reverse engineer my protective armor to enhance the Subterran version, the latter failed to maintain its integrity after an excessive assault.

Ignoring the icy glare Saera shot me, I pointed

down the road past the machines blocking it and the distribution hub that lay beyond.

"We have to advance on the perimeter," I called down. "There are still too many workers in the line of fire."

Up until then the attempt to retake Power Plant Two had gone pretty much as expected. As anticipated, workers had joined the fight and were helping us to overthrow the Tenebrae presence that had ruled these power plants for five decades.

We would probably never have risked another war fifty years after the first one. Not over some power plants that our government had willingly relinquished during the peace negotiations with the Combined Districts of Tenebrae. The information we had stolen from the ArtRep computers—one of Tenebrae's most influential corporations—had changed all that. We still wouldn't have taken the risk if it had been up to the Subterran government, but we weren't part of that government—well, at least not officially. We were rebels, and with the help of the Power Plant Resistance, we were keen to change the fate of many.

Saera nodded and raked a hand through her messy blond hair. Unfortunately, our scientist hadn't been able to reverse engineer my heads-up yet, and at the moment the device was the only one at our disposal. That's why Saera had to rely on basic communications technology that fed directly into her ear. Like most rebels, she opted not to wear a helmet, which was plain stupid but something I remembered doing myself. There was something to be said for not having your head stuck in a metal bucket.

She shouted something to a rebel soldier standing close by. I didn't need to know what she said as she pointed down the road and redirected my order. Unfortunately, we only had a handful of rebels at our disposal and had to rely on the inexperienced and untrained workers who had joined the resistance for most of the fighting.

Another loud explosion and something that sounded like a landslide drew my attention. Craning my neck, I noticed that one of the Hymag tunnels we had barricaded to stop enemy troops from using it to sneak up on us from behind had disappeared in a cloud of dust.

"What was that?" Saera shouted. I shifted my footing and leaned back to get a better look and gasped.

"Harp," I said over the communication device embedded in my heads-up. "Are you seeing this?"

Colrin Harp, the leader of our small rebel group, didn't take long to answer. Sitting in one of the Hymags we had used to get here, he monitored our progress. Knowing Harp, he would have preferred to have been in the middle of this fight, but as it was, we needed him to maintain an overview and to direct our efforts.

"Are those what I think they are?" Harp said. Because my heads-up fed directly into our monitoring systems, Harp was able to see and hear everything I could, through the device. Except that, instead of through a visor, he watched the scene unfold on a monitor.

"Maecy!" Saera shouted, and this time, along with the nickname she often used to annoy me, I could hear the anger in her voice. She'd been able to listen in on my exchange with Harp, but she hadn't seen what we had. I looked down, and perhaps it was a good thing that, because of the heads-up, she wouldn't recognize the grim expression on my face. She crossed her arms over her chest and waited for me to speak. Instead, I jumped down from the rig. The hydraulics of my suit's built-in exoskeleton easily absorbed the force of my landing, and I stood to face Saera.

"They're freaks," I said. "There are a lot of them." Saera's eyes widened as I referred to the creatures for which I didn't have a proper name.

"Like that one we met at ArtRep?" she replied. In the corner of my visor, a few images of a previous recording of our break-in of Harand Sulos's office flashed across my screen. Sulos was the owner of the ArtRep corporation and had a hand in everything evil they'd ever done and were still doing. We'd run into one of his freaks as we'd fled the building, and it had been a memorable experience. A shiver ran down my spine as I briefly reviewed the footage and remembered how only one of those things nearly had me killed.

"I wouldn't say exactly like that one," I said with a shrug, "but sort of, I guess." Freaks weren't things or monsters per se. They once had been human beings, ordinary men and women with hopes and dreams, but

ArtRep had taken that from them. The company had manipulated their bodies and rendered their minds useless by shoving them into bioprinters and turning them into fighting machines.

Looking around, I noticed the workers maneuvering vehicles and heavy machinery forward to advance on our perimeter. If it hadn't been for the breach behind us, I would have predicted a relatively smooth victory, but now I had a sinking feeling that our odds had changed.

"Harp," I asked over the coms, "have you figured it out already?" If we wanted to keep the upper hand, we'd need a strategy change, and there was no one better for that job than Harp.

"Getting final status updates," he said in his low gruff voice. "Hang on." I heard the tapping of fingers on a virtual keyboard in the background and knew Kyran, our tech guy, was doing his utmost to keep up with Harp's commands. Static assaulted my eardrums for a second, and then a different voice came on the line.

"Another sunny day down below," Reece said cheerfully, but it wasn't hard to hear the underlining tension. Still, my heart warmed at the sound of his voice; it always held a sense of mischief. I tried to suppress the smile that the thought of his blue eyes, rugged-looking face, and cheeky grin tended to draw out. Saera must have noticed because she rolled her eyes at me.

"Update," Harp said, his tone sharp. Never deterred by Harp's lack of humor, Reece must have sensed something was up because he came straight to the point.

"Sublevel two is cleared, and we've just started on sublevel one, but there are so many of them, and most of the workers have joined the fight upstairs before we could zap them," he said, now serious. "Whose stupid idea was it anyway to engage the plant without clearing all the neuro-regulators beforehand?"

By decree from ArtRep, overseers who managed the plant had inserted the workers with these neuro-regulators as a way to control them. If we wanted to successfully overtake this plant, we needed to render these devices embedded inside the workers' heads useless.

"How long?" Harp asked.

"Too long," Reece replied. "Don't forget everyone we zap is out for at least fifteen minutes, and Kelle and Riffy are doing their best to redirect everyone to a somewhat safe location to adjust to the change, but like I said, there are too many of them."

"Stop thinking about their whereabouts and move through them faster. Those workers have a better chance at survival without the regulators," Harp said. "Just zap them and render those devices useless where they stand."

The way he said it, Harp sounded heartless, but we all knew he was right. Neuro-regulators had the potential to kill a person if they had one of those things stuck in their head.

Fortunately, we'd been able to take over the plant's systems, and by destroying all of the signal boosters that connected this plant to the Feed, it would be hard for anyone to activate the neuro-regulators.

Any communication with life beyond these plant walls needed signal enhancement. The rock and the metals embedded within the ground were just too dense for any signal to penetrate. By destroying the signal boosters, we had prevented outside intervention within the plant's systems. At this point, we controlled these systems, but that could change at any time, and Harp knew it.

"Do you have any idea of what it is like down here?" Reece said. His voice, edged with anger, rose, which was unlike him. The situation on the sublevels must have been bad or else Reece would never have reacted like this. "These people are afraid." I had a sense that Reece wanted to say more, but Harp cut in.

"Keep at it and send me three people you can spare with those brain-zapper things."

"Haven't you been listening?" Reece said. "And I'm sure as hell not going to send you Kelle or Riffy."

It was hard for me to hear the anguish in Reece's voice. Usually, he clung to a note of humor as a way of self-preservation during tense situations, but I couldn't detect any of that. This could only mean things must have been terrible down there.

"Do not make me repeat myself," Harp said. Because I had an idea of what Harp had planned and sensed where this conversation was heading, I cut in.

"Reece," I said, "we've got freaks coming in." The line fell silent for a beat. Reece had been there the last time we had encountered one of those things. I had barely survived the attack, and that had been just one of them.

"All right," he finally said. "What else?"

"Keep neutralizing those neuro devices," Harp said. "We widened our sector and have more people coming your way."

"Got it," Reece replied and signed off.

"Maece, Saera," Harp started.

"Yeah," we both replied at the same time. I glanced at Saera, who had been uncharacteristically quiet. She didn't even look at me as Harp continued.

"I've already sent in another team. I need you two to help them stop those freaks from getting a foothold," he said. "See if you can use those brain-zapping things or whatever they're called to put them out of their misery." I shook my head at Harp's reference to the device designed to disrupt the neuro-regulators implanted in people's heads. He was never that into technical stuff.

"Got it," we again both said at the same time. Saera turned to me and nodded in the direction we needed to go.

"Lead the way," she said.

With an easiness that came from growing up together, and having each other's backs since we were kids, we fell into step. Weapons drawn, we zigzagged through the crowd of people who were trying to get away from the frontline. Anticipating Saera's every move and her doing the same with me, we acted as one. That familiarity intensified as a stray enforcer, who had somehow made it past the line, stepped into my path.

Although the memories of being an enforcer once myself had been erased from my mind, the instincts I'd gained seemed engrained in my soul. Within a hundredth of a second, my heads-up scanned the area. Metal structures that were part of the inner workings of this plant enclosed the narrow alley as we ran. The increased chance of weapons fire bouncing off the conductive material and striking one of the plant's citizens limited my assault options.

Numbers scrolled across my screen as I aimed my weapon. The enforcer had no intention of sparing any of the people fleeing the crossfire. The moment he had detected our approach, his weapon pointed in our direction. He fired several times, and a woman who was unable to escape his line of fire screamed before she crumpled to the ground.

Unable to help her, I jumped over her unmoving body and headed straight for the enforcers. He fired again, but my heads-up had already anticipated his intent, and I dodged the magnetic blast. A direct hit would instantly kill someone without the protection of an exoskeleton suit. Still, even while wearing a suit, the blast could cause severe pain and would surely give the enforcer the upper hand. I couldn't tell what was happening behind me, but my heads-up registered Saera's footsteps and her heavy breathing, meaning she hadn't been hit, which was enough for me.

Up close, I noticed a slight hesitation in the

enforcer's reaction and used it to knock the weapon from his hand. He struck out with the other, but I managed to deflect his blow. In one swift move, I grabbed his heads-up and yanked it from his head. I didn't recognize the person behind the mask, but I knew I couldn't hurt him—not much anyway. Similar to the freaks, enforcers were just as much victims as the men, women, and children living within these plants.

Eyes that held a strange glow looked at me seemingly confused. Enforcers depended on the information fed to them by their heads-up, and without it, they had trouble functioning. It wasn't that they couldn't perform; it just wasn't in their natures anymore.

The ArtRep corporation was located in Umbras, one of the cities that belonged to the Combined Districts of Tenebrae, and it had created these mindless soldiers. The rest of the world thought of enforcers as being artificial representations or ARs that were built to serve and maintain order.

Little did the citizens of Tenebrae know that ArtRep kidnapped people and then had their brains and physical bodies altered inside a bioprinter. After the procedure, which left them with neuro-regulators inside their heads, these enforcers had no idea of who they once had been. They lived and breathed what ArtRep told them to be. The thought nearly made my stomach roll, knowing that at one time I had been one of them.

Using the opportunity his lack of reaction gave

me, I hit him on the head with the weapon I was holding. Apparently, I hadn't struck him hard enough because he tried to grab me, but before he could get a firm hold, I hit him again. Shifting my body, I caught his arm and threw him over my shoulder.

He landed with a thud, and within seconds, Saera knelt beside him. She pressed an orange device to the back of his neck, and as she flipped the switch, the man's body began to convulse as if he were being electrocuted. In a sense, he was. The device Saera held to the man's neck sent a strong magnetic pulse, not unlike the power emitted by a Hymag line at the exact moment the high-speed transport would pass. The neuro-regulator disrupter was the device that Harp had called a brain zapper ever since he'd introduced it to us.

With the help of what I had experienced, Spiro, our resident genius, had designed the device explicitly to render the neuro-regulators that sat lodged in the back of an enforcer's head useless. It also knocked them unconscious, which gave us one less enforcer to worry about.

The device beeped, and Saera withdrew it from the man's neck before she stood and holstered the orange device. She looked at the guy for a moment longer and then knelt again to retrieve his weapon. The weapon was identical to mine and could fire more powerful rounds than our Subterran versions of a magnetic blaster. She appraised the weapon with an almost evil-looking grin before turning to me.

Her demeanor instantly changed, and I noticed a

combination of curiosity and amazement in her expression as she shook her head.

"What?" I asked, and my curiosity piqued. Her reaction also sparked a shimmer of hope. We hadn't talked, at least not really. Ever since I'd told her about the real reason behind my enforcer adventure, it had felt as if she was stonewalling me. I'd never seen her so angry, and it was going to take time for her to put it aside. We had been down these roads before, but I knew I had taken it too far this time. I hoped that sooner rather than later we could act like sisters again and not talk in the civil but cold way we'd been communicating these past few weeks, but it would have to be enough for now.

Looking surprised, she raised an eyebrow and opened her mouth as if to say something. My heads-up detected her elevated heart rate, but that could have been from the excitement a moment ago. Her pupils had fully dilated as if she had just witnessed something incredible, although I did read some concern in her eyes as she bit her lower lip. Before I could fully analyze her initial reaction, it shifted as fast as it had occurred. As if something had spooked her, she donned a mask, and her eyes grew cold as she shrugged it off.

"Nothing," she said. "Let's keep going."

Sidestepping the enforcer's unmoving form, she bumped my shoulder harder than necessary and took up a firm stride in the direction of the barricades. Unsure of what had triggered her latest reaction, I hurried after her. For the past few weeks, it seemed

Saera had needed her distance, and I had honored that by letting her be. This time, though, I couldn't help myself as I asked, "But there is something."

She ignored me and kept looking in the direction in which we were going. "Saera, please—" I started to say, but the hard look she gave me made me swallow the rest.

"Not now," she said in a firm voice, "and stop scanning me."

My step faltered as she continued and walked up to one of the workers. Shit! She must have noticed the little green light on my heads-up that indicated a scan was in progress. I hadn't even meant to scan her— well, not consciously anyway.

It seemed that these days our only way to communicate was either through hard glares or by avoiding each other. *How else was I supposed to figure out what was going on with her when she refused to talk to me?*

Exhaling slowly, I pushed the thought aside; this wasn't the time or place to fix our problems, and I needed to focus on the battle. Moving in behind Saera, I caught the tail end of her introduction as she said my name and pointed with her thumb over her shoulder.

I stared up at the worker towering over us. It wasn't as if the man was that much taller than us. It had more to do with the metal contraption he sat in. The piece of machinery looked like an extension of his body, holding him tightly secure within his seat. The technology used was similar to our exoskeleton suits except for being a lot bigger. This suit made the worker at least ten feet tall, and instead of hands, it had these large clamps for hauling around crates and other stuff.

"The name's Clyde," he said in what almost sounded like a growl. His face sat covered in streaks of grime, and dirt and a thick beard hid most of his features. What stood out were his gleaming gray eyes that shone like tiny beacons in the smoke-filled surroundings. As with the enforcer I had struck down, those eyes were a sure betrayal that Clyde still had his neuro-regulator inserted in the back of his head.

Not as invasive as the enforcer version of the device, these neuro-regulators were used to maintain order within the power plants. Even though the occupants of these plants were allowed to move freely, the devices gave overseers employed by the districts information of the workers' whereabouts and their work ethics.

Similar to the enforcer devices, though, the neuro-regulators embedded within the workers' heads could also be used to administer a high-voltage shock directly into their brains. This would effectively kill a person, and it provided the overseers with another measure of control.

Because of this kill switch, we had taken our time infiltrating Power Plant One. Disrupting the regulators inside the workers' heads had been our primary objective before we'd even initiated a full-blown attack. The same tactics should've been applied to this plant, but someone had decided on a different course.

I just hoped that wouldn't become a problem for Clyde later on.

Hinges creaked, and hydraulics hissed as Clyde raised an arm and pointed beyond the barricade. "I'm not sure what those things are that just broke through, but they seem to be in a holding pattern."

"They're ArtRep's new pets," Saera said as she started to walk toward the barricade. I followed as she climbed the struts that led to the top of a vehicle blocking the road. The machine used for garbage disposal stood on wheels as tall as me and should give us a good view of the situation.

I joined Saera on the vehicle's roof and saw Clyde's assessment of the freaks still applied. Five of them stood in a line as dust and smoke swirled around them. They held still like a bunch of drones waiting for someone to command them what to do. One of them looked female, due to certain exposed parts, but otherwise, I couldn't tell anything about who they used to be. Their faces looked ashen, and their skin bulged unnaturally with mechanical components occupying their bodies. With two of them, oversized hydraulic limbs replaced their legs to make them stand taller than the others. All of them had either one or both arms replaced. They looked ominous standing there in the gloom, surrounded by a cloud of dust and smoke with only the occasional glint bouncing off their metal constructs.

From the corner of my eye, I noticed three bodies in Subterran armor maneuvering across a scaffold as they made their way to us. They had to be the men

Harp had requested from Reece. I hadn't noticed any of the other rebels Harp had assigned, but I knew for sure we were going to need them with these five.

"Odd," Saera said, and I had a feeling that she was talking more to herself than to me. "They're not even doing anything."

Saera shifted her newly found enforcer weapon from one hand to the other. The piece was heavier than her regular gun, but I knew she'd be able to handle it. I just wondered how effective it would be on these freaks.

The ArtRep corporation built those weapons— including the enforcer armor—and these freaks. *Wouldn't they design those freaks to withstand those weapons?* My enforcer suit could take several hits before its integrity started to waver.

"Let's see if we can take advantage of that," I said, referring to the fact that the freaks still hadn't moved. I looked down at Clyde and called out to him. "Got any more of those?" I gestured to his cargo-carrier suit. He nodded, and a couple of hinges squeaked.

"Sure," he said. "I'll round up some of the workers."

"See if you can circle that way and start work on building up that barrier again. I don't want any more enemy troops using that Hymag line to get to us," I said and pointed in the direction where the explosion had occurred.

Until now we had managed to keep this area isolated and only had to deal with the enforcers and overseers stationed here. Considering the underground nature of this base, that hadn't been so hard. All the connecting Hymag lines had been blocked, which should have given us enough time to take over this plant, but we hadn't anticipated that we'd be busy removing neuro-regulators during the assault. I didn't understand why Harp had allowed this to happen.

"Will do," he answered gruffly.

"Oh, and Clyde," I added. Hinges shifted as he looked up at me. "Be careful; these things are bad news."

Without a reply, he lifted his arm. Hydraulics hissed, and metal parts ground as Clyde pointedly displayed the massive clamp before snapping it shut. I flinched at the loud clank of metal. It wasn't hard to imagine what those clamps could do to a person if caught in there. The suit would surely give him an advantage in fighting the freaks, but I feared it wouldn't be enough. Still, it was better than nothing. With a wicked grin on his face, Clyde nodded and set his cargo carrier in motion.

Saera was chewing her lower lip again. She looked anxious, and I couldn't blame her. I had a clear memory of what those things were capable of, and so had she.

"This ought to be fun," she said under her breath. I gave her a sideways glance, unsure if I should even reply. Before, we would never have stepped into a situation like this without some form of reassurance that we had each other's back or telling the other one to be careful. Although Saera's steely gaze gave me the answer, I could have done without, and I took a step forward.

A hand on my upper arm stopped me from jumping to the next vehicle to get to the other side of the barricade.

"Hey," Saera said in a timid voice. I turned to face her, feeling a bit shocked at the sound of that single word, and I wasn't even sure why. "Be safe." I suddenly had the urge to scan her again. It felt as if I was getting conflicting orders that didn't make sense.

"I, uh…," I said, feeling confused and sounding like a babbling idiot. Maybe being an enforcer had rubbed off on me, although I couldn't remember much about it.

Saera shook her head in disbelief as if something was wrong with me. She grabbed me in a hug as she repeated, "Just be safe."

"Be safe," I echoed.

TWO
SAERA

My fists clenched as I watched Maece jump to the next vehicle and then the next until she reached the front of the barricade. She crouched to peer over the edge of the transport as magnetic blasts whizzed over her head. There was no need to form a plan of attack because there was only one option, and that was to confront these freaks—preferably outside the perimeter to avoid civilian casualties as much as possible. Besides, there was only one person for the job, and that was Maece—she was the only one who had ever faced one of these things.

The concern I felt for her started to get in the way of me being mad at her, and it frustrated the hell out of me. She raised her weapon and fired at what must have been an enforcer before she jumped from the makeshift barricade.

Maece had always been more adept in these kinds of situations. She was stronger, could run faster, and almost seemed to have a sixth sense for assessing a situation. I, on the other hand, wasn't much of a soldier.

Groaning, I took an unsteady leap to the next vehicle in an attempt to keep up. I stumbled and clumsily fell to my stomach. Only then I noticed the magnetic blast that had been coming straight at me. With a curse word or two stuck in my throat, I crawled to the edge of the vehicle and peeked over the side. Maece had engaged two enforcers. From within the perimeter, it had seemed as if the number of enforcers had dwindled, but there were plenty still out there.

I internally cursed Maece for not having waited for me as I swung my legs over the edge, dropped to the ground, and landed in a crouch. As I checked my surroundings, I spotted Maece again and stopped to blink. The two enforcers were down, and she had engaged a third. Her arms reacted in a blur of motions, blocking every punch the enforcer threw at her. It was a crazy thing to watch her move that fast. She whirled around placing a backspin kick to the enforcer's head, dislodging his heads-up device and sending it flying.

I had seen Maece fight before, and she'd always been good, especially with all the enforcer techniques ingrained in her brain. But ever since the doctors had removed that neuro-regulator from her head, it seemed as if she was progressively getting better. As if every fight that she engaged in left her with some new move. Amazed, I had to force myself to snap out of it as I spotted the next man in an exoskeleton suit.

As if he had all the time in the world, the enforcer fiddled with his weapon, and I instantly knew what he was doing. He was changing ammunition, and he was planning to shoot Maece with a special round. An enforcer suit could withstand most weapons fire, to a degree, but the suit didn't stand a chance against the special explosive rounds only enforcers carried. I was shouting for Maece as the enforcer raised his weapon, and I raised the weapon I had stolen earlier. Before I could even pull the trigger, Maece had turned and fired several times. The enforcer hadn't even had the time to twitch a muscle as she rushed toward him and knocked him out cold.

I exhaled in relief and got to my feet. As I ran to the unconscious form, I secured my new weapon and retrieved the neuro-disruptor. Because of the heads-up, I could only see the lower half of Maece's face where perspiration coated her dark skin and her short, black hair poking out as she gave me a brief nod. Before I could drop to my knees at the enforcer's side, she was already on the move again. I pressed the disruptor to the back of the man's neck and zapped him. As I watched the man convulse, it seemed Harp's description of the device wasn't as inappropriate as I had first thought.

Looking up, I saw Maece talking to one of three men who belonged to our group. The other two each hovered over an enforcer and pressed orange-colored devices of their own to the necks of the men laying in front of them.

I quickly turned my head to the right as I heard

shouts coming from that direction but breathed more easily again when I recognized their Subterran-made suits. Six of them ran straight past me to join Maece and the others.

I stood and left the enforcer to fend for himself. He'd have to get around on his own after he woke up. With a little luck, one of the workers would bring him in without killing him. After a zap to the brain, most subjects tended to be a bit confused—especially if they had most of their lives erased. Blocking people's memories made it easier for ArtRep to control them, but the mind was a tricky thing. If these enforcers were lucky, then their memories might find their way back to them, but there was always a risk of losing them altogether. I couldn't imagine what that would do to a person, to have everything you were and once knew wiped from your mind, but at least they would no longer be susceptible to ArtRep's control.

A shiver ran down my spine as I watched Maece issuing commands to the newly arrived troops. Maece had to endure all of that. Not just the physical torture of having your body altered in a bioprinter, but also the emotional despair of not knowing who or what you are—and she had done it willingly.

The thought still angered me. Maece had abandoned all of us. She had left me believing she'd died. My stomach churned, and I knew I had to stop thinking like that. If Maece hadn't done what she did, we would never have found out about Sulos's plan. These people working here at the plant would never have had a chance at a normal life, and it would have just been a matter of time until Sulos had enough of this planet and flipped the switch that would have killed us all.

He was the reason for all of this. He and the company that he had built. ArtRep was the old man's brainchild, and with it, he wanted to create a world that fitted his image. He had built an enforcer army, and even though the districts might think that these enhanced soldiers produced by a bioprinter served the people, they only served one man, and that was Harand Sulos. In fairness, Sulos was still in a position to kill us all, but at least we were trying to do something about it.

I walked over to the others and noticed Maece staring off into space. As I had done so often these past few weeks, I wondered what was going on in that head of hers. Even though she had returned—and I couldn't have been happier about that—it felt as if we had lost something in the almost two years that she had been away.

Sure, I was still mad about what she'd done, but I've been mad at her before, and it usually didn't take me that long to get over things. I probably had gotten over it, but for some reason, it seemed harder to get that across. I only needed to look at her, and I could feel the tension rise between us. Her defenses would go up, and I felt a need to respond in a similar manner.

Maece stepped forward and signaled with a hand for the others to stay. I followed her gaze and spotted the five freaks standing there like a bunch of statues.

Maybe this wasn't going to be as bad as we thought after all—except the freaks were staring at Maece.

Ignoring her signal to stay put, I followed and stopped at her side. The freaks were still standing at some distance, and if we'd had weapons capable of destroying them, we might have used them as target practice. As it was, I doubted that even the special rounds that enforcers carried would make a dent in their armor-plated and structurally enhanced bodies.

"I hear you," she said. I frowned and stared at her. *I hadn't said anything, had I?* I couldn't see her eyes because of the heads-up device strapped to her head, but her body radiated tension, and I figured she was listening to someone talking over the coms, but I wasn't getting any interesting chatter myself. Taking a few steps back, I opened my own communications channel.

"Harp," I said. For some reason, I whispered, although I didn't know why; it seemed appropriate. "You there."

"Why haven't you engaged the freaks?" he asked. His straight to business attitude always managed to calm my nerves, although he had a way of triggering my outrage at the same time.

"Maece has an incoming transmission," I replied. He didn't ask for further explanation, and I could hear his muffled voice converse with someone.

"Found it," I heard a different disembodied voice say over the coms, and I recognized Kyran. I could already picture him with his messy hair, sitting all wide-eyed behind his monitor as his fingers danced on a virtual keypad. A moment later, I heard static followed by a voice that sent a chill down my spine.

"Your council had assured me of their cooperation," Sulos said in a calm, almost soothing, tone. His voice sounded far away and born out of static. I took in the five mutilated statues staring in our direction and figured Sulos must use them as a relay and Maece's heads-up had picked up the signal.

ArtRep, the company that belonged to Sulos and that had once taken Maece, also produced the device strapped to her head. It would have been easy for them to send out a signal that Maece would be able to pick up. *But how were these freaks getting a signal?*

Contact with underground facilities was difficult. Similar to Subterra or any other location underground, any communication with life beyond the surrounding walls needed signal enhancement. Communication wasn't impossible, though. We had old-fashioned signal boosters that used cables to send any signal to a relay station, and from there we could get access to the Feed. Except we had destroyed every signal booster and relay station in the vicinity before we even joined this campaign. Kyran would probably know by now, but I didn't dare to ask, and I held my breath as I listened to the man who didn't care whether he needed to destroy an entire planet if it meant saving his ass.

"They had promised me to do nothing and withhold the information of my New World," he said and sounded genuinely disappointed. "But now you and your little band of rebels have already disrupted power output at Power Plant One and will do the same for Two."

Briefly turning toward the plant, I watched the flames rise from one of the structures. The fight was still ongoing, but Sulos was right. Even if we lost, we would have severely disrupted Two's power output. The thought of screwing up Sulos's plans should have given rise to a smile on my face if it wasn't for the fact that just crossing him wasn't enough. Sulos had cost these people so much, and he needed to be stopped once and for all.

We didn't know Sulos's exact location, although we figured he might be hiding out on his space station. For years he'd worked on building a station that orbited some distant planet. He eventually planned to terraform the planet and create his New World. His plan was still decades away from completion, but once he finished his space station, he had no more use for the earth and its people. Sulos had already threatened to open up a wormhole near the sun's core. In doing so, he would expedite the sun's transition into a red giant, and that would mean the end of Earth.

We didn't expect him to act on his threat anytime soon because he still needed the resources this planet had to offer, but we didn't just want to sit around and wait for it to happen. That was one of the reasons our plan to liberate the plants was set in motion. Our primary objective was to free all the workers and even the enforcers bound to slavery, but also to control the power output of the plants. If Sulos ever decided to open a wormhole close to the sun, he would have to use the wormhole generator, and that thing needed power.

"What do you want?" Maece asked. It was easy for me to hear the tension in her voice, but I doubted anyone else would notice.

"As I'd explained to your council, I would like to make use of the resources your little planet still has to offer, and to do that, nothing would have been in need of change. Life would have continued as it always had," he said, "but you decided to take things into your own hands, and now I must send you a message."

One the freaks took a step forward. Without taking her eyes off the things, Maece lifted a hand and made a waving motion. The six rebels that had joined us just stood there ogling each other. As it became apparent that I'd been the only one to understand her command, I stepped in.

"Hey, you, skinny guy," I said to the rebel that Maece had been talking to before. With the information displayed on her heads-up, Maece probably had detailed information on the guys, but I had no way of knowing their names. "Take your men…," I started to say but paused as my eyes scanned the faces staring back at me. With their shaved heads, they all looked the same. Among the faces I spotted a smaller figure with big baby doll eyes who was clearly female, and next to her stood a person with a beautifully sculpted face I couldn't decide on. Not all men, I thought as I spotted workers in cargo-carrier suits approaching the Hymag entrance.

"Take your people and have them take up

positions around our targets," I said. "You won't be any match for them, so load your weapons with the biggest impact rounds you've got and take your shots from a distance."

"Ma'am," the skinny guy said, "you want us to stay clear?" He gave me a look that told me that he thought I was insane, but then he didn't know what these things were capable of. I nodded and pointed at the workers who had started lifting heavy materials and dragging them toward the entrance of the Hymag line.

"Two of you get over there and provide backup," I said. The skinny guy nodded and didn't seem to have a problem with that. He turned to face his people and sent two them off in the direction of the workers.

As he turned back to me, he said, "Ma'am, I'm not sure if I can let you engage these..." As his eyes turned to the freaks, his voice trailed off.

"Trust me: you can," I said. "Get into position and mind your targets. I don't want to get shot by any of you."

Officially, it wasn't my place to submit orders—those usually came from Harp—but over the years our group had gained seniority over the rest of the rebels, and as long as Harp didn't intervene, they would do as I said. They all nodded, and I spotted the rebel with the sculpted face again. They looked nothing alike, except for the shaved head, but still, he or she reminded me of Kelle.

Kelle was somewhere on a sublevel doing her best to remove neuro-regulators from the workers before they could kill them. She should be fine, but I also knew she was going to be utterly irked and was probably going to kick my ass if I didn't make it through whatever was coming next.

"Why would you destroy the thing you need the most?" Maece said over the coms. The conversation with Sulos was still playing out, but I'd been listening with only half an ear. Sulos had threatened to flip the kill switch on the people within this plant. This meant he would send out a signal powerful enough to engage the neuro-regulators, similar to how our brain zappers worked. Except, Sulos's signal would cause anyone with such a device stuck in the back of their heads to have their brains fried. They would die instantly.

"Look around you, Miss Lux," Sulos said. "You have destroyed most of the facility. It's of no use to me anymore, and neither are its people." He paused a moment and seemed to be going for the dramatic effect. "But you have a use for these people, don't you?" As I listened to Sulos's words, a sinking feeling grew in my gut that he was planning to set an example. That he intended to show us what would happen if we crossed him.

Maece hadn't moved an inch, but Sulos's earlier comment about the destruction done to the plant made me look around as I walked up to the three remaining rebels with their brain zappers in hand. *How was he getting his information?* We had destroyed all the signal boosters and relay stations in the vicinity of the plant, and I couldn't imagine Sulos being anyplace nearby. *How could they have reached Maece's heads-up and sent her Sulos's transmission without a signal booster or a relay station to connect them to the Feed unless they had brought their own?*

I told the three remaining rebels to get out of sight, but to stay close. If Maece and I managed to destroy them—well to be honest, probably only Maece would be able to take out one of these freaks—then I'd want the devices stuck in their heads rendered useless. At least, if they had devices stuck in their heads.

Keeping my distance, I kept a close eye on Maece. Sulos just kept talking on and on about what he was doing was for the sake of humanity and whatnot. How the government had complied with his wishes by keeping the general public in the dark about his New World and that we, with our actions, had jeopardized everything because rumors were already spreading. That if we agreed to cooperate from now on, we'd be rewarded for doing so. I had heard these things before, and they didn't make any sense to me in this context until I noticed those freaks take a step to close the distance between us.

"Harp," I said over the coms. I didn't dare to chance Sulos overhearing us through Maece's heads-up, and I moved further away from her.

"What?" Harp said in his minimalistic, none-too-conversational tone.

"The stuff he's saying doesn't make any sense," I said.

"He's buying time," Harp said. I should have known Harp would pick up on that.

"Time for what?" I asked. "Can he even do what he's yammering on about?" Without a signal booster, Sulos would have a hard time coming through on his threats. *How would the kill-switch signal even reach us without a connection to the Feed?* On top of that, we had rendered control of the system, and I figured he'd have a hard time getting past Kyran's security measures.

"The connection he's using to communicate with Maece is weak," Kyran said. His words sounded muffled, and I imagined him sitting behind his virtual keypad with a heads-up device analyzer, or had, stuck between his teeth.

Kyran had a habit of chewing on the cylindrical device. He had kept it as a souvenir after a short stint of working undercover at the Tenebrae Enforcer Department. Kyran had played an intricate part in Maece's escape, and I trusted his skills. In working order, the tool would be used in the field to analyze faulty headsets and other technical stuff, but the time spent between Kyran's teeth had rendered it useless. Except maybe for giving Kyran something to fiddle with.

The words had barely left Kyran's mouth when the freaks took another step closer. Their action made something click inside my head while Kyran babbled on. "I doubt he'd be able to reach the plant, let alone the sublevels."

"Oh shit," I said. Maece, who must have monitored my conversation with the others through her heads-up, turned to face me. I closed the gap between us and grabbed her arm. She shot the freaks another glance but then let me pull her away.

The five mutilated figures reacted in the same instance as if they had anticipated our move. In the background, I still heard Sulos's voice, but I couldn't make out his words.

"It's the heads-up," I said. "It is linked to our systems, which in turn are directly connected to the plant."

"Yeah," Maece said. She must have been reading my mind, because as she continued, she said, "We have to get the heads-up out of range of those freaks. If they manage a direct linkup, Sulos can use it to connect to the Feed and flip the switch."

"Kyran," I heard Harp bellow into my ear, "break the connection."

I looked over my shoulder, hoping to see some distance between us and those things, but I couldn't have been further from the truth. Those things moved faster than we ever could, and if we didn't hurry, they'd be on us in seconds.

Maece fired off a few rounds, but the magnetic blasts were instantly absorbed by the freaks' armor. In a change of tactic, we ran as fast as we could in the direction of the barricades. If we could create some distance between us and those freaks, the rebels might be able to take a shot at them. The thought had barely crossed my mind before I heard a barrage of magnetic explosions. Looking over my shoulder, I noticed the rebels who had joined us emerge from their positions and fire their weapons at the freaks. I could tell the magnetic impacts slowed the freaks' progress, and I felt an urge to stop, to draw my newly acquired enforcer weapon. I wanted to join them in the fight, but it wouldn't be enough to stop the freaks. We needed to get that heads-up as far away from them as possible, and to do that, I needed to focus on getting back behind the perimeter.

Resistance fighters had gathered on the barricade and watched our approach with their weapons raised. It felt odd running toward an array of weapons that pointed straight at me, and I could only hope that they were good shots.

As if at some great distance, I heard Kyran curse in the background. I was still receiving Harp's communications feed over the coms, and it didn't sound promising. Kyran still hadn't been able to cut the connection to Maece's heads-up.

Midrun, Maece grabbed me just before she removed the heads-up and shoved it into my hands.

"Destroy it," she said. For a second, I could see the worry in her hazel eyes and the creases that marred her dark skin. She already started to turn before I could do anything but grab the device.

"Maece," I called after her. She knew as well as I did that she needed the device's fast calculations if she wanted to make even a dent in these things. She also knew that we couldn't allow the freaks to make a direct connection with the device, especially not while

Kyran was still trying to break the link with the plant and ultimately, the worker's neuro devices. From my peripheral vision, I could see her well-protected body slam into one of the freaks and take down another in the same movement.

Sensing one of the freaks right behind me, I focused on pushing my legs as fast as they would go. The added strength that my suit provided helped me to find a fast-paced rhythm. As I neared the barricades, I realized that I was still holding Maece's heads-up and grabbed my weapon from its holster. I needed to destroy this thing before those freaks could do with it whatever they needed to do with it.

Just as I raised my weapon and pointed it at the device, something forced the air from my lungs. Unable to keep upright, I hit the ground hard and landed on my stomach. My vision turned to black for a second, and all the sound around me faded into nothingness. My heart pounded frantically, and the noise reverberated so loudly in my head that I thought it might have taken up residence in there. Forcing myself to snap out of it, I blinked. Fortunately, I had held on to the heads-up and my weapon, but as I tried to get to my feet, it seemed as if my legs didn't work anymore. Half turning, I gasped as I saw the mutilated figure pin my legs to the ground.

In a desperate attempt, I whirled my weapon around and pointed it at the freak. Its mouth pulled into a nasty sneer as I fired several times. I struck everything from its chest, neck, and even managed to skim its skull, but I might as well have been throwing rocks at the creature because my magnetic blasts did nothing to deter the thing from holding me down. It lifted its robotic arm, which up close looked massive, and I cried out as it came barreling down on me. Its metal fist knocked the weapon from my hand. Still lying on my stomach, I had a hard time tracking the freak's movement until I felt cold clamps wrap around the back of my neck, and it pushed my face into the dirt.

Unable to do anything else, I focused on the device still clasped in my left hand. I raised my arm and slammed the thing into the ground in the hope of breaking it. Just as I wanted to bring my arm up again, the hold around my neck increased, and metal fingers dug into my skin. I would have screamed, but long metal digits wrapped around my throat and squeezed hard enough to stop the air from getting to my lungs.

As my vision started to fade, I could barely make out the freak's other mechanical hand wrap its tentacles around the heads-up. With a hiss and a click, something shot out from the freak's appendage and connected with the device. Somewhere deep within my subconscious, something told me to fight, but my limbs weren't listening to me anymore. I needed air; I needed to breathe. A shrill beeping sound broke my final resolve, and my eyes started to close.

The sound of weapons fire close by pulled me out of my haze, and my eyes shot open. The claw around my neck was gone, and I could breathe again. Coughing, I pushed myself up on my elbows, desperate to suck air into my longs. I glanced sideways and then up to see the black form of an enforcer standing by my side with its back turned to me. My vision was blurry, and I didn't think my body was in any condition to run or fight this enforcer. In some strange attempt to refocus, my eyes roamed up along the suit's exoskeleton. Hydraulics, metal alloys, and electronics all came together to create an ominous-looking piece of armor that lacked the usual headgear.

Relief washed over me as I realized it was Maece standing by my side. She stood motionless staring down at the body of one of the freaks. *Was it over?*

With a groan, I managed to get on my knees and looked around. Bodies lay scattered across the area, and two of the rebels holding brain zappers hovered over one of the freaks. The remaining four, including the one lying at Maece's feet, still holding on to a heads-up device, crushed beyond repair, appeared to be dead.

I stumbled getting to my feet and felt Maece grab my waist to hold me steady.

"I'm okay," I said, but words were no more than a hoarse croak. It hurt to swallow, and as I placed a hand on my throat, it felt tender. Maece didn't reply, and as our eyes met, it didn't matter that my throat hurt because I couldn't help but swallow hard. The pained expression on her face cut right through me, and I felt the dread that we had failed wrap around me.

The loud hum of a Hymag arriving and then the engines powering down drew my eyes to the Hymag entrance. Cargo carriers stood motionless near the opening with heavy loads still clamped in their mechanical arms. The bodies of the men driving the machines hung slumped in their cabins. They were all dead—Clyde was dead.

As the noise of the Hymag engines faded, shouting reached us from within the darkness of the tunnel. Moments later, enforcers moved out of the dark and quickly started to clear the debris obstructing the Hymag line. It wouldn't take them long before they would ride the transport loaded with enforcers into the center of the plant.

"Call Harp," Maece said. I turned to her in confusion, but as I met her hazel eyes that looked darker than usual, I realized her heads-up had been destroyed and she couldn't make the call herself. "Tell him we need to evacuate."

THREE
MAECE

Removing the suit felt like a relief, but not in a way it used to feel. Still, I was glad to be wearing my own clothes again, and I walked to the corner of the room where I sank down on the small cot. One look at the pillow told me that I felt dead tired, but I also knew sleep wouldn't come. Not tonight and probably not for a long time. Maybe I should have accepted Reece's advice about getting drunk to the point of no return. A drink might have taken the edge off a little, but it would have never erased the horror of the past few hours. Besides, I doubted if Reece and the others had even left. On the Hymag ride back to the rebel base, they had looked as drained as I felt.

I rubbed my hands over my face and fell backward to lean against the wall. Tears stung my eyes, and I didn't know if I wanted to cry, scream, or kill someone. I searched the tiny room but found nothing that felt worth getting up for and trash. This small room was the same one they had taken me after the doctor had "fixed part of my brain." At least that's what Saera had called it.

It felt as if it had only been yesterday that Saera and the others had coaxed me out from ArtRep's grasp and had brought me home. Not that this place was home, but the rebel base underneath the City of Umbras was where we spend most of our days, so it might as well be home. Besides, our home hadn't been what I remembered it to be for a while now, and even the ride on the Hymag back to the base had confirmed that.

The silence on the ride back wasn't that surprising, not after losing so many. Sulos had come through on his threat—he had flipped the switch. Reece, Riffy, and Kelle had worked so hard to disrupt as many neuro-regulators as they could, but in the end, it hadn't been enough. Thousands had died, and it was all my fault. *Why hadn't I seen through Sulos's ruse? Why didn't I realize he needed to use my heads-up to send the signal?*

None of them had said anything, and I wondered if they blamed me for what had happened. After all, it had been my heads-up that had caused all these deaths, and I had been too slow to stop it.

A soft knock on the door pulled me out of my self-recrimination, and I looked up to see Kelle. As always, her expression was downcast, but although I read more than the regular amount of hurt in her eyes and the tension in her jaw looked painful, she appeared to be her usual self.

"Hey," she said, sounding timid. "Can I come in?"

I nodded in answer. She closed the door behind her and briefly took in the room. Except for a dresser and nightstand with a lamp standing next to my cot, the place was bare, and soon her eyes landed on me. A finger on her right hand twitched. The soft hum of hydraulics and mechanics buzzed in the small room as Kelle balled her fist and then flexed her fingers. The residual tension in her body often exhibited itself through her prosthetic. Even though the robotic replacement of her lower right arm would give some child nightmares, Kelle very much looked like a kid herself. At the age of twenty-one, she looked fragile and on the short side, but I knew better than to underestimate her.

She rubbed a hand over the three millimeters of black hair that covered her head, and shifted from foot to foot. I scooted sideways to give her a place to sit on the cot. To her credit, she didn't hesitate, and she sat down with a long sigh.

"You all right?" I asked tentatively. She grimaced and shook her head. I waited for a beat to see if she'd say anything else, and when she didn't, I added, "Wanna talk about it?"

She shook her head again and then kept her eyes firmly on some spot on the floor. With Saera, a simple question would usually be reciprocated with a barrage of words, and I felt unaccustomed to the uneasy silence. Unsure what else to do, I searched out the same rough area on the floor and joined Kelle in staring at it.

I had no idea how much time had passed when Kelle shifted, and our eyes met.

"You know, you shouldn't be in here alone," she said.

"It's probably better that way," I said.

"Why?"

I returned to looking at the spot on the floor to avoid the intensity in her dark eyes. It had become harder for me to look people in the eye—even Saera. Fear of what they might reveal overtook me every time. "I have a feeling the others wouldn't want me there," I said and hated the note of self-pity in my voice.

"You know that's not true," she replied. Kelle's voice sounded even and just as stoic as that mask she always managed to uphold; it rarely betrayed any kind of emotion. For some reason, with her placid demeanor, she could take the edge off my racing thoughts. I seemed to be analyzing anything and everything these days even without my heads-up.

"What happened was my fault," I said, "and everyone knows it." My words came out harsher than I'd intended, but I looked up to see that, except for a raised eyebrow, Kelle's expression hadn't changed.

"Are you drunk?" she asked without a hint of humor. "Because I don't see how this could be your fault."

"I should've done something, moved faster. It seems so obvious to me now what Sulos had planned, and I should've seen it coming. Now they are all dead because of me." I had to take a breath after I finished.

Kelle actually looked surprised before she replied, "Oh, c'mon, if anyone is to blame it's Sulos and perhaps that idiot that decided to stray from the plan and mess things up for everyone."

I shifted, feeling nervous, and clamped my fingers around the edge of the cot to stop them from shaking. I hated this feeling of uncertainty. After taking a deep breath to calm my nerves, I shook my head and looked up to face Kelle.

"You weren't out there," I said. "You don't know–"

"Don't you dare. I saw it all, and believe me…" Her voice broke, and she took a breath before she added, "and I still don't blame you."

Her jaw flexed as if she were grinding her teeth, and I could see moist gather in her eyes as she fought back tears. The person sitting in front of me wasn't anything like the Kelle I knew. That Kelle always looked stoic and very much in control, but it seemed that the mask she always wore had started to crumble a bit.

"Thanks," I said and felt grateful for this moment. Kelle wasn't one to show much of her inner self, especially not to me. For reasons that were mostly my doing, I'd been the last one in our group to bond with Kelle after Harp showed up with her on our doorstep. It had taken a few years for us to trust one another. And while I'd basically grown up with the others, it was Kelle sitting here now, and I appreciated that. Still, that didn't mean she was right about all this.

"You're wrong, though," I said. "I did this. Sulos wouldn't have been able to do this if I hadn't been there, and if I hadn't run off on some stupid mission, thinking I could make a difference, then these people would still be alive."

"Is that what this is about?" she said. This time I heard a note of disbelief in her tone, and it was as if all my senses went into full alert. "Or could it be that you're feeling guilty about making decisions without us. About leaving us."

As if some strange voice in my head had warned me to be wary of anything Kelle did or said, I shifted on the bed to create some distance between us and watched her. Her stoic mask had returned, and I couldn't read her face. Feeling confused, I stood and paced to the other side of the room.

Feeling Kelle's eyes following me, I kept my gaze riveted to the floor.

"Either way, what you're thinking is just plain dumb. You know that, right?" she said. I gathered that she was trying to make me feel better about what had happened, but her remark only fueled the anger that started to build inside me, and I shot her a hard glare.

"It's the truth."

So many people had died by my hand, and I didn't just mean those who had perished at the plant. I had worked as an enforcer for two years, and everyone knew what they did. They held up the so-called peace by acting as judges, juries, and executioners to anyone who dared to defy the authoritarian order. My memories of that time might have been erased from my mind, but that didn't mean I was ignorant about what I had done.

The young face of a man sprang to the forefront of my mind. He had become my last official act as an enforcer and one of the few memories that had remained of that time. I had shot him twice without flinching in some dark alley surrounded by garbage and filth. The fear in his eyes had become a constant reminder and a symbol of all I had done.

Turning to face Kelle again, I noticed my reflection in a mirror bolted to the wall. The sleeveless shirt I was wearing revealed the black ink embedded in my dark skin and showed every detail of the wings tattooed on my arms. Some guardian angel I turned out to be. The only thing that I was good for was getting people killed.

I shook my head in despair and saw Kelle watching me. She stood and held my gaze. I could almost feel the intensity of her dark eyes penetrating my thoughts as she said, "I can't even imagine what's going on in that head of yours, but we would never have figured out what Sulos was up to if you hadn't gone out there and risked it all."

"Tell that to Saera," I replied.

A tinge of a smile graced Kelle's face at the mention of Saera before she said, "Saera will come around. She always does. I thought you knew her better than that."

I shook my head, unwilling to believe her, because if I let myself be convinced, that would diminish all the lives that I had destroyed.

"I think you should talk to Spiro." I gave her a questioning look as she got up from the cot. Spiro was our resident genius who had designed the neuro-disruptor. The idea had come from his own experience of having a neuro-regulator stuck inside his head as a small child. Spiro had become the first person to be freed from the device because as a twelve-year-old he had touched a Hymag line just as the transport whisked by. The incident should have killed him, but somehow, he had managed to survive. It had screwed him up, though, and he hadn't grown an inch since.

"Why?" I asked as she moved to the door and opened it.

"He's the only one that can make you see what's going on in your head."

I scoffed and said, "When has Spiro ever said anything that made sense to anyone?"

The tiniest of twitches at the corner of her mouth nearly gave way to a smile.

"I didn't say, 'said.' I said, 'make you see.'"

I wondered if she had suggested me talking to Spiro because of the similarities in our history. We both had had neuro devices stuck in our heads, and we both had managed to survive the removal of them. There hadn't been any other cases like ours, at least none that I knew of. The incident had left Spiro's body in disarray, and perhaps that was the reason Kelle wanted me to talk to him. *Did she think something was wrong with me?*

Kelle walked out, but before the door clicked shut, she added, "Oh and there is a briefing in two hours. Harp wants us all to be there."

At the click of the door, I turned back to the

mirror. I stared at my reflection as I replayed the conversation from a moment ago inside my head. It had resolved nothing, but for some reason, Kelle showing up at all made me feel a little better. It had taken me longer than the others to see her for who she was and why Saera had been so infatuated with her from the beginning. Perhaps Saera's infatuation had been the reason for that slow evolution. The fear of losing Saera to Kelle seemed stupid now that I looked back on it, and since then, I had learned to appreciate her for who she was. Her showing up like this only added to that appreciation, but I could still feel the doubts linger at the front of my mind. *I could never forgive myself for the things I'd done, so why would anyone else?*

I drew in a deep breath and held it as the urge to punch a hole in the wall threatened to overtake me. With my eyes closed, I waited for the compulsion to fade. I released the air from my lungs as I opened my eyes and stared in the mirror. Maybe Kelle was right; maybe I was reading too much into this, and I should talk to Spiro. I shook my head, afraid to trust my own thoughts. As I inspected the circles underneath my eyes, I figured that I should probably take advantage of the time allotted and get some sleep.

I should have known sleep wouldn't come and two hours wouldn't have been enough to replenish the fatigue I felt anyway. I yawned as I walked up the steps leading to the platform. Not that I had expected to sleep, not with the images of the dead haunting me. I shook my head, knowing that I wouldn't be any good to anyone if I couldn't regain my focus. We had experienced a loss, and we would probably suffer more, but that didn't mean we could abandon the fight. There were still Subterrans living under the tyrannical rule of Tenebrae, and the planet remained under the threat of destruction by Sulos.

We needed to look ahead and concentrate on our next step, but it didn't stop me from wondering what Sulos's plan would be for the power plant. *Would he just abandon it or replace the workers who had died?* I didn't want to think of the people unfortunate enough to replace the workforce that had perished, because I doubted that any free will would be involved.

Besides, the power disruption should have had repercussions within the districts. I could imagine power outages and trouble providing homes with their usual amounts of energy cylinders. Rumors of the act of resistance would have spread by now, even in the districts. *I wondered how much longer Sulos would be able to keep his secret from the general population?*

Climbing the last few steps, I paused at the top of the stairs. It didn't matter if I entered the area stepping from a Hymag or just walking up these stairs. Every time I looked up at the domed structure, it amazed me. The hidden underground base underneath the City of Umbras wasn't nearly as big as the power plant or the city itself, protected by its energy shield, but somehow this place got to me.

The round platform seemingly hovered in the

middle of the space, surrounded by an immense ditch that was wide enough that it couldn't be jumped and deep enough that you couldn't see the bottom. Four bridges connected with the platform, one of which led to a magnetic lift and gave access to the surface high above our heads, while the others were Hymag lines with access to a Hymag docking platform. Fortunately, Subterra had managed to retain some of the power plants within its borders after the war with the districts, or else we would've had a hell of a time trying to keep this base running.

The central control area looked busier than usual. Under normal circumstances only rebels under Harp's command occupied the more than a dozen workstations, tapping at their virtual keys and flipping switches. These men and women were still present and did their jobs, but some additional people mixed among their ranks. Some of them, in workers' clothes, stood clustered together, talking among themselves. I could have been just me, but I sensed a tension in the air that could be deemed understandable but felt foreign just the same.

The massive screens, which in standard operating mode hung in a circle over the workstations, had been redirected and moved to hang over a large conference table. Harp stood by the table, apparently in deep conversation with one of the newcomers. I stopped a moment to take in the scene.

The man talking to Harp wasn't a stranger to me, not at all. We had fought together to free Power Plant One, he had been there in Two, and it was he who

Kelle had referred to when she'd mentioned the idiot who'd strayed from the plan. I had to swallow hard at the memory of the loss we had suffered before I could shove the thought aside.

Darren Russ used to be a power plant worker but had joined the resistance years ago. He and Harp went way back, and I suspected he had something to do with the kids Harp had rescued from the plants. Kids like Saera and me. I had never thought Darren and Harp to be friends, more like acquaintances with similar goals. By observing Darren's animated hand gestures and him pointing a finger at Harp, I had a feeling the relationship had turned a lot more interesting. Even from this distance, it was clear that they were arguing. Well, at least Darren was. Harp just stood there with his hands folded behind his back.

Darren visibly shifted as he noticed me watching them. He wore a dark-blue overall over his strong worker's build with a heavy belt strapped around his middle. Several weapons clung to his hips and thighs, including an ax. I held his gaze as he stared at me with one eye. Two claw-like marks ran across his left eye, down his jaw and neck, making him blind on that side, but he hadn't bothered to cover up the nasty-looking scar. The mere sight of him made the blood boil inside my veins, and I realized that I had to agree with Kelle. Darren shared some of the responsibility for what had happened inside Two.

Having lost Darren's attention, Harp turned to face me. With his hands resting behind his back, he stood in his usual posture as he beckoned me over with a slight nod. From a distance, Harp still looked young and resilient, but up close I could tell that the creases around his dark eyes had deepened over the past months. Gray started to show along the temples of his black hair and trimmed beard.

As I approached the conference table, I noticed Saera sitting at some distance on the Hymag platform. She had her arms wrapped around Kelle's waist, who was standing in front of the platform, leaning back. Riffy sat at Saera's side with his face buried in his hands while Reece patted his back. The moment Reece noticed me, I tried to return his warm smile but felt like I failed miserably, and I shifted my gaze away from them. I couldn't face them, not right now. Instead, I joined Harp.

"Maece, you know Darren," Harp said. I could always trust Harp to get straight to business, and I nodded.

"Of course," I replied. Grinding my teeth to keep myself from saying something that Harp would surely not approve of, I offered my hand in greeting. We had met before and worked together, but usually, our interactions went through Harp. I couldn't say that I felt saddened by that. Besides the fact that he'd been partially responsible for what had happened in Two, there was something about Darren that reminded me too much of the past. In fact, all of the resistance folk, of which most were former plant workers, retold things I'd rather forget.

I couldn't have been more than eight years old when Saera and I had been forced to live on our own without a home. The power plants weren't an easy place to live at any age, and with Saera only being a few years older than me, we had been two kids trying to survive. Back then, I hadn't known what was the hardest, finding a safe place to sleep every night away from the predators that preyed on young children, or scavenging for food. If it hadn't been for Harp, we probably would have died on those streets.

Darren took my hand, although he didn't shake it. He just held it without releasing it. He tightened his grip as he spoke in a low but threatening voice. "What the hell went wrong out there?"

I pulled my hand away from his grasp and stared at him.

"What do you mean, what went wrong?"

"You were supposed to stop those freaks, not help them kill all of our people." His words struck me as if someone had just rammed a fist into my chest and squeezed my heart.

"What?" I said. Darren started to point that finger of his again like I'd seen him do before with Harp.

"You heard me," he said louder this time. "This is your fault." It hadn't been that long ago that I'd blamed myself for what had happened, but hearing it said by this guy didn't compute. The anger that had built inside me from the moment that I'd spotted him started to boil over, and I swatted his pointing hand away from my face. He wasn't just pointing a finger at me, as far as I was concerned. He was laying blame on everyone within the rebellion, and I wasn't going to stand for that.

"You were the one who failed in removing all the neuro-regulators before you called us in in the first place," I said in a loud enough voice that would probably be heard by everyone inside the base. "And, secondly, you conveniently forgot to mention that until we got there. Half of our people were busy doing your job."

Partly wondering why Harp wasn't putting this guy in his place, I took a step forward to invade Darren's personal space and stared into the one good eye he had left. With a pair of strong hands, Darren shoved me backward, but I managed to hold my ground.

"What is your proble—," I started to say, but before I could finish, I felt his hands on me again. I tried to jerk away from him but missed the strength of my suit. Without it, I was no match for Darren's strong build. He spun me around, and before I knew it, he twisted my arm behind my back and planted my face on the smooth surface of the conference table. I struggled against him, but he just tightened his grip to the point where he could snap the bones in my arm. I felt his warm breath on my skin as he hovered over me, and I ground my teeth as he spoke into my ear.

"Not so tough without your suit, are you, girl?"

On pure instinct, I snapped my head back and felt it connect. As Darren groaned and loosened his grip, I pushed up from the table, whirled around, and connected my fist to his face. Darren wobbled on his feet but did not go down. Intending to punch his remaining eye shut, I raised my fist again. Anticipating my move, Darren stepped back, right into Reece's arms.

The sight of Reece holding Darren in a chokehold stopped me from reconnecting my fist with his mutilated face. Darren might be strong, but Reece knew how to subdue a man.

"You okay, babe," Reece said in that cocky way of his. Reece helping out didn't abate the annoyance I felt for getting myself into such a stupid situation in the first place. Reece must have seen something in my reaction because he shot me a lopsided grin.

Darren struggled so he could get some precious air into his lungs, and Reece turned his attention to the man clawing at his arm.

"Now are you going to behave, or am I going to have to stick a wet finger in your ear?" Reece said as he stuck his index finger into his mouth to prove his resolve.

Voices rose in Darren's defense. Other members of the resistance had gathered around us and were stirring up even more of a fuss. Saera, Kelle, and Riffy had also joined us at the table and had stepped in between the men in worker overalls and Reece, trying to sooth the situation.

Riffy's face looked flushed as he stood ready to pounce on anyone who threatened to get close to his friend. With his chubby face and oversized belly that showed a little where his shirt didn't manage to cover it, he stood in pale comparison to the broad-shouldered workers who towered over him, but he held his ground.

Even though of even shorter stature than Riffy, Kelle had no problem keeping the men who had come to Darren's aid at bay. She had removed the glove from her prosthetic hand and only needed to flex her fingers for the workers to keep their distance. Anyone would know the power that could be placed behind a blow from a mechanical limb.

In her sleeveless shirt, Saera showed off the tattoos on her slim but muscular arms. The flames etched into her skin flexed along with her muscles as she shoved one of the men and shouted, "Back off!"

"Enough!" Harp's voice echoed in the open space before everyone fell quiet. He stepped closer to Reece, who was still holding Darren.

"Will you be able to act civilly?" Harp asked. Darren jerked his body, probably to see if Reece had loosened his grip, but he couldn't free himself. Relenting, Darren nodded.

With a gesture from Harp, Reece instantly released the big man from his hold. Darren coughed and then drew in a couple of deep breaths. With his sleeve, he wiped at the blood that trickled from his nose before he shot me a deadly glare. I couldn't care less about the way Darren looked at me, because I could only marvel at the way my friends had stood up for me. How Saera had come to my defense even though I knew she was still mad at me.

Harp waited until he had Darren's attention again. With a short nod, Harp gestured at the men in overalls, telling Darren in not so many words to have them stand down. Darren waved a hand to his men, who hesitated only slightly before they backed off.

"Now, let's try this again," Harp said.

Harp waited patiently until the crowd that had gathered around the conference table dispersed. Darren and one of his lieutenants, a young man named Miguel, stood at one side of the table, while the five of us stood on the other. Harp had positioned himself at the head of the table, ignoring all of us. He kept his eyes fixed on the screens hanging over our heads. Numbers scrolled down those screens, and a chill ran down my spine as he started to cite the information, "We've extracted two hundred and forty-two souls from the plant, including six enforcers and one freak that our scientists are dying to get their hands on," he said. "We have twenty-five injured resistance members and..." Harp paused as his eyes met every one of us until they landed on Darren. "And thirty-two hundred dead."

"You were supposed to secure the system, so the kill switch couldn't be activated and get those regulators deactivated," Darren said. He didn't in the least seem deterred by the number of deaths Harp had mentioned. He might have already known the numbers, but still, I would have welcomed any reaction that made him appear at least a bit human. As it were, he might as well have been an enforcer. "Those deaths are on you and your little puppet over

here. It was her heads-up that lead to all of this."
Darren pointed another accusing finger in my
direction, and I struggled not to cringe.

"I really don't like that guy," Riffy said from
somewhere behind me.

"That's an understatement," Reece replied to
Riffy's remark.

A steadying hand moved to my back, but I didn't
turn to see whose it was. Instead, I balled my fists and
tried to remember how to breathe. The tension in my
chest eased a little as I noticed the slight tremor in
Darren's pointing hand. His jaw flexed, which
coincided with the anger he wanted to project, but
something in his eye betrayed it wasn't just that.
Miguel, Darren's aide, stood motionless by his side
with his gaze fixed on the ground.

Harp eased forward and placed his palms flat on
the table. He narrowed his dark gaze on Darren and
waited until the man lowered his accusing finger.

"The original plan, which had proven itself
successful in liberating One," Harp said in a gravelly
but calm voice, "what was it?"

When Darren failed to make a sound, it seemed
his lieutenant felt compelled to answer the question.

"To infiltrate the plant and to disrupt as many of
the regulators before implementing the final attack
strategy," Miguel said. The young man looked
nervous, and his eyes shot straight back to the ground
after he had finished.

"At least someone got something right," Reece
muttered from behind me, and his remark was

followed by a chuckle that could only have come from Riffy.

"Right," Harp said without even trying to hide his disapproval. He straightened and took up his usual posture, by clasping his hands behind his back. "You went early and didn't bother to tell us. Why?"

Darren crossed his arms over his chest as if he wasn't impressed, but a small twitch underneath his eye told me he was. He shot Miguel a disapproving look and cleared his throat.

"Getting rid of all the neuro devices beforehand would have taken too long, and besides, Sulos would never have had the means to trigger them if you hadn't delivered it to him."

Harp tilted his head to the side, but his eyes never wavered from Darren. He waited to see if Darren added anything else, and when he didn't, Harp said, "Let me rephrase that. You jumped the gun. Why?"

"We have intel that suggests Sulos is moving up the timetable," Darren said, and to his credit, he sounded confident. "He is not going to wait the full year, and we expect him to activate the wormhole generator sooner rather than later. Bringing down the plants means bringing down the wormhole generator."

Darren even managed a smug expression as he attempted to hold Harp's gaze but failed miserably. Harp kept a sharp eye on Darren as he absorbed the information. Because the plants provided the power needed to energize the shields protecting the city and anything else that needed a spark, Darren's assessment that they also sustained the wormhole generator rang true to me. What Darren hadn't mentioned was why he suspected Sulos might move up the timetable.

"I would like to know who has graced you with that knowledge, because we have enough information to know that Sulos's space station is far from finished, and I'm not even mentioning this New World he wants to terraform," Harp said as he referred to the information Saera and I had downloaded from the ArtRep mainframe. Information we had intended to spread among the population, but unfortunately, we had failed.

The council, which was supposedly on our side, had changed its mind and decided to comply with Sulos's demands instead. Although not many dared to say it aloud, we all knew they were gunning for a one-way ticket to this New World once Sulos finished it. Nobody wanted to stay on this dying planet.

"I cannot tell you how I've obtained this information—" Darren started to say.

"That doesn't come as a surprise," Riffy piped in. Startled by his disruptive comment, I peeked over my shoulder and watched Reece give Riffy a playful yet deliberate whack on the head.

"What did I tell you about timing," Reece muttered.

"Sorry," Riffy added as he rubbed his head.

Darren looked annoyed as I turned back to him, but his spiteful gaze was directed at me instead of at the guys behind me.

"As I was saying, I cannot divulge my sources, but trust me when I say that one of the primary resources he needs to succeed is power," Darren continued. "The process of shipping energy cylinders via space freighters is taking too long, so he's going to use the wormhole generator to take what he needs from the sun and leave us all for dead."

I wasn't a scientist, but that statement didn't make much sense to me, and I shot Harp a questioning look. Harp didn't show it, but I knew he would have been as confused as I was by Darren's reasoning. He might be a great leader and strategist, but he wasn't very tech savvy.

"Kyran," he called out. Harp's voiced thundered in the open space. Looking over my shoulder toward the workstations, I noticed Kyran scrambling to get up from his desk chair. One foot had found the floor, but the other still rested on his desk. Half stumbling, he grabbed a pad and hurried over.

As I turned back to the table, I locked eyes with Saera. She must have been the one to place her hand on my back for support earlier. She shifted uneasily before returning her attention back to the screens. It was as if she didn't even want to look at me, and I had to quell the urge to scream at her. Fortunately, Kyran provided a welcome distraction.

"Kyran," Harp said, "pull up the intel on Sulos's space station." Without hesitation, Kyran switched on the device in his hands and started tapping on the small pad. The screens hovering over the table came to life and replaced one set of data with a bunch of different numbers. When no one spoke, Kyran looked nervous, as Harp returned his questioning gaze with an impatient raised eyebrow.

"Oh, you mean me!" Kyran said. He raked a hand through his messy hair before his fingers returned to the pad and he started tapping.

The same images that I had seen before, when we first came across the information in Sulos's office, popped up on the screens. The darkness of space, accentuated with tiny bright specks, caught my eyes as Kyran expanded the image and zoomed out. The earth disappeared among all the different stars until I couldn't tell where it had been. Shifting the image, he zoomed back in, and Kyran indicated a planet surrounded by two moons and what by now we had come to know as Sulos's space station.

The station was still a mere speck on the screen compared to the two moons and the planet itself, but it had to be enormous. For a moment we watched as the man-made structure drifted in orbit of the planet that Sulos had picked to become his New World.

"As you can see," Kyran said, "the space station is still far from completion, and at this point, we don't think Sulos is even close to starting the terraforming process on the planet. According to our calculations, he won't even make the time line he has set for us."

About six months ago, Sulos had given us a warning that if we didn't comply with his demand, which was basically to keep our mouths shut and do nothing, he would destroy the earth by opening another wormhole close to the sun. Scientists had managed to open wormholes before and, with it, had nearly killed the human race.

Driven by a desire to reach beyond the capabilities that standard space travel allowed, these scientists had succeeded to build a wormhole generator. The idea was to travel further than the unviable planets or gas giants that our race had managed to reach until then. At first, it had all seemed fine, and numerous tests had been successful until that one disastrous attempt that opened a wormhole too close to the sun's core.

By doing so, these scientists had unintentionally opened up the sun's fuel valve and vented the precious content out through the space conduit. They'd managed to close the lid but not before the incident had hastened the sun's transition toward the red giant phase. As the star started to burn brighter, the ice caps permanently melted, and oceans turned into vast wastelands. Only the shield technology that was available at the time and the move to live underground had saved humanity from extinction. If Sulos were to open up that wormhole again, nothing would prevent the sun from turning into a red giant, billions of years before it was supposed to. The earth would die.

"We don't have any current data on the structure of the station, but we have been monitoring the outer rims for any travel activity," Kyran continued. The outer rim was basically a term for everything located outside the city or, more exactly, outside the shield's borders. Just outside the City of Umbras several landing platforms had been build where space freighters could dock to load or unload their cargo.

Usually, smaller ships commuted between the earth, and the more massive space freighters remained in orbit. Although the Umbras outer rim was known to accommodate the bigger freighters, there could be months in between such arrivals and departures.

"We've had an increase in arrivals and departures," Kyran said.

"How much of an increase?" Harp asked.

"Oh, about five times as much," Kyran replied. There wasn't much of a reaction to the news as I took stock of the people standing around the table. There should have been. Space travel wasn't new, and it hadn't been for centuries, but that was kind of the problem.

Since the wormhole incident, our focus as a race had been more about survival and not just because of the expanding sun hovering over our heads. Turmoil and wars had plagued the lands, setting our space program way back. Sure, there had been the occasional formation of governments that had promised a wide-scale search for a planet viable enough to sustain human life, but funds for such undertakings usually dried up pretty quickly.

The only reason that Sulos had managed to get as far as he had was that he had used ArtRep's funds and influence to play his dirty games within the government and the way he had subjected everyone to his cruelty. He had enslaved people and had turned them into enforcers. The technology belonged to ArtRep, which gave them control of a physically enhanced security force, and Sulos owned ArtRep.

With the help of this army of his, he had become one of the most influential men within the districts. After that, it hadn't been that hard for him to take control of the power plants and all the other production facilities that produced the resources that he needed.

"Do we know what they are carrying?" Harp asked.

Kyran checked his pad before he said, "The usual, energy cylinders, raw material, workers, but mostly processed fungi and mushrooms." He pulled up a bunch of numbers, and we all stared at them for a while. A chart displayed on a different screen revealed the amounts of all the transported goods and workforce over the past year in colorful lines. As an afterthought Kyran added, "Oh, and it seems they've been receiving an enormous amount of medical supplies, which in itself wouldn't be suspicious until I spotted the name Icordia on one of the manifests."

I flinched at the mention of the name of the hospital located on the edge of Subterran territory. People disappearing under suspicious circumstances had launched Harp into an investigation of the institution and eventually had led me to willingly set foot inside the place, knowing I might never leave.

The memory of being restrained and shoved into a bioprinter over two years ago sent a shiver down my spine. The hospital had linked Sulos to the abducted Subterrans, and that's how we'd found out how he had managed to build his enforcer army. It seemed Icordia had remained active all this time. I didn't dare to think what kind of business they had ventured into.

"That says it all," Darren exclaimed, unaware of my discomfort and ignoring the information Kyran had provided about Icordia. All eyes turned to him, and he smirked as if he'd just solved the most intricate puzzle of all time. Even Harp raised an eyebrow at his exclamation.

"Explain," Harp merely said after he had lowered his brow to its usual frowning position. Darren pointed at the screen displaying the colorful chart.

"Just look at the numbers," he said, and he almost sounded excited. "There has been a significant decrease in the number of energy cylinders being transported."

Looking at the numbers, I realized he was right. There had indeed been a decrease in the number of transported energy cylinders, but that could mean anything. Harp voiced as much.

"Which means?"

Darren raised his hands, palms up, and shook his head as if he were addressing a bunch of idiots. "He's going to use alternative means to get the energy he needs."

"Which is?" Harp said, sounding dimwitted, as if he had no idea of what Darren was talking about, which in all honesty might have been the case.

"He's going to use the wormhole generator," Darren said. "He's going to open up a hole, suck out the sun's energy, and use it to power that damn station of his, and eventually use it to terraform the planet itself."

Harp didn't respond for the longest time. At his

side, Kyran stood biting a nail, probably as a substitute for the heads-up device analyzer he had usually stuck between his teeth.

"Kyran," Harp said. As if he'd been waiting for the opportunity to speak, Kyran jumped to attention.

"That is very unlikely," he said. "In fact, I would say impossible."

Darren opened his mouth, no doubt wanting to disagree, but Kyran was on a roll.

"The mere infancy of the wormhole generator and the historical reports of the initial test indicate as much. Scientists might have been able to open a wormhole, but there are no reports that they had even the slightest idea where it went. Even the placement of the opening turned out to be problematic—that's what has gotten us into trouble in the first place. Even if Sulos did manage to open a hole near the sun and managed to suck out its hydrogen, what would he do with it?"

Kyran drew in a breath and almost as an afterthought added, "Besides, there are still plenty resources that he needs besides energy, and he can only get those here."

This time it was Kyran who looked smug, but Darren didn't relent. He pointed at Harp as he spoke.

"Is this what the council has taught you—to ignore your instincts and trust what these little pencil pushers tell you?"

Harp didn't move a muscle as he listened to Darren spew his venom. Any other rebel would have lashed out at the council reference. We might have worked for them at one time, but by going along with Sulos's plan to keep silent and not inform the citizens of this planet, they had betrayed our people and not just the ones working at the plants or the ones who had lost family members. They had betrayed all of us. Despite the accusation, Harp remained as calm as ever.

"He is going to use the generator, and we need to destroy it before he destroys us all and that's why I sped up the attack on the power plant," Darren said. "And this is exactly the reason why I didn't let you in on it, because you're too weak to make the hard decisions."

Harp's gaze narrowed on Darren. A muscle flexed in his jaw as Harp took his time to address the one-eyed man.

"So, your priorities went from helping the plant workers to sacrificing them in the name of stupidity."

I had a feeling Darren didn't agree with Harp's assessment from the way that he puffed up his chest and balled his fist.

"You have no right—" Darren started to say but was soon interrupted by a commanding yet warm voice.

"Perhaps it is time for a break."

We all turned in the direction that the voice had come from, and I wasn't surprised to see Monroe step out from the shadows of a parked Hymag. As always, he wore a tailored suit designed to accentuate his broad shoulders, in a soft yellow that made his dark skin stand out. Gray overruled what must have once been jet-black hair, but the lack of lines on his face made it impossible to guess his age. He must have been watching us from a distance for a while now.

"Great," Darren said, "the council is here." The disdain in his voice was evident, but Monroe chose to ignore it.

"We have all suffered a great loss, and we shouldn't draw any hasty conclusions," Monroe said as he approached the table. He stopped at Harp's side, but their eyes never met. Instead, they kept their gazes directed at Darren, who tried not to squirm under their scrutiny.

Apparently annoyed, Darren said, "We have to go back and retake Two before Sulos has a chance to strengthen his presence. If we don't, he'll use it to power the generator, and we'll all be dead before you know it."

It was clear that Kyran's words hadn't made much of an impression on Darren. He was still hell-bent on stopping Sulos from using the generator. Darren had one good point, though.

Power Plant Two stood closest to the City of Nebula and the generator was located on the city's outer rim. Massive amounts of energy would be needed to create a wormhole, and taking out Two would have provided a strategic advantage. The reason that we hadn't gone straight after the generator came down to pure logistics. It was hard maneuvering platoons of rebels underground, especially with a limited number of Hymags at our disposal. Besides, we didn't have the rebels to spare, and by focusing on the plants, we had the advantage of working alongside the Power Plant Resistance.

If Darren had himself convinced that Sulos was about to destroy us using the generator, it made sense that he had jumped the gun on Two, but I had to agree with Harp that it wouldn't be likely for Sulos to use it just yet. There had to be a different reason for cutting back on transporting energy cylinders. *Maybe Sulos needed room on the freighters for something else—but what?* Kyran's mention of Icordia didn't sit right with me, and I wondered what they had to do with all this.

"You have heard what the young man has just explained," Monroe said and raised a hand to indicate Kyran. "There is no need to make overhast—"

"That is exactly your problem, you and that council of yours. You refuse to make the hard decisions, and it's us workers that have to suffer in the end," Darren said in a loud voice that hovered on the brink of yelling. "I'll bet that you have already booked your ticket for the first flight out of here."

Monroe sighed, he looked weary, and I couldn't blame him. He did not need to defend his presence within the council. We needed eyes and ears on what the council, and therefore what the government, was doing and with Monroe being third alderman to the City of Subterra, he had a front-row seat. Of course, the council had no idea of Monroe's connection to the rebels and the fact that he was the one feeding us crucial information.

"You have no idea what you're dealing with," Monroe said.

"If you don't help us, then we'll do it ourselves," Darren continued. "We are going to stop Sulos from using that generator with or without you."

Darren opened his mouth in a likely attempt to keep his argument with Monroe going, but I interjected before he could.

"Is there any word from Two?" I asked. "What's the status of the operation?"

Darren had no qualm about projecting his annoyance of my interruption on his face, and while the others looked at me stupefied, Harp eyed me with suspicion.

"It looks like no efforts have been put into resuming energy production," Kyran replied.

"Any repercussions up top?" I continued. I didn't need to explain that I meant maintaining the shields to protect the cities and its people.

Kyran ran his fingers over his pad and frowned before he said, "From what I can tell, none whatsoever, but it does seem our government has stepped in by rerouting our own power output to help sustain the districts' needs."

"What!" Darren exclaimed as he shot Monroe an accusing glare. "You are all traitors."

"Something else is going on here," I said, ignoring Darren and his outburst. "Sulos wants us to believe that he doesn't care about the earth, that it is dead anyway, that all he cares about is getting what he needs from this place. The threat of opening up a wormhole was just a way to get the Subterran government to play along."

I wasn't sure if anyone had even paid attention to what I'd said with Darren vocalizing his discontent, but Kelle, who was standing silently at Saera's side, crossed her arms over her chest as she said, "And by killing all those people in Two, he proved that he isn't afraid to come through on that threat." The bitterness in her words was palpable and her mask was in place, but it wasn't hard for me to see she had trouble holding up her stoic appearance.

"Everyone knows now what he is willing to do," Saera said, stepping closer to Kelle. "By now they'll have pledged their full support."

"And if Henkel finds out we had anything to do with what happened in Two," Reece added, "then the rebels are screwed."

Reece referred to Elise Henkel, second alderman to Subterra and member of the council. The woman had been part of the government for as long as I could remember, and it wouldn't surprise me if she'd be the one who had initiated helping the districts by supplying them with energy to sustain the shields.

We had only met briefly after we had obtained the information from the ArtRep computers and had failed to distribute this data among the main population. It turned out that the woman with the long white hair and wrinkles who had shown the years on her face was partly responsible for holding back that information. I had always suspected that she must have struck some kind of deal with Sulos, but there was no way to prove that.

"The question is," Harp said, "what is it that Sulos

is after?"

We all turned in Harp's direction. Despite Darren's ongoing tirade, Harp had followed our conversation. I had no answer to his question, though, and I wondered if Harp had figured it out and just wasn't telling us. The expression on Harp's face was unreadable to me as he turned back to face the others.

"Enough!" For a second time, Harp's voice boomed inside the domed space. If I didn't know any better, he looked like he might have lost his temper. "You," he said with his gaze fixed on me and the others standing behind me, "go home and get some rest."

Feeling a bit shocked, I glanced over my shoulder and noticed the others had similar wide-eyed expressions.

"And you, follow me," Harp said to Darren. "We're going to talk this out in a more private setting."

Harp turned to face Monroe and nodded. "Please join us," he said.

"I will join you in a moment," Monroe replied. Harp raised an eyebrow but didn't add anything else before he nodded and stomped away.

I watched as Darren took a moment to talk to his lieutenant and then reluctantly followed Harp. My body still reeled with tension as I just stood there. The accusations going back and forth didn't sound that promising for the alliance that our group of rebels had formed with the Power Plant Resistance. The fact was that we needed each other if we wanted any chance of defeating Sulos, and I hoped Harp would manage to talk some reason into Darren or at least calm things down.

"Could I have a word with you, Ms. Lux?" a warm-sounding voice said. Despite the soft-spoken words, I flinched as I realized who had uttered them. A kind smile graced Monroe's face as he gestured with a hand for me to join him.

We walked a few steps away from the table and the others. I briefly checked behind me and noticed Saera and the rest of our group huddled up together. I probably had a little time before we left.

"What is it that I can help you with?" I asked as I came face-to-face with Monroe.

He smiled again, but this time, it didn't reach his eyes. "I was just wondering how you were doing," he said.

I blinked in surprise, not sure of what to make of his question. It seemed harmless enough and it would even be appropriate among friends, but it wasn't as if Monroe and I were friends. In fact, I hardly knew him at all. I was aware that he had some longtime relation with Harp and that he played an intricate part in this rebellion. He was the one who kept us informed of all the actions taken by the Subterran government. As third alderman of Subterra and along with a seat on the council, he had a strong influence and often used it to our advantage.

"I, uh...I'm fine, thank you," I said without

stumbling too much over my own words.

Monroe stared directly into my eyes as he asked, "No residual aftereffects of the procedure?" This time he had me at a loss for words.

"Wha-what?"

He blinked and shook his head as if he realized the intrusiveness of his question.

"I'm sorry," he said, "but I'm curious." He shot me a hesitant smile before he continued. "You see, my son…he, too, has been taken, and you have given me hope that one day he might come back to us."

Apparently, my brain needed to play catchup to what Monroe had just told me because I could only glare at him for the longest time. *Had he just said to me that his son had been turned into an enforcer?*

"How?" was all I could think to ask. Monroe looked over my shoulder seemingly staring off into space and shrugged.

"One day, he left for work, and he never came home," he said before he blinked and returned his attention back to me. "I want to tell his wife and children that there is still hope."

"How did you find out about him being an enforcer?" I asked.

Monroe gestured in the direction in which Harp and Darren had disappeared as he said, "Harp, of course."

"Ah," I said and couldn't hide a knowing smile. Monroe instantly shook his head.

"It is not what you think," he said. "Yes, Harp informed me about my son, but I was the one to offer my assistance to the rebels for his help. That was five years ago."

"That's a long time," I muttered more to myself than to Monroe. That was already three years longer in the service of the Tenebrae Enforcer Department than I had been.

"I apologize," Monroe as he inclined his head. "I do not wish to bother you with this, but I could not help my curiosity and just wanted to speak to you."

He turned to leave, but before he could walk away, I asked, "What's his name?"

Monroe bowed his head and kept his back turned to me as he replied, "Akiyo."

"Akiyo," I said under my breath as Monroe walked off.

It seemed everyone had their own reasons for doing the things they did, although they didn't seem to be so different from one another.

It all came down to missing loved ones. *Wasn't that the reason why I had volunteered in the first place?* Memories are strange things. I had lost mine for a while, because of a safety feature ArtRep had built into its artificial representations or ARs. Enforcers could be better controlled without those pesky memories.

After Saera and the others had pulled me out of that world, there was nothing more that I wanted than getting my memories back. I had my wish granted after doctors removed the neuro-regulator from my head. Except for the enforcer memories, everything had returned, including the memories I could have done without.

Memories that dealt with loss and grief. Memories that after all these years could still break my heart as if it had happened yesterday. My parent's death was one of those memories. A memory that had turned out to be false and one of the reasons I had volunteered to become an enforcer.

Saera's dad and my parents hadn't died in a plant mishap; they'd been taken. Harp had warned beforehand that there was no indication that they had served as enforcers or that they were still alive, but that didn't stop me from hoping. Somewhere deep inside me, I had held on to the idea that maybe my parents were still out there. This had driven me to do things that may or may not have been the right thing, but either way had cost me dearly. The same could be said for Monroe.

His actions could lead to being tried for treason if he were ever found out. Although, if Sulos had his way, there wouldn't be much of life left on this planet, let alone a government or a court to convict him.

I watched him leave and wondered if he would ever get his son back at all. Five years of maintaining order within the districts meant Akiyo would have caused a lot of hurt to a lot of people whose only faults often were that they were trying to stay alive.

Kyran had erased most of the atrocities that I had committed from my mind, and they still haunted me. I just hoped someone would be able to do the same thing for Akiyo—if he managed to get out at all. The thought sent a shiver down my spine.

FOUR

SAERA

MAECE LOOKED a bit shell-shocked as Harp left us standing there around the conference table and even more so after she had had a talk with Monroe. I had no idea what the alderman had to discuss with Maece, but from the gloomy expressions on their faces, it appeared to have been an intense conversation.

The way Maece stood there she reminded me of that skinny, frizzy-haired little kid who'd managed to coerce that bear away from me. She looked so lost, and all I wanted to do was throw my arms around her and hug her, but everything that had happened these past two years kept me from doing just that. Kyran mentioning Icordia only fueled those memories.

Believing she had died had nearly destroyed me. If it hadn't been for Kelle and the guys, I didn't think I'd have been able to go on. Since I'd been six years old, she'd been my best friend and confidante. We might not have had the same biological parents, and we might not look anything alike, but we'd been sisters in every other sense of the word.

The relief and joy I had felt after we'd found out she hadn't died seemed bigger than anything I had ever felt in my life, and even with her mind all wiped and memories gone, I knew we would find that bond again. I could never have imagined that Maece would have chosen that path for herself. That she would have decided to become an enforcer and left us all thinking she had died.

Remembering the day that she had disappeared still brought tears to my eyes, but that didn't mean I hadn't forgiven her. She had placed her life on the line for all of us and that had to count for something.

Still, I didn't seem to be able to bridge the chasm that had formed between us. Something had shifted ever since she had come back, and the change threatened the bond we once shared. It felt as if some unseen force was trying to pull her away from me and all I could do was watch. Nothing I did seemed to resonate with her in the way I wanted to, so I kept my distance as I watched her standing there staring into space like a confused little kid while all I wanted to do was to comfort her.

"That was so not informative—at all," Reece said. I turned to face him and met a pair of weary eyes. His eyes shifted to where Maece stood behind me, and he plastered a grin on his face like only Reece could. "What do you say we go to the Bolder Bar and get wasted?"

I recognized his attempt to lighten the mood and

figured we could use the distraction.

"Haven't you killed enough brain cells drinking mushroom ale?" I said raising an eyebrow. "It's not as if you had plenty to begin with."

"Oh," Reece said, jabbing a fist to his chest as if he were going to stab himself. "Saera, you hurt my feelings; you coming?"

"Can I come?" Riffy asked, still looking a bit dazed after having been berated by Reece.

"Your presence is always required," Reece said to him before turning back to me. I sighed as I considered his proposition, but it didn't seem right at a time like this. Fortunately, it wasn't me who had to be the voice of reason.

"How about we just go home?" Kelle said. Her voice sounded even more timid than usual. In fact, none of them had been very vocal in the hours since we'd returned from the plant. Considering what had happened, that wasn't strange. I had seen the bodies of all those people. Even though I had only met him briefly, the sight of Clyde's body hanging in his harness had shaken me. All those deaths seemed so futile. Bile rose up in my throat, and my stomach churned as I thought about it, but it wasn't as if it was something we'd never seen before.

We'd all grown up inside those plants, and death was part of everyday life. If it wasn't an accidental explosion that killed dozens, or an overeager enforcer beating people down, then dying of hunger would keep the whitewasher employed. Someone needed to keep the streets from filling up with the dead.

Back at Two, I hadn't been underground with Reece, Kelle, and Riffy, but it seemed something had happened down on those lower levels that had affected them to the core. Kelle looked up with pleading eyes that told me she wanted to go home. I placed a hand on the back of her neck and let my fingers brush along the fine stubble of her shaved head.

"All right," Reece said, sounding like a whining kid, "let's go home—Maece?" Reece's loud voice had no trouble reaching Maece, who still stood separated from our group where Monroe had left her. She jerked her head as if she'd awoken from a bad dream and turned to face us. The intensity of her gaze made me feel uncomfortable, as if she were reading my mind somehow, and I looked away.

Reece pretended to cough after a moment of uncomfortable silence, and I wondered if he felt as uneasy as I did.

It turned out that he wasn't, as he casually walked over to her. I couldn't hear what was being said, but Maece smiled shyly as her eyes grew bright. Reece had a way of doing that to her. He reached out a tentative hand, and as their fingers met, the smile on Maece's face grew.

The two of them acted nothing like the couple I would catch making out in every room of our tiny home. From this distance, I got the sense that Reece was afraid to break her. Still, they had rekindled their ties, and I couldn't help feeling a bit jealous.

Things had changed after Maece had returned from her deliberate mission to join the enforcers. I hadn't noticed at first, but the more time passed, the more apparent it became.

The change might have had something to do with her telling me that she'd been stupid enough to have volunteered for the mission. Once the neuro-regulator had been removed from her head, the memories of her life before had returned, while Kyran had made sure that she couldn't recall anything from her time as an enforcer, but I remembered for the both of us.

What I couldn't remember was the last time that I'd been that angry with her. It didn't help that Reece had known all along, but I had a feeling it wasn't that, and I didn't think it was me. After all, I had a right to be angry, and Maece knew me well enough to know that I would eventually turn around. I just needed some time. Still, Maece seemed to take it harder than any other time we had fallen out. She kept probing me with that intense gaze of hers while keeping her distance as if she was afraid of me.

What was even worse was that she kept taking these risks, like when she handed me that heads-up device and, without warning, charged five freaks. *Hadn't she learned from the last time that she had confronted one of those things?* She had nearly died. Sure, it had worked out in the end, but I couldn't bear the thought of losing her again. Maece, on the other hand, didn't seem to care about any of that.

I couldn't figure out why she acted this way, and sometimes her attitude just infuriated me. *Why couldn't we just go back to the way we were?*

Maece and Reece walked over and at my side, I

noticed, Kelle had no problem with the underlying tension as I perceived it. She held Maece's gaze and nodded.

"Let's go home," Maece said in a subdued tone. Without another word, she walked in the direction of the Hymag platform.

"Yeah, go ahead. Don't worry about us," I called after her. "We'll be right behind you." I regretted the note of sarcasm as soon as it had left my mouth. *How was it that I could go from being worried about her to being pissed off at her within a fraction of a second?*

As soon as Maece was out of earshot, Reece said, "You know, you might want to give her a break."

I shot him a look that loosely translated to "Back off."

"Two years," I said with enough venom in my voice to make Reece flinch. "Both of you played us for two years."

I wasn't sure if it had been Reece that had triggered it or the events of the day, but I felt as if someone had pressed the vent button, and words poured out of me.

"And then she comes back, and everything seems fine until she drops that little bombshell on me like, *'Oh, I faked my own death. Sorry about that.'*"

I threw my hands up in the air as if that would clarify how I felt. "And I get it. I really do. I understand why she did what she did and I'm trying my damnedest to get past it, but this…"

My voice broke, and I had to swallow. Tears stung at my eyes as I pointed a finger in the direction

Maece had gone. "I don't know who that is anymore."

Reece visibly swallowed as I held his gaze. He opened his mouth, but no sound came out. He seemed dumbstruck, which was something I hadn't ever witnessed from Reece. A hand on my arm forced me to look down into dark eyes filled with concern.

"Saera," Kelle said. Her voice barely rose above a whisper. She didn't have to add that I needed to calm down.

"I know. I know," I replied, blowing out a breath before turning to Reece. "Sorry."

"That's okay," he said with a shrug. He cocked his head as if he was considering something before opening his mouth again. "At the risk of getting my head ripped off," he said and took a tentative step back, "maybe you're asking for too much." The words had barely left his mouth before he grabbed Riffy by the shoulders and positioned him between us.

"Hey," Riffy said in surprise as he tried to wriggle from Reece's grasp.

Ignoring Riffy, I stared at Reece. I opened my mouth to reply but was unable to manage a quick retort. With a shrug Kelle told me that she agreed with Reece.

"I…," I started to say but stopped myself. A thin smile formed on Reece's lips, and it wasn't like the all-or-nothing charm offense that I was used to, which was probably for the best. In this rare moment, he looked sincere.

"I know she's been a bit off-kilter, but I'm glad

she's back, and it's not like you've welcomed her with open arms after her confession," Reece said.

"I think I've had the right to be angry," I snapped. "And if she continues to go head-to-head with those freaks, we'll probably have to organize another wake, and that's just…" The words to convey what I wanted to say eluded me, and I took a shuddering breath.

"She seems to know what she's doing though," Kelle said.

"You have to admit that she kicks ass," Reece added, and the look of pride on his face felt endearing and aggravating at the same time.

"Besides," Riffy said, still wedged in the middle, "she did have a neuro device stuck in her brain that messed with her head. We all know how that changed Spiro. Maybe Maece's change is just different."

My eyes shot to Riffy, and he shrugged. Behind him, Reece mimicked Riffy's gesture.

I groaned in frustration. Maece had been gone for two years, and I didn't want to settle for a different version. *Was it so wrong that I wanted my sister back?*

"I don't think she's changed that much," Kelle said and squeezed my arm, "but I do think Riffy's right. That device has messed with her head. Besides, she feels guilty about what she's done and thinks she's the reason for what happened in Two."

"That is just plain ridiculous," I said as I wondered about Kelle's insight. "Did she talk to you about this?"

Kelle nodded, and I threw up my arms in despair.

"That's just great," I muttered. Instead of talking to me, Maece was talking to the most unlikely person in our group. Yes, Kelle was everything to me, but even though their bond had grown over the years, it wasn't like Kelle was Maece's go-to person to talk about stuff—that was me. We shared things she didn't even want Reece to know.

"I think she's jealous," Reece said with a wink in Kelle's direction. Kelle's eyebrow rose as I pointed a finger at Reece.

"You have a big mouth, you know that," I said just before Kelle grabbed my hand.

"She just needs time," she said as her fingers entwined with mine.

"I agree," Riffy added.

"And I," Reece chimed in.

Taking a deep breath, I nodded and could only hope that they were right. Patience had never been my strong suit, but it seemed I had no choice.

"Besides," Reece said with a grin that could only mean mischief, "it's kind of nice having some peace and quiet at home."

I glared at him. He had clearly made a dig at me talking too much, but his remark seemed so out of place that again I couldn't think of a quick retort. The longer it took for me to reply, the more extensive the grin on Reece's face became.

"You should talk," I finally managed and intended to stab a finger into his chest. As soon as I came close enough, though, he used Riffy for cover. "You drive the whole neighborhood insane with your pranks." I tried to keep a firm tone but had to smile at Reece's antics to keep Riffy positioned between us.

I finally gave up and found myself staring in the direction that Maece had gone. She was nowhere to be seen.

"She'll find her way," Reece said, sounding serious again. Our eyes met, and I sighed. As usually, Reece had managed to defuse the situation, and I wasn't ungrateful for that. Perhaps I should also take his advice and give Maece a break.

"I hope so."

"Trust me," Reece added. As I looked into his blue eyes, I knew that he believed what he was saying. I figured he had as much riding on this as I had. He still loved Maece, but he didn't seem as concerned about the situation as I was.

Those two had dabbled around each other from the moment they had met. The relationship had turned serious about a year before Maece had left. I clearly remembered the first time that I had caught her sneaking out of Reece's room. The combination of embarrassment and bliss plastered on her face was unforgettable. I couldn't even fathom how Reece had been able to let her go. On the other hand, I knew better than anyone that, once Maece had made up her mind, there was no turning back.

Maybe it was just me, and I was asking too much. For some reason, Maece and I had found ourselves on opposite sides of a chasm, and we had to find a way to bridge it.

"He's right, Saera," Kelle said. I smiled as I looked down at Kelle and pulled her closer. Even though she put on a brave face, I had a feeling

Maece wouldn't be my only concern after today's events.

"Let's go find Tyrel and see if she can arrange a trip home," I said as I kissed the top of her head. Riffy's head perked up at the mention Tyrel's name. It seemed our friend had created a special interest in the young woman who had often saved our butts with all her technical skills. Like with Kyran, we often depended on Tyrel and her quick thinking to help us to execute our missions. Both Kyran and Tyrel might be tech geeks and often only accompanied us as a voice over the communications feed, but they're very much part of the team.

"I'll do it," he said, and before I could reply, he hurried off in the direction of the workstations.

As we walked up to the workstations, we found Tyrel where I'd expected her to be. The young woman with shades of red and green in her hair looked utterly engaged with the screen in front of her, and her fingers typed ferociously. We also found someone we hadn't expected, and Riffy didn't appear very happy about it.

Miguel, Darren's lieutenant, sat with his butt perched on Tyrel's workplace, supporting a toothy grin. Tyrel ignored him, though, and kept her eyes fixed on the monitor. She typed something and then turned her gaze to Riffy.

"You'll be able to depart in thirty minutes," she

said. At the shy smile she gave him, Riffy's face turned red.

"Oh, uh…," he stammered. "Thanks." Tyrel returned her attention to the screen, but not before her cheeks turned a similar color red. Reece poked me in the arm and, our previous interaction apparently forgotten, grinned like an idiot as he gestured with his chin in the direction of the two.

"So," Miguel started to say, drawing out the word. "Once your friends depart, maybe you and I could go and find something to eat?"

The smile on his face widened, showing even more of his incredibly white teeth. Miguel turned out to be a cocky fellow, and I had to admit he looked the part. He seemed to know it, too, judging by the way he pulled a hand through his wavy black hair and how he gave Tyrel a grin that could have been right out of Reece's how-to-swoon-a-girl textbook.

Riffy recognized it, and he shifted uncomfortably while his eyes held a particular kind of dread that made me smile and feel for him at the same time. Tyrel returned her attention to her fingers on the keyboard as if to hide her face, which had turned as red as the color she'd dyed her hair.

"Oh, I'm sorry," Reece exclaimed as he threw himself against the desk and pretended to grab Miguel to maintain his balance. In a move that was anything but clumsy, Reece took Miguel by the shoulders and maneuvered him away from the desk. "Listen, Mike— it was Mike, right?"

Miguel looked a little abashed by the intervention.

There was no way that Reece did not know the young man's name. We had met him on several occasions, and he was never very far from Darren's side. Still, Miguel managed to stay polite as he replied, "It's Miguel."

"Oh, I'm sorry," Reece said again, "but listen, I wanted to talk to you…you're like Darren's little minion—I mean, right-hand man, right."

Miguel's demeanor changed as he raised an eyebrow and gave Reece an annoyed look. Reece ignored him and kept talking nonsense as he guided Miguel away from the table.

The four of us stared after them, and I noticed a big smile on Tyrel's face. Riffy fiddled with his jacket, not having a clue what to do next. It seemed so obvious that the two of them were into each other, and it would be so much easier if just one of them gathered the nerves to say it. As it was, they both were too shy to talk to each other. Maybe they were just being shy with all of us around, and I figured we'd give them some time alone.

"Riffy, why don't you finish up, and we'll meet you in the Hymag?" I said and took Kelle's arm.

Riffy gave me a wide-eyed look that would've had me laughing aloud if I weren't biting my lip to prevent me from doing just that. As if that wasn't enough, Kelle gave him a little push with her prosthetic arm. The mechanical appendix worked similarly to the exoskeleton suit, providing additional strength, and that little nudge had Riffy nearly tumbling into Tyrel's lap. Unable to contain myself for long, I tugged on

Kelle's arm and dragged her away from the scene before I would burst out laughing.

"Now don't say I never help you with your little schemes," Kelle said. There was a hint of a smile on her face that made me sigh in relief, but I had a feeling something still lay heavily on her shoulders.

This feeling became apparent as she fell silent on the walk across the platform. Kelle kept her eyes downcast as if she were hiding from me.

I hadn't had a chance to talk to her yet about what had happened on those lower levels at the time Sulos had flipped the kill switch. Of course, I could imagine what had happened; I had seen it with my own eyes, but something had hit Kelle hard, seemingly harder than the rest of us, because I'd never seen her this withdrawn.

We neared the Hymag, and I couldn't see Maece but decided to wait before talking to Kelle. She wasn't a person to easily open up, and I knew she'd shut down if someone else were present. This would have to wait until we got home.

Kelle climbed up onto the platform and held out a hand to help me up. I took it, but she didn't release my grip after we were both standing on the platform. Instead, she pulled me to her and wrapped her arms around my waist. Her action surprised me a little. On the Hymag platform, shadow enveloped us because of the lack of light, but it wasn't as if we were hidden from the people working at the control stations. Not that I cared who saw us, but Kelle wasn't usually like this. She rested her head on my chest, and being taller than her, I pressed my cheek to her forehead. In return, I held her tight, and as I caressed the stubble on her head with the tips of my fingers, I took a moment to enjoy the intimate embrace, but I also knew this wasn't about that.

"Hey, what's wrong?" I asked and pulled away a bit to take her face in my hands, forcing her to look into my eyes. What I saw in those eyes, nearly broke my heart. She appeared to be on the brink of tears. I'd known Kelle for years, and I don't think I had ever seen her this distraught.

"Baby, you've gotta talk to me," I said in a gentle tone. "You're hurting and I…" I hesitated, not sure what to say. In the time we'd been together it was usually Kelle comforting me over the loss of Maece. This turnaround was new to me. She shook her head, breaking my grip on her face, but she didn't let go of my waist as she placed her head on my chest again.

"He's dead," she said a moment later. I wasn't sure who she was talking about, so I decide to wait her out and gently stroked the back of her neck. "This kid." Her words came out on half a sob, and I kissed the top of her head but kept silent. This wasn't the easiest thing to do for me as I had a tendency to talk during intense moments.

"His name was Daely, and he was so scared," she said at barely a whisper. "I knew we were running out of time, but the kid was so scared of getting zapped." I felt my heart sink as I realized where this was heading. "I was fooling around a bit, to put him more at ease. I just wanted…"

"You were trying to help him," I said, leaning into her. Kelle shook her head fervidly and nearly choked on her next words.

"I got him killed. He died in my arms because I screwed up."

Maybe that was the reason Maece had talked to Kelle because they felt a similar burden. As she cried, I knew there wasn't anything I could say to ease her pain and that she probably wouldn't even listen to me, but I had to try.

"I'm so sorry, baby," I said as I caressed the back of her neck. "This wasn't your fault."

I held her tight as I repeated the words over and over again. It must have taken a while for Kelle to calm down, but for all I cared, time might as well have stopped. It was only when I spotted Reece and Riffy waiting patiently as they sat on the conference table that I noticed that time had passed. I couldn't help a faint smile at the fact that we knew each other this well and that they knew Kelle would need some space.

From the corner of my eye, I saw Maece standing in the doorway of the Hymag, silently watching us. All the awkwardness that had occurred between us vanished from my mind as I held her gaze for the first time in a long time. I needed her there. She was my sister, and we had always dealt with these things together, and somehow in this moment the weirdness that plagued our relationship seemed to belong to the past. She didn't come any closer but gave a brief nod as she stood there in that doorway watching us, where I needed her to be—in silent support.

FIVE
MAECE

FOR A BRIEF MOMENT, everything had seemed fine. As if nothing had happened, I felt connected to Saera even though she had her hands full comforting Kelle. That's where her focus stayed as the Hymag brought us back to Subterra and I felt our connection slip again. Nobody felt like talking, and that was fine by me. My mind was too occupied, and I couldn't even decide why. *What the hell was wrong with me?*

At the central Hymag station in Subterra, we met a flurry of activity. We all knew what was going on, and we kept our heads down as we stepped from the Hymag and onto the platform. Men and women of the different branches of the government were getting themselves ready to receive the few refugees that had made it out of the power plant alive, those few that we had managed to evacuate before the enforcers had overrun our perimeter. Soldiers guarded the area and aid workers set up their medical gear to give the refugees a quick once-over before they shipped them to a different location.

As far as the members of the government or the council were concerned, we had nothing to do with the attacks on the power plants. Along with Darren and Monroe, Harp had created a trail that led all evidence to the Power Plant Resistance. According to official records, no rebels had taken part in the failed attempt to liberate Plant Number Two. This meant we could move around freely and didn't have to hide our faces, although it wouldn't be wise to stand out or draw attention to ourselves.

Maybe that's why Darren had been so angry. The lack of support from the government or the council limited the number of resources and manpower Harp had available. However, for some reason, his anger seemed directed at me, which seemed unreasonable —*or was it?* The fact that Darren had gone in without disclosing it first had meant even fewer boots on the ground within the plant, and that was on him, but still, if I'd been paying better attention, I might have seen through Sulos's plan sooner.

"Watch it," Saera said as she tugged on my arm. Four armed guards marched by, and I would have bumped into them if Saera hadn't redirected me.

"Sorry," I replied and pulled away from her. Avoiding her, I kept my gaze riveted on the ground until I reached the exit. Perhaps I should've exploited the moment and built on that brief connection I had sensed back at the base, but the stupidity of almost bumping into a guard could have cost us a lot. It would have drawn attention to us, and that would not have been good.

If Harp hadn't created this deception that none of the rebels had been involved in the liberation of Two, we wouldn't have been able to come home. We had mostly Monroe to thank for that because of the information he fed the council. As third alderman to Subterra, he risked a lot on the feeble notion that maybe one day he might see his son again, and I felt grateful for that. I needed the reassurance of being able to go home without the fear of getting arrested. Something stupid like bumping into a guard could elicit a whole bunch of questions raining down on us, because even though the council supported by the government endorsed the existence of a rebel force operating in secret, officially we were branded as outlaws. The government would never admit that they had anything to do with us, especially not since the districts viewed us as terrorists. If questioned, Harp would surely clear things up, but that would take time and lots of paperwork, and I didn't want to be responsible for that. I had done enough.

Within the confines of our small apartment, the silence felt even more palpable. Despite the fact that we all had our own private space, the place wasn't that big and, with the likes of Reece and Riffy present, usually filled with a lot of noise. It wasn't that uncommon to have a neighbor standing at the front door complaining about one thing or another, but that hadn't happened in a while. It seemed everything had changed after I had told my friends and sister the truth about what had happened.

I rubbed the back of my neck as I walked down the hall toward our main living room. After my absence, I'd spent a lot of time in my bedroom, especially after I'd told the others the reasons for me becoming an enforcer. It all just felt too overwhelming, and I couldn't handle the looks. Saera was still angry with me, and she had a right to be, but something in the back of my mind told me that this had more to do with me than with her. I just had to figure out what.

Unfortunately, at this point, everyone else seemed to have decided that they wanted to be alone. Reece's door was closed, and so was Saera's, or should I say, Kelle's. Somewhere along the way, Saera had moved from hers to Kelle's room.

I stopped at the entrance to the living room and was surprised to see it wasn't empty. Riffy sat on the couch and looked to be in a captivating conversation with Spiro. He nodded his head and smiled at something Spiro had said. It was good to see some of that glint back in Riffy's eyes and the dimples that graced his chubby cheeks as he smiled.

Spiro had this ability to make everyone around him feel at ease. His presence oozed a calm that rubbed off on people. Even watching the man trapped in a child's body as he managed to create a smile on Riffy's face made me smile. He might have looked like a twelve-year-old boy, but as Reece liked to put it, "Spiro has the mind of a god." But then Reece had always had a flair for the overdramatic. The thought made me grin, and I felt more at ease than I had in a long while.

Something had shifted; I could sense it. Ever since I had seen Saera comfort Kelle on that Hymag platform and our eyes had met. The anger I had faced for weeks now hadn't been there. All I could sense was fear that came with her concern for Kelle, and I couldn't help but foster hope from that.

I had almost felt comfortable enough to knock on Reece's door. Like with Saera, a distance had formed between us, but it hadn't been out of anger or regret. Reece wouldn't be Reece if he didn't make it clear to me what he wanted, and with every smile and sometimes a not-so-subtle remark, he had hinted that the door was open, so to speak. The space he allowed me was because he knew I needed it, not because he wanted to keep his distance. He always seemed to know what I needed. Whether it was a stupid joke to make me smile or a listening ear as I ranted about a fallout I'd had with Harp while drinking shots at a local bar, he always seemed to know.

"You'd be more comfortable sitting down," a voice said, pulling me from my thoughts. Riffy looked up and smiled as he saw me standing at the door. Spiro was sitting with his back to me and hadn't turned around. I hadn't made any noise, but it didn't come as a surprise that he had sensed my approach. Spiro had this way of knowing things. I didn't know how it worked. All I knew was that ever since that neuro device had been removed from Spiro's head, his synapses fired at inhuman speeds inside his brain, and because of that, his neurons were capable of efficient, lightning-fast thinking and communication. He couldn't just do this within his own head, but also within the minds of others. Even though his abilities should have been familiar enough to me because I'd known him for so many years, they still baffled me.

"Do not fear what you do not know and come join us." His words echoed in my head, and I didn't need to have seen his mouth to know it hadn't moved.

"I do not wish to disturb." The thought that formed my reply came naturally. Riffy sat on the couch, eyeing me expectantly, unaware of the silent communication between Spiro and me. Spiro turned, and a smile lit up his round face.

"Please, come join us," he said in a soothing voice, using his vocal cords this time.

I shifted an uncertain gaze between the two men sitting on the couch. I might have been looking for company, but I suddenly felt unsure about it. I couldn't help feeling as if this entire situation was my fault and that I didn't deserve to be here. *So many people had died because of my wrongdoing and now what? Was I supposed to pretend it never happened and just hope that the others would accept that?* Still, I found nothing confronting in their expressions and made my way over to them.

Riffy shifted to make room, but with the couch too small to accommodate all three of us and it not being much of a comfortable seat anyway, I opted to sit on the block of concrete that we used as a side table.

"Riffy tells me you've all suffered a great loss," Spiro said.

"Yeah, you might say that," I said and shot Riffy a comforting smile. "It's been a bad day."

"Great loss is accompanied by experience," Spiro replied.

I dropped my chin to my chest and managed to contain a groan. Spiro's tendency to talk in riddles could be utterly frustrating at times, but I knew he couldn't help himself. I guessed it was how his brain worked.

I figured he was right, though. We had suffered a significant loss, and it had been an experience. Not one, I would like to repeat, though. *But how would we ever be able to avoid it?*

With the debacle in Two, we had lost our only chance to make a dent in Sulos's plans. Instead of helping the plant workers we had ended up killing them–I had ended up killing them. We had resolved nothing and only made things worse.

Initially, we wanted to figure out what had happened to all those people who had somehow, mysteriously, died. After Harp had learned that these people hadn't died but were taken to serve as enforcers, I wanted to help. Especially after I had found out that my parents and Saera's dad might have suffered the same fate. As a child, I never questioned the deaths that plagued our existence. It was just our way of life. People died and disappeared all the time. Once I was old enough and had learned about what ArtRep was doing to these people, a twisted sense of hope rose inside me that maybe there was still hope for our parents. Only after some nagging persistence on my part, Harp had shared what he knew about the procedures a person would be subjected to in the early days of creating artificial representations that weren't exactly artificial.

The knowledge I gained evaporated that remaining hope and replaced it with a need for revenge, and it seemed so obvious for me to do what I did. I was fully aware of the stakes and knew what it would mean for me to join the Tenebrae Enforcer Department and what they would demand from me, but it seemed worth it. All those deaths that I'd caused as an enforcer might have seemed worth it if we'd managed to stop ArtRep. *But what was it that we had achieved? Nothing!* And now even more people had died. The only thing that I had ended up doing besides getting people killed was hurting my friends.

"It's all my fault," I muttered under my breath as I rubbed my temples.

I hadn't intended to say the words, the act only registered after I heard Riffy ask, "What is?"

I looked up in surprise and noticed his worried expression. His mouth hung half open in an O, and as his eyes grew wide, I quickly added, "Nothing, I was just–"

I was unable to finish my sentence as Riffy interjected, "You don't believe that crap Darren's been spewing, do ya?" I flinched unaccustomed by the harshness in Riffy's voice. "Because he's just trying to hide his own screwup." Riffy jumped to his feet, his face flushed and pointing a finger at me. "That guy is just an idiot, and there is no way that you should feel—"

A small hand gripped Riffy's wrist and interrupted his rant.

"Responsibility can only be professed by oneself," Spiro said. Riffy turned to the childlike figure sitting on the couch and glared at him. The confused expression on his face along with his attempt to defend me made me smile, but I had a feeling that I understood what Spiro was saying. It wasn't Darren's accusation that had me feeling this way—the feeling of guilt was my own.

Riffy plopped back down on the couch and apparently hit the solid surface harder than intended.

"Ouch," he muttered and then rubbed his butt.

A high-pitched beep sounded inside the apartment and Riffy jumped up from the couch again.

"I should get that," he said. Before he could move to open the front door, I called out to him.

"Riff." He froze and shot me a wide-eyed look. I stood, opened my arms, feeling appreciative of my friend for the way he wanted to stick up for me, and hugged him. "Thanks."

"For what?" he asked as he returned the hug.

"For being you." Riffy grinned from ear to ear as he gazed up at me.

"That's easy," he said and then set off to open the door and let in whoever was visiting at this late hour.

"Absolution can only come from the heart that can be most difficult to convince," Spiro said. I turned to the couch where he was still sitting, his face marred by concentration and his eyes closed. I was hearing him in my head again. He opened his eyes and smiled at what I assumed to be at the look of confusion on my face.

I had trouble deciphering Spiro's words most of the time, and I often wondered if he actually had some higher form of speech or if his brain had gotten jumbled up so much that he had trouble making sense.

Reading the question from my face, he added, "No amount of forgiveness will absolve without one's own permission."

Seeing my raised eyebrow, Spiro shot me another knowing smile before he added, "Maybe you shouldn't be so hard on yourself."

Harp walked into the living room and put an end to my conversation with Spiro. He stopped at the large block of concrete that served as the dining table and let his eyes roam over us. To anyone else, Harp looked in control with his face deprived of any expression, his shoulders straight and his hands laced behind his back, but something was off. His eyes blazed with anger, and I didn't think I'd like what he had to say.

"Get them all in here," he said over his shoulder to Riffy.

———

I was right; I didn't like what Harp had to say at all. Once he had gathered us around the dining table, he had explained about the conversation he'd had with Darren and Monroe.

"You want us to do what?" Reece, who was sitting to my right, asked, appalled. Voices careened on and over each other after that.

Sitting across from me, Saera threw an arm up and nearly smacked Kelle in the face as she exclaimed, "That's the dumbest thing I've ever heard."

"Why is Darren dictating our next moves?" Kelle asked.

"I don't understand," Riffy said.

All around me, frustration rose, and I needed a moment to let it all sink in. Harp held his hands folded on the smooth surface of the rock as he sat at the head of the table. He appeared to be patiently waiting for the ruckus to die down, but I could tell he wasn't happy with the situation.

It seemed as if Darren Russ had left him without a choice, and all he could do was follow. Darren had threatened to move in on the remaining power plants without the rebels. Over the years, the Power Plant Resistance had grown quite a following, and cells had emerged in every plant located within district territory. I didn't doubt that he had the manpower to pull it off, but his fear of Sulos caused him to make rash decisions. He seemed convinced that Sulos would strike the sun with a wormhole within weeks, and he wasn't going to sit around and wait for that to happen. I just feared that the people working inside those plants would be the ones to pay the price.

Like Harp, I waited for the voices to die down and for the initial shock of the plan to fade before I spoke.

"Why would Darren want to hit the plants if he knows it won't do him any good in the first place?"

"Yeah," Reece chimed in, "it's not like that would stop Sulos from using the wormhole generator."

"He thinks that disrupting the power flow will render the generator useless," Harp replied in answer to Reece's question.

"And kill everyone living in the cities above ground," Saera chimed in.

"It doesn't make sense for Sulos to use the generator in the first place," Kelle said.

She was right. Sulos's space station wasn't near finished and would still need the space freighters to supply him with the resources to complete it. Resources he could only find on this planet. Besides, I doubted if Sulos even intended to destroy the earth. *Why would he even bother while he was tucked away at his own private space station?* He just needed the wormhole generator as a means to threaten our government to keep them from informing the public. The intel we had gathered on Sulos would cause riots, even in the districts and that meant he wouldn't be getting his precious resources.

"Because Darren is an idiot," Harp said. "But that doesn't mean our plan won't work." His eyes roamed across the table, searching out every one of us. "Darren is right about one thing: sitting around and doing nothing won't help us in the long run. That's why we need to take action now before Darren ruins everything, and Sulos would never expect a preemptive strike."

"Well, technically, it's your plan," Reece said, "and I have several problems with it." He sat up straighter as he started counting down on his fingers. "For one, you want to split up the team again." Reece shook his head. "Always a bad idea."

"Damn right, it is," Saera said under her breath. Reece nodded in Saera's direction before he gave Harp a look that basically said: "See, I'm not the only one," and then he continued.

"Two, you want us to steal a space freighter—bad idea. Three, you want us to fly that freighter and attack Sulos's space station—I'm not sure how to do that with an unarmed freighter anyhow. And in the meantime, you want us to sneak into the City of Nebula, infiltrate its outer rim and blow up a wormhole generator." Reece looked at his hand. "I'm running out of fingers here."

Although he'd done it in less than a minute, it seemed Reece had made an excellent summation of all the things Harp had intended for this team.

"This plan sucks," Saera said. As if she had just voiced all of our concerns with those few words, the room fell silent. She looked deflated as she slumped in her seat, while next to her, Kelle's body seemed to hold enough tension for the both of them. Riffy just looked shell-shocked, and I could hear Reece grind his teeth from where he was sitting next to me.

Spiro, who sat across from Harp, looked somewhat pensive to me. His eyes never veered from Harp, and I wondered if they might be having some private conversation between the two of them. I wouldn't put it past Harp, and Spiro was indeed capable of it. It made me wonder what else might have been said in all those briefings that had occurred before this one. Those times that I knew what Spiro could do, but never actually figured he would use his abilities to this degree.

"Let's go over the plan," Harp said. He cleared his throat and looked at us as we sat around the table before he drew in a breath and continued. "We have three objectives. The first one is to confiscate a space freighter capable of reaching Sulos's space station. This will be a joint venture where this team accompanied by a platoon of rebels will travel by Hymag to the outer rim of the City of Umbras. We have intel on a freighter that has been out of commission because of maintenance. By now the vessel should be in optimum condition for the trip."

Harp paused, probably because he knew that he had just explained the relatively easy part of the plan. That's why he took his time, and I realized that this must be eating at him too. We were his kids after all.

"What about the council?" I asked. "I'm sure deploying an entire platoon will come to their attention."

"If we pull this off, a shift in power will be unavoidable," Harp replied, "and then it won't matter what the council and, with them, the Subterran government thinks or does."

"*If* we pull this off," Reece said with emphasis on the first word.

"The remaining objectives will require splitting up the team," Harp started again, ignoring Reece and letting his gaze shift to me. "After obtaining the first objective, Maece, Reece, and Riffy will travel to the City of Nebula. The wormhole generator is located on its outer rim. Now, I know we all have our doubts that Sulos will use that generator, but that doesn't mean that the perception of the threat is any less to our government and Darren. Besides, some people might have additional agendas as it comes to their compliance with Sulos. So even though the compound is reportedly not heavily guarded, I doubt that information is correct. The plan is to execute a surgical strike. Infiltrate, plant explosives, and get the hell out."

Harp had a way of simplifying things that made the plan sound straightforward enough and not unlike operations we'd done before. But back then we would've had the whole team on one specific mission. An ominous feeling settled in the pit of my stomach, and I had a suspicion it wouldn't let up for a long time.

Harp waited for a beat, no doubt expecting a smart-ass remark of some kind, but none came. As he continued, he turned to Saera. "You, Kelle, and Kyran will board the freighter with the majority of the rebel platoon and proceed to the system Sulos occupies."

"Then what?" Saera asked. Harp shifted nearly

imperceptibly, but enough for me to see. The movement made my breath catch, and my stomach clenched. Even before he answered, I knew what he was going to say.

"We have no up-to-date intel on the station, and we'll need to withhold on the follow-up plan until we do," Harp said. "To do that we'll need to be able to communicate and that's why you will be dropping modified relay stations with built-in boosters along the way."

"Wait, what?" Reece said. "You're sending them out there without a plan. What kind of show are you running here?"

"You can't expect us to go out there blind!" Saera said as her blue eyes grew cold.

"We need to assess the situation first," Harp said, undeterred by Saera's gaze. I watched them both in their silent standoff and could almost feel the underlining current of tension build between them.

"I don't like this," Reece said under his breath. Leaning forward he added, "The moment that ship takes off, Sulos will know and what? You think he'll just sit around and wait for it to arrive?"

"He'll probably open fire the moment we show up on his radar," Kelle said. "There is no way that Sulos will let us just sit there and scope out the place." The fingers on Kelle's prosthetic hand twitched as she shot Saera a quick glance before returning her attention back to Harp. It seemed the young woman had also sensed the underlining tension.

"The station is not capable of that kind of firepower," Harp said.

"Sure, that makes sense," Reece said and sounded a bit condescending. "And he probably doesn't have any fighter crafts either—as in, armed fighter crafts." Harp slowly turned to Reece and narrowed his gaze. I had a feeling he might be losing his patience with us.

"From what Kyran has learned, the station is still fragile. Sulos won't risk—" Harp started to say as Saera spoke up.

"A fragile space station, you say." I could almost taste the bitterness in her tone as she added, "So, what? You want us to ram it?" Her steely gaze was still focused on Harp, who did not waver under her scrutiny. Saera's remark seemed a bit excessive, but I couldn't condemn her anger. I fully understood why Harp wanted us to go after the wormhole generator, because of the threat it posed, but the space station seemed an unnecessary objective.

"Since when do I need to explain—"

Sensing this conversation might get out of hand, I was about to interrupt when a voice I hadn't heard in a while drew all our attention to the other end of the table as Spiro said, "Harp, my old friend, considering the ramifications, perhaps it is wise to enlighten our young friends." Spiro's brows furrowed as the room fell silent. The moment stretched out, and from the look on Harp's face, I felt sure there was some fierce arguing going on between the two even though the rest of us could not hear it.

Neither of them looked pleased as Harp cleared

his throat before he said, "We have someone on the inside, and depending on the information, we'll either take actions to destroy the station or take over the entire operation."

As if his words broke the spell, Saera twitched, and her eyes swiftly shot to the young woman beside her before she turned to me. Her eyes held a determination that sent a chill down my spine. Her sharp-edged jaw clenched and the blue in her eyes appeared like ice, but for some reason I didn't feel that her anger was directed at me. Apart from that, her face showed nothing, although it seemed obvious she had something on her mind. I had a feeling she wasn't going to lay out her cards during this meeting, but I knew I was going to find out soon.

"So, while we are all risking our lives, what does our friend Darren intent to do?" Reece asked. The venom in his voice sounded obvious as he held Harp's gaze.

Without a hint of discomfort, Harp replied, "He is determined to go on with his plan. That is why we need to move fast."

"And you are just going to let him get away with that?" I asked and felt a bit surprised at the disdain in my voice.

"Darren has agreed to wait until the generator is destroyed," Harp said.

"You don't say," Reece said. "And what did you have to offer in return—your soul?" Harp shot Reece a look that made me think that Reece might not have been that far off with his remark.

"I told him we would release the intel on Sulos and transmit it on the Feed for everyone to see."

The room fell silent for a moment. This had been our initial plan, but Sulos's threat to the government had made a stop to that.

The Feed wasn't just a means to communicate; most of the information, like the news and official government announcements, were broadcast across the Feed. ArtRep maintained the underlying infrastructure and controlled the central network, although it was a known fact that anyone with enough knowledge of the system would be able to link up. Basically, anyone could tap into the vast communication network and download or upload anything they wanted or needed to know or share. Substantial penalties were put in place to discourage people with malicious intent to hack the system and undermine the government, but that didn't stop them from trying, and it wouldn't stop us rebels.

Getting the information out there wasn't the problem, and even though we had decided on releasing the information the first time, the decision wouldn't be any easier this time around. If word got out that Sulos had been using Subterrans abducted from their homes to build his enforcer army, it could cause riots and not just underground. He had used precious resources to build that space station of his, and he had no intention of letting anyone on, except for the few he had selected. We could safely assume that the citizens of the districts would not agree.

"Yeah right," Reece said elated, "good luck with that."

"I know we'd agreed on that before, but things have changed," Saera said. "We did all right on the first plant, so why can't we do that again and help our people that way? Releasing that information will only cause more disarray and more death."

"Hasn't Darren done enough?" Kelle said through clenched teeth. "You can't trust him." Kelle's hand, which had been resting on the table, had formed a white-knuckled fist, and Saera placed her hand over it.

"I don't," Harp said, "but this isn't just about the people in the plants."

"People serving as enforcers and those being turned into freaks are just as much a part of this," I said. All heads turned in my direction. A tiny part of me expected them to disagree or perhaps be indifferent, but I should have known we were of one mind on this.

"I agree," Harp said. For a long moment, no one spoke until an unexpected voice broke the silence.

"Uh…," Riffy said as he raised a careful hand. With that, he drew our immediate attention. Riffy wasn't one to speak up during meetings, but I guessed the stakes had never been this high before. "Sorry," he said, "I know I can be slow on the uptake, but I still don't get it."

Harp managed a few words in repeating the plan, but Riffy waved him off. "No, I don't mean about the what, but about the why," he said.

Raising an eyebrow, I sat up straighter, intrigued

by what was to come next. Reece shot me a look and mouthed the word, "What!"

"I mean, I get that taking down the generator will stop Sulos from threatening the planet, but why go up there at all?" he asked and pointed a finger at the ceiling. "And why is Darren holding all the cards?" Riffy's cheeks flushed red, but he stubbornly held Harp's gaze. A sense of pride rushed through me at the sight of the chubby-faced kid that had turned into a man during my absence.

Harp sat back without breaking eye contact with Riffy.

"That's a good question," Harp said and nodded appreciatively in Riffy's direction. Riffy's face nearly turned a shade of purple at Harp's gesture.

"Because Darren is just the excuse," Kelle said. "Isn't he?" There was a hardness in her voice that I had heard before, but not often directed at Harp. Kelle had always shown the utmost respect for Harp, and if there had been moments that she might have doubted his command, she had never voiced them. "You just want to go after Sulos and kill him."

I couldn't decide who to focus on as I shifted my attention from Kelle to Harp and back again as their silent standoff continued. Kelle might have a point. The plan to go after a space station with an unarmed freighter did not sound promising, and Harp had wanted to take Sulos down for years. Knowing Sulos, he would probably be hiding out on that station. However, in my opinion, the fault in Kelle's reasoning was that I couldn't believe that Harp would risk any of us on a futile mission.

"Do you have any idea of the scope of Darren's operation?" Harp said in a sharp tone.

The young woman didn't flinch and held his gaze as she slowly shook her head.

"He has hundreds of followers, and they don't give a shit about the people living up top. All they want is to get back some sense of control over their lives." As if to grab our attention Harp slammed his palm flat on the table. I flinched at the sound of his raised voice.

"This isn't just about the plant workers or about the resistance or even you and me. This is about all of us and something needs to be done."

Harp stood and leaned forward with his hands flat on the stone surface of the table as he said, "I do not enjoy sending good people into harm's way, and believe it or not, you are good people. Above all that, you are my people, but something needs to be done, or do you want to live out your lives in fear that Sulos can kill thousands with the flick of a switch? And I'm not even talking about the wormhole generator. How many still walk around with those neuro devices stuck in the back of their necks? Are you willing to risk those lives by doing nothing?" He paused to let his eyes roam around the table. "Are you?"

We all stared at him as we sat motionless in our seats. I had no idea what to make of Harp's outburst and had to remind myself to breathe. I'd never seen him like this. The silence seemed to build until the only person able to break it spoke up.

"Good people, ha," Reece said nodding his head. "I'm so touched." I shifted my gaze to Reece and noticed the pursed lower lip he had added for dramatic effect. An unintentional smile curved my mouth, and I shoved an elbow into Reece's side as he raised his hands and began to applaud. "Great speech, Harp. I'm so motivated right now. When can we go?"

For a moment I feared Reece had gone too far with his clapping, but the tiniest of twitches at the corner of Harp's mouth told me he was safe. Harp shook his head in disbelief and sat back down.

"Why do I bother with you all?" he grumbled, but I doubted the others had heard.

Reece's comments had lifted some of the tension in the room, but it wasn't long after that silence took over again. It gave me a chance to reminisce over Harp's words. He had spoken of good people, and although I felt touched by his reference to us, I knew this wasn't about us. Like he had said, this was about every single person on this planet. Still, it seemed as if he had successfully avoided Riffy's initial question and circumvented Kelle's remark. He was hiding something, and I needed to find out what.

I noticed Harp watching me, wide-eyed. His reaction only strengthened the feeling he was keeping something from us.

He still hadn't explained why he wanted to send the freighter. In his speech, Harp had hinted at being more concerned about the neuro devices than the wormhole generator. *Was that why he was planning the trip?* The generator could easily be destroyed but removing those neuro-regulators would take a lot more time. *Was Harp afraid that Sulos would do what he had in Two?* Not only thousands of workers had those devices embedded in the back of theirs heads but also enforcers working for Tenebrae. Subterrans who had their lives stolen.

I kept a close eye on Harp and wished I knew what he was thinking. It wasn't unusual for him to keep things from us and I felt pretty sure that he hadn't told us everything. If he kept things from us it would be in our best interest. I trusted him that much; how could I not?

He had rescued us from the plants in the same way that he had helped hundreds of kids in similar situations, but he had also taken us in when no one else wanted us. Subterra had systems in place that helped our people to live comfortably. There were none of the luxuries that I had seen in the districts, but there also none of the direness that the workers at the plants had to endure. Despite all this, not everyone was willing to take in a stranger's child. Especially not if there happened to be two who broke every rule just to be together.

The thought of Saera showing up at my new caretaker's home in the middle of the night made me smile, although the lovely lady who had taken me in hadn't been so happy about the fact that Saera had brought the authorities to her doorstep. We weren't exactly legal citizens, and Saera had unknowingly brought a whole heap of trouble down on the woman.

Fortunately, Harp had cleaned up the mess and,

after a couple of related incidents, had decided it was best to keep us close to him. Later, I'd found out something similar had occurred after he'd brought Riffy and Reece back from one of his plant visits.

Those kinds of selfless acts had ingrained my trust in Harp and made it difficult to believe he had any ill intent, but I couldn't help feeling that something was off.

A beep sounded, and Harp glanced at his wrist device.

"I have to go," he said as he stood. "Talk it over. I'll meet you at the base tomorrow morning and inform you about any other developments."

Harp inclined his head and then turned. He left the room without another word, and as if in agreement, we all stayed silent until I heard the front door click shut behind him.

SIX

SAERA

THE URGE TO jump up and scream profanities grew as a combination of rage and despair ran through my veins. I stopped myself, though, because at the same time I felt as if I was about to throw up. Harp had us backed into a corner this time, and I wasn't sure how to handle it.

"Does he really expect us to go through with this," I said. "I mean, I get it—greater good and all, but…" My voice trailed off, and I wasn't sure what I was trying to say. I glanced at Kelle who sat motionless by my side, her eyes glued to the surface of the table. "Don't we have a right to our own lives?" I was rambling, but I couldn't help myself. Unlike the others, I'd never been the perfect soldier. I just followed the rest.

"I don't think we have a choice," Maece said. I glanced up to where Maece stood in the center of the living room. She'd gotten up after Harp had left and had been staring down the hallway for a while. She turned with her arms folded across her chest.

"That seems to be your answer for everything, consequences be damned." Maece flinched at my hard words, and I instantly regretted them. In an attempt to compose myself, I closed my eyes for a second. Without turning away, I drew in a breath and opened my eyes to face her.

"Sorry," I said, "that was out of line." Relief washed over me as she nodded to accept my apology. I wasn't sure what had gotten over me, although the fact that Harp had just presented me with a suicide mission might have something to do with it. *What else could it be? Why would he send an unarmed freighter to go seek out a space station that, knowing Sulos would probably be armed to the teeth?*

Maece and I had enough issues to work out, so I shouldn't let my emotions get the best of me and lay blame where it didn't belong. Besides, I wasn't about to let Harp ruin all our lives, and I needed Maece's help with that.

"I don't know about you guys, but I'm in serious need of a drink," Reece said as he rose from his seat. He grinned, but I didn't sense any of the mischief that tended to twinkle behind those blue eyes. "Anyone else?"

"Shouldn't we at least talk about this," I said.

"Why?" he asked. "Is anyone planning on not going tomorrow?" Reece made sure to meet all of our gazes and when none of us replied he said, "Then what's the point. We're all just going to do as he says and we all know why that is, so…"

His voice trailed off as if he were giving us another chance to object before he added, "Drinks?"

Again, the room remained silent, and Reece shrugged as if he didn't care and turned to leave. "Suit yourself," he said over his shoulder. "If you change your mind, I'll be at the Bolder Bar."

He stopped at Maece's side, and placing a hand on her hip, he leaned in and whispered something in her ear. She nodded and shot him a brief smile before he turned to leave. As Reece made his way down the short hallway, Riffy shot up from his seat.

"Reece, wait up," he called out after the retreating form. "I'm coming with." Nearly stumbling over his own feet, Riffy stopped and turned around to face us. "See you guys later," he said. I wasn't sure if he'd meant it as a statement or a question, but I felt a reason to assure him.

"Count on it," I said, and my words collided with Maece.

"See you soon, Riff," she said. Riffy threw us a dimpled smile and took off after Reece. In the seat next to me, Kelle shifted, and I stood as she did. She looked weary, and the dark circles under her red-rimmed eyes confirmed it. This day had been unusually hard for her, and it showed on her face.

I internally cursed Harp. *Why couldn't he have waited a day or two before hitting us with this stupid plan of his?*

"I'm tired and going to bed," she said. She sounded a bit rough around the edges, but the plea in her voice nearly broke my heart as she added, "You coming?"

I wanted to go with her so badly, but I knew I had to take care of something first. Something that couldn't wait until morning. I brushed the back of my hand along her cheek before I pulled her close.

Near her ear I said, "I need to talk to Maece, and then I'll be right there." Her arms around my waist gripped me tighter. Then she released me and pulled back. A look of understanding graced her face.

She knew as well as I did that if we were going to go through with this mad plan, I might not have another chance to make things right. Kelle stood on her tiptoes and leaned in to kiss me. Her lips barely brushed mine, but I had to ball my hands into fists at my sides to stop myself from holding on to her as she pulled back and walked away from me.

As Kelle walked past Spiro, she squeezed his arm and nodded as he looked at her with a loving smile. She stopped and looked up to face Maece. The intensity in Kelle's dark gaze was apparent, but Maece didn't seem fazed by it. They gave each other a knowing nod before Kelle left without uttering a word.

I watched until Kelle's form disappeared down the connecting hallway and then turned to Maece. I needed to talk to her—I had a request that only she could grant me. But I couldn't do that if we didn't solve this thing that kept pushing us apart. This thing that I didn't even understand.

Nothing ever came easy. That was something I had learned at an early age. Living on the streets, surviving on scraps of food that we'd found inside the dumpsters behind the food distribution center taught you that. You even learned to live in the face of death.

The first time I had nearly lost Maece, she had snuck away while I was asleep. Mom had died after a short-term illness. It was only later that I realized that malnourishment must have contributed to her rapid demise.

Within the plants, there weren't any food distribution outlets as generous as the ones we had in Subterra. Our government might not be the greatest in making choices as it came to Sulos, but at least they provided for their people and divided resources evenly among citizens.

People working at the plants under the districts rule weren't so lucky. Sure, the overseers provided rations, but they were so meager that they were barely enough to keep a person going. Because she worked at one of the plants, we were granted rations for our household, which officially contained two. It didn't matter to overseers that we had taken in an orphaned child. If it were up to them, Maece would have been out on the streets at the age of five after her parents had died in an explosion that was deemed a plant mishap. Mom wouldn't stand for it and had taken her in. This had eventually sealed her fate because she'd given every ounce of food she could acquire to Maece and me.

After Mom had died, we found shelter in an abandoned warehouse, although it wasn't that abandoned. A bunch of homeless folks had found their way to the building. That, at least, kept us off the streets and out of the hands of the enforcers.

One night—Maece must have been seven or eight years old—she had snuck out, and I'd nearly lost it when I couldn't find her the next morning. It had taken me almost all day before I'd eventually found her stuck in a defecation receptacle near the edge of the plant. She had fallen in and couldn't get back out. She had wanted to surprise me, hoping to find food. Instead of surprising me, she had scared the shit out of me. Having spent most of the day inside that thing had drained the strength from her small form, and she would have drowned if I hadn't found her when I had.

That was one of the few times I'd actually lost my temper with her. I understood after she had explained that she had been trying to help, and I had to admit those crap buckets did have the same color as the dumpsters behind the food distribution center. I could still vividly remember the pained expression she had held, and it hadn't that different from what I had seen those past few months. She had only tried to help, and back then I could see that after an hour or so.

How she had missed the smell wafting off those things still remained a mystery to me, though. That same smell had been what had us kicked out of the warehouse. I had tried to wash her and her clothes the best I could, but the nasty smell had lingered. The odor had actually permeated every room that Maece had ventured into, and after a while, the other residents holing up at the warehouse had not so kindly asked us to leave. That turned out to be a positive thing because I didn't think we would've run into Harp otherwise.

"Can I talk to you?" I said under my breath and felt tears stinging my eyes. As with the crap bucket, Maece had tried to do the right thing when she joined the Tenebrae Enforcer Department. I knew that, and maybe it was time that I told her that.

Maece nodded but not after searching eye contact with Spiro as if she needed his approval. The manchild stood there watching us with an expression of glee on his face. I knew him well enough to know that he would never invade our minds without our permission, but I suddenly felt uncomfortable in his presence.

"I…uh," she said as she shifted from one foot to another. "I was thinking about meeting up with Reece. You guys wanna come?" With that she spared me having to ask Spiro to leave, although I wasn't exactly in the mood for drinks.

Her gaze traveled from me to Spiro, but I already guessed his answer. The rare occasions that he had accompanied us to one of the bars over the years could be counted on one hand. He never felt comfortable with large crowds-they made a too big an impression on his senses.

"I shall remain," he said, "but thank you for the offer."

"I should stay with Kelle," I said. "She, uh…" I didn't know how much Maece had overheard of what Kelle had said as we stood on that Hymag platform, but from the way she looked at me in understanding now, I figured pretty much everything. "I need to talk to you, though."

She shot me a thin smile, but as she shifted from foot to foot and her eyes kept darting from me to Spiro and back again, I could tell Maece was worried. *Was she nervous about meeting Reece?*

The two of them had been rebuilding their bond, and although it had been slow going, like Kelle had said, she needed time. If there was anyone in this world willing to give her that, then it would be Reece. He had waited for her for two years, after all. Reece had mentioned that Maece was a bit off-kilter, as he had put it, and that I hadn't exactly welcomed her back with open arms after her confession of choosing to become an enforcer. So, maybe it wasn't Reece that she was acting all nervous about—perhaps it was me.

"Can we talk on the way?" I asked. That way I didn't have to be rude to Spiro. Besides the Bolder Bar was only a short walk, and I should be back before Kelle started to miss me.

"Yeah, sure," she said, but the hesitation in her voice was obvious.

Maece said her goodbye to Spiro, and I patted him on the back as I passed him and muttered, "You keep out of trouble." I was already at the door as he replied.

"Sometimes it cannot be avoided," he said. "Destiny will always find you."

"Yeah, yeah," I called back over my shoulder. "And sometimes a fortune cookie just needs to be eaten."

I followed Maece out of the building and looked up to be greeted by the gray-blue color of rock as it stretched over the city as far as the eye could see. Located deep underground, far beneath the surface and its destructive sun, Subterra wasn't the most beautiful place to look at, but it was home.

The air was humid but clean due to an intricate ventilation system. Street lamps cast blueish lights that gave the surrounding buildings an ominous feel. Especially at these late hours when the streets were mostly empty, the atmosphere felt claustrophobic.

"Hey, wait up," I called after Maece and ran to catch up. As I approached her, I glanced up at the square blocks that could rise to five stories and were homes to many. They all looked the same. Even the narrow streets looked the same, and if one wasn't careful, it'd be easy to get turned around. Maece slowed her pace for me to catch up.

"So," I said as we walked shoulder to shoulder. Maece shot me a quick sideways glance before diverting her eyes back to the ground.

"So…what was it you wanted to talk about?"

I grinned at this small sign that we were falling back into our old routine. It was this thing that we'd done since childhood to keep ourselves occupied or to keep nerves or fear at bay. Maece would ask the questions, and I'd talk.

Still, we weren't back to our old selves yet, far from

it even, and maybe it was up to me to make that first step.

"I'm sorry," I said in a tentative voice and playfully nudged her shoulder.

"There's nothing for you to be sorry about," Maece said briskly and crossed the street without even checking it. Admittedly the chance of running into a vehicle was slim, but to me it was more proof of her carelessness.

"Hey," I said as she reached the sidewalk and I grabbed an arm to pull her to a stop. "Stop acting like a reckless kid."

Maece's eyebrows rose in disbelief as I gestured at the street and said, "Do you wanna get yourself killed?"

The moment the words fell from my mouth I felt stupid for conjuring them up, and the anger in Maece expression reflected as much.

"That is still how you see me, isn't it?" she said. "As some stupid kid that you need to take care of." She wrenched her arm away from me and tried to walk away. Anger that I knew wasn't going to help but that I was unable to stop surged through my veins. I sidestepped to block her path and shoved her in the shoulders.

"What," Maece exclaimed as she straightened. She looked ready for a fight, and I was about to give her one.

"Considering what you've put me through, I figure I have a right to think that," I said with enough venom that my own words should have tasted sour. "Have you ever stopped to think how your death would affect me! It damn near killed me, and if it hadn't been for the others, it would have. You left us behind, and you didn't even trust me enough to tell me what you were doing. After everything we've been through, you trusted Reece and Harp more than you trusted me." Memories of living on the streets after our parents had died flooded my mind, and my voice broke.

Maece's mouth opened and closed as if at a loss for words. She took a step back, and her shoulders sagged as our eyes met. The light from a streetlamp revealed the dark circles underneath her eyes, and her cheeks appeared hollow. She had lost weight, and I felt stupid for not having noticed that before. A man passing spared us a glance, but quickly moved on.

Maece's eyes grew wide, looking confused as she stared at me.

"It was never…," she said, shaking her head. "Trust had nothing to do with it. I…I didn't want to give you…" This time it was her voice that broke.

"Give me what?" I asked gently.

"Hope," she said as she dropped her chin to her chest and pinched the bridge of her nose. I wasn't sure what Maece was trying to tell me, but I didn't want to push her, and so I waited. She took a breath as she faced me again.

"Those people disappearing, the reason I joined TED," she said, "that wasn't just happening in Subterra; it happened inside the plants, too, and it had been going on for a long time."

My chest felt tight as if someone was squeezing my

heart as I watched a stray tear trail down her cheek. Bile rose up my throat, and I felt nausea stir up my stomach as I feared what she was going to say next.

"They didn't die in some stupid plant accident. They took them. Sulos took them and…" Maece's voice trailed off, but she didn't have to explain the rest.

She didn't have to tell me that the overseers that had come to our home to tell us that Maece's parents along with my dad had died in some plant accident had lied. That instead of them being dead they had been taken to one of Sulos's facilities and shoved into a bioprinter to become ArtRep slaves and work for the Tenebrae Enforcer Department.

It was hard to look at her with so much pain gathered behind those dark eyes.

"You thought you could find them," I said.

Maece nodded and added, "At the least I wanted to find out what had happened to them." I blew out a long breath to steel myself for my next question and the answer that seemed unavoidable.

"Did you?"

Maece shook her head as she said, "The program was still very young back then, and a lot of mistakes were made. The chance of them…"

She didn't finish her sentence, and she didn't have too. All of this had happened many years ago, and the chance of them lasting this long would be nonexistent.

I tilted my head to stare at the rock protecting us from the world above. I had stopped mourning for my parents a long time ago; I still missed them, but over the years the pain had faded. With Harp's help,

Maece and I had found a new family. People that cared about each other and depended on us. People like Kelle, Reece, and Riffy—even Harp with his unconventional approach to parenting.

"I'm sorry," she said, and her words pulled me out of my thoughts. "I messed everything up. People died because of me and I…" Her voice broke as I met Maece's tear-streaked face and sensed my own eyes were filling up as well. "I never meant for any of this, and I know what happened in Two is my fault and that I'll never be able to make up for it, but—"

I raised my hand to stop Maece from rambling on, and realized I was holding my breath. After exhaling a long sigh, I said, "Look…" I hesitated as I recognized that Kelle had been on point. Maece did blame herself for all that had been going on, and I felt ashamed that I had contributed to that. She shouldn't have to bear that weight when all she had tried to do was the right thing. I realized that now as I was about to venture along a similar path.

My thoughts were still all over the place, and I wanted this to sound right. "I can't pretend that I wasn't angry. In fact, I'm still angry-you left us, and you let me believe you were dead." Maece visible swallowed and her dark skin paled. "Do you have any idea what that did to me—what it did to all of us?"

A few buildings down from where we stood a door swung open and drew my attention. Two figures who looked to be a couple walked arm in arm and talked in low voices as they came our way. Grateful for the interruption, I waited until they passed before I continued.

"I can't just erase that, and once in a while, it'll show. I can't help that, but you have to know that all of this that is going on isn't your fault." My voice rose an octave as I drove a fist into Maece's chest.

My strike forced Maece to take a step back, and her eyes grew wide as she stared at me in shock. "There is only one person to blame, and that is Sulos, and we're going to make him pay."

I hadn't finished talking yet, but I couldn't just stand there motionless anymore, and I pulled her into a hug.

"Doing dumb stuff doesn't erase the fact that you are my family, I thought we both should know that by now," I said as I eased back and held her at arm's length, "but don't ever do it again because I will kick your ass."

A smile formed on Maece's face before she hugged me again and even slightly lifted me off the ground. "You can kick my ass anytime," she said.

"Yeah, well, maybe I should rethink that," I replied as we started walking again and I tried to conjure up a way to address why I had come along in the first place.

The bombshell of a mission that Harp had dropped on us didn't sit well with me. My conversation with Maece had shown a light on Harp's reason, though. He must have known for a long time what ArtRep was doing. Harp had pulled hundreds of orphaned kids from the plants, and somewhere along the way, he must have figured out what had happened to their parents. If the basis of his plan was to get revenge on Sulos, then I could understand that.

Harp had seen the consequences of the old man's actions firsthand. I could only hope that it hadn't clouded Harp's judgment, and even though this mission of finding Sulos's space station reeked like a suicide mission, I was willing to take that chance, but that didn't mean I was willing to let someone I loved take that chance.

We crossed another street and neared the area where a couple of Reece's favorite drink holes, including the Bolder Bar, were located. Although it was late, lights illuminated the sidewalks from inside the establishments, and the noise levels started to rise.

"What's on your mind?" Maece asked, a few buildings short of the Bolder Bar.

I looked up and caught her watching me. "What, why?" I said evasively.

"Because you've been quiet for like three minutes."

I replied with a faint smile and stopped in front of the bar. Laughter reached us from inside, and it wasn't hard to recognize Reece's voice among the crowd. Maece must have heard him too because she smiled and turned her head to watch the door. It seemed she was eager to get inside. She didn't, though, and instead focused on me.

"Back home, you said you wanted to talk to me," she said, "and I saw the look you gave me at the table."

She was right. There had been something on my

mind ever since Harp had dropped his plan on us. The fact that he hadn't supplied a definitive answer about why he wanted us to go up there and what we were supposed to do once we reached Sulos's space station hadn't gone unnoticed by me. Revenge might be an explanation, but with Harp, one could never know, and as Reece had pointed out, sending a space freighter didn't make any sense since a craft like that didn't carry any weapons. *What were we supposed to do, just wait, and see?*

I had this nagging feeling that wasn't what Harp had in mind. The only option I could think of would be to use the ship as a battering ram. It seemed unimaginable that Harp would request such a thing, but considering the desperation I had witnessed while he had given his speech, I had my doubts, and I couldn't take that risk—not when Kelle was aboard.

"Talk to me," Maece said with a hint of a smile, "or else I'll run back and drag Spiro out here."

I wanted to laugh at her threat to have the man-child pry the thoughts from my mind, but the tightness in my chest stopped me from doing so. It also made it kind of hard to breathe, and I felt sick to my stomach. Of course, Maece sensed something was up as she eyed me suspiciously. I shoved my hands in my pockets to stop them from fidgeting and then faced Maece head-on.

"I need you to look after Kelle," I said and was surprised at the strength of my voice. Maece tilted her head slightly back and raised an eyebrow. "I don't want her to come on the ship." I didn't have the heart to tell Maece what I suspected the outcome of the mission would be and decided to approach the subject from a different angle. I just hoped she wouldn't read the lie off my face.

"But…," Maece started to say, and as she searched for words, I quickly interjected.

"I know both plans suck and will probably get us all killed, but with you, she might have a chance—you can protect her."

Maece shook her head.

"What makes you think I'll be able to protect her?" she asked.

I choked out a nervous laugh, knowing that I was using the truth to hide a lie.

"You do remember that you took out five of those freaks, right!" Maece gave me a look that told me she hadn't even considered what had happened. "Removing that regulator from the back of your head has done a number on your body, because you move faster than I have ever seen anyone move, and you react to things as if you knew what was going to happen in the first place."

I could see her thinking behind those dark eyes. Thoughts that I felt sure had crossed my mind. Neither mission held guarantees. *Would it matter on which job we would die? Wouldn't you rather be with Kelle?*

I couldn't just tell her that I had a strong feeling that anyone aboard that ship would never come home. I felt convinced Harp was sending us on a suicide mission and he didn't have the heart to tell us.

"Please," I said. Hot tears started to roll down my

cheeks as I begged her to do as I asked. "I can't watch her die."

Maece closed her eyes as if she couldn't bear to watch the agony on my face and nodded. As she opened them again, I was sobbing, and I couldn't stop myself. Embarrassed, I turned away from her, but she grabbed my shoulder and pulled me close.

"Kelle is going to be so pissed at me," she said with a sigh. I managed to choke out a laugh at that as I frantically wiped at my tears.

"You can't tell her," I said in a note of desperation. Maece shook her head.

"Are you sure this is what you want, I mean—" Maece said. She broke off her sentence as if she didn't want to utter the words. Her dark eyes seemed to bore into me as if she could read my soul, and I knew what she was trying to tell me. If I did this, it wouldn't be that much different from what Maece had done when she had chosen to become an enforcer and leave us all behind. Doing this meant betraying Kelle's trust but having her hate me was better than having her dead.

"Please...I...I don't want her on that ship." I knew I sounded desperate, and I could only imagine what Maece would be thinking. The rapid movement of her eyes told me she was probably going over the entire mission plan, trying to figure out the implications. "I know what I'm asking," I said and held my breath as I waited for a reply. Maece blinked before holding my gaze for a long time.

"Okay," she said and nodded to emphasize her

answer. A moment later, she added, "Remember to breathe."

I drew in a shuddering breath and sniffed as I whipped a hand along my nose. There was still a note of uncertainty in my voice as I asked for confirmation.

"Yeah?"

"Yeah, I'll figure something out," she said before she puffed up her cheeks and blew out a long breath as her gaze turned to the bar's entrance. "I'd say it's time for a drink."

I followed her gaze and felt my heart sink. Having a drink would have been our usual routine before any mission. Hang out and enjoy each other's company because it could be the last time. The challenge that Harp had laid out before us could very well be that last time, but still, I shook my head.

"I can't," I said. My voice barely reached over the noise that came from the bar, but the faint smile that curved her lips told me Maece had heard.

"Good choice," she said. I shrugged and shoved my hands back into my pockets.

"You don't mind," I asked.

"Go be with your girl," she said and then kissed my temple. "I'll see you in the morning. And don't worry: I'll figure something out. I owe you at least that much."

With that, Maece released her grip on my shoulder and walked to the entrance of the bar. Shrugging off a cold shiver that I refused to see as a bad omen, I watched Maece give me a final wave and disappear inside. Taking a deep breath, I made my first step in the direction of home.

My breathing felt labored as I stood in the tiny hallway and stared at the closed door of Kelle's room. I couldn't remember if I had run the entire way back or just the stairs in our apartment building.

With most of us out, silence hung around me like an unwelcome blanket. I preferred the sound of banter even though it drove me out of my mind sometimes. Anything seemed better than this silence.

I took a minute to catch my breath and then eased the door open. It wouldn't surprise me if Kelle was still awake. I hadn't been gone that long, but I didn't want to take the chance of waking her up. We were going to need all the sleep we could get.

A streak of blue light cast by a streetlamp entered the room through a small window. The sliver of light penetrated the darkness across the bed underneath as I watched the form hidden underneath the covers.

I couldn't tell whether Kelle was asleep, so as soundlessly as possible, I closed the door and stripped off my clothes. On tiptoes, I snuck across the room and slipped underneath the sheets.

Kelle hadn't moved, and for a second, I pondered what to do, but in the next moment, the choice was taken away from me. Kelle shifted in the bed and pressed her back against my side. Permission granted, I turned on my side and fitted my body behind hers.

She took my hand as I slid it across her abdomen and pressed it to her chest.

"You worked things out?" she asked. Instead of the issues Maece and I had dealt with, and what Kelle would likely be referring to, my mind shot to the request I had made only a few minutes ago. I felt my heart rate speed up and feared Kelle would feel it pound against her back. Nuzzling Kelle's neck, I drew in a slow, deliberate breath and inhaled her essence in the hope it would calm my raging heart.

"Yeah, I think we're good," I replied and fought to keep the tension from my voice. Kelle sighed and squeezed my hand.

"That's good."

In the silence that followed, I searched for words, something that would make it all right, but all I could think of was that all of this was about to end. Perhaps I just lacked the courage to say what needed to be said. As Kelle's breathing evened out, I felt a loss even worse than when they told me Maece had died. I shivered and tighten my hold on the slumbering woman. Kissing her shoulder, I closed my eyes but knew sleep would not come.

SEVEN

MAECE

THE SOUNDS I had heard coming from the bar as I had stood outside with Saera did not measure up to the ten or so people occupying the space. Unlike its square facade on the outside, the bar had a cave-like look to it. The lighting was soft, and the walls were draped in tapestry to hide the depressing effect of the gray-blue rock that surrounded us.

A couple of the booths carved straight out of the stone had occupants nursing their drinks and laughing. The atmosphere seemed amicable, although most of the patrons looked as if you shouldn't mess with them. If they even had jobs, I could see most of them doing hard labor without breaking a sweat.

I spotted Reece and Riffy sitting at the bar having an animated conversation with the bartender. The old lady behind the bar spotted me as I approached.

"Oh, oh," she said and patted Reece on the arm. "Here comes trouble." Reece's eyes were a little hazy as he looked up and saw me walk over to his table. I would have thought a few too many shots of mushroom ale would have caused the clouded eyes, but as soon as he saw me, Reece blinked and sat up straighter. Blue eyes with a hint of uncertainty stared back at me as I grabbed a stool and sat down next to him.

"So, are you going to offer a girl a drink or what?" I said. Without taking my eyes off Reece, I waved a hand at Riffy. "Hey, Riff."

"Hey," Riffy replied. Silence fell between us as Reece stared at me with his mouth slightly open, and I stared back, forcing myself not to smile. It stretched for a long time until the older woman decided it to be enough.

"Maybe you should move a little further down here while I fix the lady and your friend a drink," the old lady said as a smile formed deep creases on her face. She gestured for Riffy to follow her. "C'mon, young man, and then you can tell me little more about this girl with the colorful hair that you're crazy about."

Reece must have registered some of what the old lady had said because his face twitched, and for a moment his eyes shifted to where the woman had stood a moment ago.

"I…," he started after realizing the woman had left. "I mean…you're here." The baffled look on his face made it impossible for me not to grin. I waited for the old lady to place the drink in front of me and leave us again.

"Are you all right?" I asked, but I sounded less

confident than I had before. "You look a bit shell-shocked." His eyes widened, and his mouth twitched before he shot me one of those heart-melting grins.

"Yeah," he said and shook his head as if to clear it. "I just wasn't expecting you here tonight. Did something happen?" He seemed tense as he waited for my reply but visibly relaxed as I blew out a breath and smiled.

"Saera and I talked," I said.

"Really," he said as he raised his glass. "Can I assume this was a positive talk?"

I nodded in agreement and raised my glass.

"Well, it's about time," he said and drank the ale in one gulp.

"I'm sorry if things had been weird," I said after emptying my drink. The situation with Saera had been a strain on all of us, but Reece had been caught in the middle, and I had feared the underlying tension might have jeopardized his friendship with Kelle.

"Weird," Reece said, feigning confusion. "Things didn't get weird." He turned and called out, "Riffy, did things get weird?"

Riffy pulled away from his conversation with the old lady, looking flustered. His face turned a dark crimson as he stared at us with his mouth ajar.

"Huh," he more or less grunted. Reece turned back with an easy grin on his rugged-looking face. He hadn't shaven in a while, and it showed, but I couldn't remember him looking more handsome than he did right now.

I relayed part of the conversation I had with Saera

and also some of the things Spiro had mentioned. As he listened, I could see the change in Reece's eyes. They grew brighter, and some of the mischief behind those eyes started to return.

"So, are you gonna stop blaming yourself for everything?" he said. I stared at him wide-eyed, and Reece grinned as he added, "Don't look so surprised, babe. I kind of know how your mind works."

I blew out a breath and shook my head. "I don't think that's possible."

"No, I didn't think so, but I'm glad you sorted things out with Saera," Reece said, "and just know that we all have your back–always."

"I guess," I said under my breath and perched my head up on my elbow. I studied his face while his eyes locked on mine. "I'm sorry."

This time, it was Reece who looked surprised.

"For what?" he asked and waved at the bartender.

"For…I don't know, being weird and distant," I said after he ordered another round of drinks.

"I hate to break it to you, Maece, but you've always been a bit weird," he said, "and it takes a whole lot more to get rid of me."

"Why are you so patient with me?" I asked.

Reece tilted his head to a side and watched me like that for the longest time. If he let me, I could drown in those blue depths as he seemed to take in every aspect of my being. When he looked at me like that, it felt as if I was the only thing in the world that mattered to him.

"I would think you'd know that by now," he said, sounding uncharacteristically serious.

"Here ya go," the old lady said, pulling us out of the moment as she placed fresh drinks in front of us. I cleared my throat as the old lady gave me a knowing smile.

Looking a bit dazed, Reece reached for his drink and lifted it for a toast, but then stopped. He shot me a questioning look before he asked, "So, if things are sort of okay now, why didn't you bring Saera along, and Kelle for that matter?"

"Uh…," I started to say but then had to swallow hard. Reece raised an eyebrow as he watched me searching for words. "I think Saera might have found herself on our side of the fence—if that makes any sense."

My words were cryptic in part because I didn't want to say out loud that Saera had contrived a plan that might affect Kelle as much as my plan of becoming an enforcer had touched her. I didn't think it was my place to do that.

Reece's eyes narrowed, and the lightest of creases formed between his eyes as he mulled over what I had said.

"Should we be preparing for another storm?" he asked.

I didn't know what Reece had been thinking at that point. The oncoming mission would be enough of a storm for me, but the thing with Kelle could cause another set of problems. Still, I shook my head and said, "Not now. I don't think I'd be able to do anything else tonight except having a quiet drink among friends."

Reece raised an eyebrow and set his drink down. He cleared his throat as he inched closer while his eyes never trailed away from my face.

"Are you sure about that?" Reece asked in a voice that held an edge of desire.

"Why?" I asked as if I didn't know what he was hinting at. "Did you make plans for tonight?"

Reece lifted his drink again and waited for me to do the same. "I might," he said as he downed the shot in one swallow.

I followed his example and grimaced at the taste. It had been a while since I had tasted the strong mushroom concoction, and I felt it burn at the back of my throat. Reece grinned at my reaction and leaned in.

"It looks like you're out of practice," he murmured into my ear. His warm breath tickled my skin and seemed to work as a catalyst, heating up my cheeks. "Therefore, I feel it is my duty to reacquaint you with all the pleasantries that this fine establishment has to offer." He eased back to look into my eyes, and I had to swallow hard at the wanting look he gave me.

He lifted a hand and swirled his finger in the air to request another round of drinks without taking his eyes off me. Instead of lowering his hand, he let his finger trail up along my jaw and caught a strand of hair that he tugged behind my ear. I closed my eyes, and even though it had been the briefest touch of a finger, I felt its warmth radiating along my skin.

As I opened my eyes again, I stared into demanding blue eyes that I felt sure could read my soul. I hadn't even noticed that I had closed the distance between us. The kiss that followed didn't feel as if it originated in a bar surrounded by drunk and half-drunk people. It felt as if Reece and I were the only ones inside this cave-like space and everything around us had disappeared.

It seemed too soon when Reece pulled his lips away from mine, and I only vaguely registered the loud whistle that someone had felt necessary to let out.

Clearing his throat again, Reece shifted uneasily until his eyes landed on the drinks that apparently had been placed there without us noticing. As if it might run away from him, he snatched up the drink and threw it back before he called out to old lady behind the bar.

"I think I need another drink," he said, and I smiled at his antics as he added with a wave of his hand, "Riffy, get over here."

Riffy seemed a bit hesitant at first. I had a feeling he didn't want to disturb us, but it wouldn't be right without him. Drinks flowed while laughter ensued, and for a short time, I could almost forget about what tomorrow had in store for us. I just wished Saera and Kelle would have been here to join us.

As the hour grew later, the bar started to empty out and I watched the old lady yawn as she cleaned up. Riffy had also taken his leave, claiming that he needed his beauty rest, but it had been evident to me from the way Reece had talked into his ear a few minutes before he left that Reece might have suggested that Riffy should leave.

"Are you ready to go?" Reece asked. The sadness in his eyes wasn't hard to overlook as he stood and offered me his arm. The night was coming to an end, and what remained was the unknown racing toward us like a Hymag at full speed. I figured we still had some time and linked my arm with his as he guided me outside and down the street—home.

"So," Reece said as we neared our building. He'd been quiet for most of the short walk home, and I was expecting a question of some kind. He cleared his throat as if he wasn't sure how to phrase what he was about to say.

"This thing…about Saera being on the other side of the fence, might that by any chance have anything to do with a certain brooding young lady?"

I should have known Reece would come back to that previous remark and I gave him a sideways glance as I left his question hanging for a bit. Saera had confided in me, and I wasn't sure if I should tell Reece about what she had asked of me.

It wasn't that I didn't trust Reece. On the contrary, I trusted him with my life, and he had kept my secret for two years. He hadn't said anything to Saera or the others about what had happened to me and was even forced to let them believe that I had died. I couldn't even imagine how difficult that must have been for him.

I sighed as I stopped in front of the entrance and looked up to meet his gaze.

As if he read my mind he said, "You don't have to tell me if you can't."

I smiled at him, but then diverted my gaze and swept it down the empty street. It wasn't just Saera's wishes and Kelle I had to consider here. Changing the plan in mid-execution might jeopardize anyone involved. I drew in a breath and leaned against the wall as I redirected my attention back to Reece.

"She wants me to keep Kelle from boarding that freighter," I said.

Reece's eyes never veered from mine as he said, "Ah."

"That's it?" I said as moments passed. "All you have to say is, ah."

He looked up at the rock ceiling that loomed over us as if he was gazing at the stars. With a contemplative expression, he scratched the stubble on his cheek before his focus returned to me.

"Yep," he said, "that's pretty much it."

I shook my head, unable to hide a smile.

"I just told you that I might compromise the mission and you say, ah."

He grinned at me and with a step closed the gap between us. "I guess it explains why she suddenly changed her mind about finally working things out with you," he said.

"That's not fair," I said, pushing off the wall in an attempt to reach for the door.

Reece stopped me by caging me with his arms while his hands rested on the wall on either side of me. The move forced me to lean back again. "She would never let something slide just because she wants something from me."

"She wouldn't?" he said with a voice that had dropped an octave.

"No," I said with a hint of agitation. "Although I do think she realizes that what she is planning will come pretty damn close to what I have done. Maybe it helps her understand my reasons even though I still doubt them."

Reece grinned and inched closer.

"Yeah, that's pretty much the conclusion I had come to," he said before he brushed his lips against mine. "I don't understand why you even think of doubting me on those things." He kissed me again, but with a bit more effort, and I took hold of the back of his neck just in case my legs caved.

"I don't," I said as we came up for air. Breathing heavily, I added, "But I need you...to erase my doubts."

"Ah," he said again, followed by a toothy grin.

Trying to resist him, I said, "So, what am I supposed to do?"

"Well," he said as he leaned in again, but this time he lowered his mouth to explore my neck. I tilted my head to give him better access as he alternated between speaking and kissing my neck and jaw. "We'll figure out a way to keep Kelle from boarding that freighter that won't jeopardize the mission."

"How?" I managed to voice as I sighed.

"I'm thinking about it," he said in a warm breath near my ear as he pressed his body firmer into mine. I held on to him as his hands released the wall and slipped underneath my jacket.

"Maybe we should think about it upstairs," I replied.

"Now that's the best idea you've had all day."

"I don't wanna get up," Reece mumbled as I extracted myself from his arms. One of his eyes opened, and he grinned as he saw me. A moment later, he groaned and added, "I think my brain might have melted."

"I'm sure Riffy will have something in his arsenal that'll help with that," I said as I bent down to kiss the top of his head. "Poor baby."

These days, drugs were made to aid in almost any kind of illness or injury. If something hadn't killed you, there was probably something available that would help you get back on your feet in no time at all. We were all trained to administer these types of drugs and to handle the medical equipment that came along with them, but Riffy was usually the one who had to carry the supplies. This had kind of turned him into our field medic, as it were, and it had transitioned to our home.

As Reece lay on his stomach, I caught a glimpse of

the tattoo of a mythical creature called a dragon on his back. I couldn't stop my fingers from trailing over the intricate details of the design. The creature symbolized his strength, but because the animal looked a bit cross-eyed from a particular vantage point, I always liked to think it also represented the craziness inside Reece.

"You still have a few minutes," I said.

"Then stay," he said in groggy voice and threw out a clumsy arm to reach for me.

I scrambled away from him because with Reece, a few minutes usually weren't enough.

"That's probably a bad idea," I said as I reached for my pants and fumbled to get them on. Reece's room only held the tiniest of mirrors that he used for shaving, and his shaggy hair didn't need much nurturing. Without anything to help me, I finger-combed my hair and grabbed my shirt and jacket off the floor.

An elaborate sigh made me turn to Reece, who had shifted onto his back with his arms supporting his head as he watched.

"I love watching you dress," he said, "but then, I can't wait to remove those layers again."

"Don't even think about it," I said, shaking my head. "Now get your ass out of bed."

"Yes, ma'am," he said as I moved to the door.

Glancing over my shoulder, I noticed Reece stretch and paused as my eyes lingered on his abs. He must have realized I was watching because he shifted into a deliberate pose that gave me an even better view of his toned physique. I shook my head as he extravagantly waggled his eyebrows, but I could not hide a smile as I resumed my way out the door.

I stepped into the hallway at the same time as Saera, and she shot me a grin that reminded me of the one she shot me the first time she had caught me sneaking out Reece's room. It felt as if fate needed for us to have this moment, however brief.

I barely managed to return the gesture as the grin on Saera's face faded, and we jumped back to reality.

"Hey," she said sounding subdued, "you ready?" The simple question might have referred to any number of things. Ready to save our people, confiscate a space freighter, ready to deceive my lover, ready to die. It could have meant all of the above, but there always could only be one answer.

"Yeah," I replied. Reece and I had briefly spoken about how we were going to keep Kelle from boarding the freighter, but when it came down to deciding on how to keep the mission from going sour, he kept distracting me. Admittedly those had been pleasant distractions, but I still had no clue of how we were going to handle it.

Harp would only have divided us the way he had because he needed our skills in certain places for the separate missions to succeed. He hadn't explained as much, but I suspected he needed the people capable of inflicting the more brute-force approach on the ground, which meant Riffy, Reece, and me.

Saera usually took my lead, so I wasn't sure why he had chosen to split us up, but Kelle was the thinker of the bunch. She might not say all that much or all that often, but she listened and noticed things. She had been the one to first suggest exposing Sulos's secret by putting it out there on the Feed for everyone to see—a plan that apparently was still in play. With a follow-up plan still hanging in the air, I had a pretty good idea why he would want her up there, and we were about to mess that up.

EIGHT

SAERA

DESPITE THE FACT that I had gotten myself to bed nice and early, I felt like Maece and Reece looked. They had both dark circles under their eyes and moved as if someone had placed an extra sixty pounds on their shoulders, but at least their mood was light. Even though we all felt the weight of the mission hanging over our heads, and I could almost taste the tension in the air, they seemed to handle it like they'd always had.

"So," Reece said with a note of excitement in his voice, "are you ready to see Ty again?" He poked Riffy in his round belly and gave him a playful shove.

"Get away from me," Riffy said and punched the air where Reece had been standing, but he had managed to dart away from the incoming fist.

"You want me to hit him, Riff?" Maece asked. That remark sparked a devious grin on Riffy's face.

Reece turned to walk backward and slammed a fist to his own chest.

"Argh," he cried out. "Babe, you're killing me here."

The three of them walked in front of me as we headed to the Hymag station. The lights dotting the street shined brighter to give the illusion of day, but to me, everything seemed sober and gray and perhaps even more so than usual.

Although I enjoyed watching the banter playing out in front of me, I didn't feel like participating. Kelle walked by my side with her hands shoved into her pockets and her eyes glued to the concrete beneath our feet. I knew better than to ask what was on her mind, but I had given her every opportunity to open up. She had a tendency to work things out on her own before sharing them with me. At times, this frustrated the hell out of me, but it was also one of the things that made me fall for her in the first place. She had survived within the plants on her own longer than most of us combined and had learned to do things on her own.

Something was up, though, and I couldn't help wondering if she had figured out that I was up to something. I wasn't exactly acting like myself, but pretending to do that would have felt like even more of a betrayal. That was how I felt. As if I was about to betray her trust. Hell, I already betrayed her trust; she just didn't know it yet.

Ahead, Maece shot me a worried look over her

shoulder. *Was she worried about me, or did she have doubts about my request?*

It had occurred to me as I had lain awake last night and pondered over the consequences of what I had asked of her. If Maece managed to keep Kelle from boarding the freighter—I was sure she would— then that would change the dynamics of the mission, and Harp would be furious. He might have to make some changes to the plan. But Harp could deal with that, and he might pretend to be a hard-ass, but I had dealt with him before. I just hoped I wouldn't endanger the mission. Maece would have come to the same conclusion. *Was that what had her looking so anxious?*

Shouts pulled me out of my rambling thoughts as we neared the central Hymag station. A large section of a transshipment area had been cleared out. Instead of boxes, crates, and containers the fenced-off area now held beds—lots of beds.

Following the other's leads, I stopped at the fortified fence where heavily armed guards patrolled the perimeter.

"Just give me a sec," Reece said as he gestured for us to stay. He jogged in the direction of one of the guards and greeted him as if he knew him. That didn't surprise me because sometimes it seemed as if Reece knew every person in Subterra.

Bile rose in my throat as I gazed into the gaunt faces locked behind the fence. People who were mostly skin and bones shuffled between the rows of beds while others stood in line to reach small shacks that appeared to be distributing food. An even longer row of men and women led to restroom facilities. A handful of medical personnel walked along the rows in an attempt to give first aid to the people unable to get out of bed, but from the cries for help, it was easy to determine that it wasn't enough.

Reece returned, and the grim expression on his face told me that I wasn't going to like what he had learned.

"They're from One and Two," he said as we gathered around him. This didn't come as a surprise; these people had to have come from the power plants.

"But why are they detained?" I asked. "It's not like they're prisoners of war or something."

"Apparently, they are," Reece said.

"What!" I said appalled.

"How come?" Maece asked.

Reece shrugged and moved further away from the fence and its guards. "Well, not prisoners per se, but according to Subterran law, they are citizens of the districts," he said in a hushed tone as he kept a careful eye on the guards.

"But they're Subterran," Riffy said.

"Those power plants have belonged to the districts for a long time. I doubt the government sees these people as Subterran anymore," Reece said.

"So, what is going to happen to them?" Kelle asked, sounding subdued while her eyes seemed fixed on the men, women, and children locked behind the fence.

"The guard I just spoke with, he thinks they'll be shipped across the borders after our government finishes with their groveling to the districts," Reece said with a hint of disgust.

"They're probably trying to convince the districts, as we speak, that Subterra had nothing to do with the extraction," Maece chimed in.

Even if our government had been aware of the rebels' involvement or even if the council had approved our actions, they would never admit that to the districts. Subterra would have disavowed all participation. If not, the Combined Districts of Tenebrae would see what we had done as an act of war. I figured it to be the reason why the Subterran government had incarcerated the remaining survivors of the plants.

"They can't do that," Kelle said in a loud voice. "They can't just send—"

Aware that she was drawing attention to us that we couldn't use right now, I grabbed her roughly by the shoulder and pulled her further away from the fence. Over my shoulder, I saw Reece shrug in the direction of the guard he knew and swirled a finger near his temple before he came after us together with the others.

"All right, all right," Kelle said with obvious anger in her voice. "Let go of me!"

She pulled away and gave me a shove in the chest that sent me flying, and I landed on my butt. Pain shot through my chest, and I rubbed my breastbone. Catching the breath that Kelle had knocked out of me, I could only stare at her in disbelief.

"Kelle," Riffy said, sounding aghast, as he shifted

his gaze from her to me sitting on the ground. Maece and Reece pulled me up by the arms until I could get my feet under me. They all looked as shocked as I felt. I also felt a spark of anger shimmer in my gut, but it quickly turned to acid and made me feel sick to my stomach as I met Kelle's pain-filled eyes.

Her prosthetic—and the reason my chest hurt as much as it did—twitched as if she weren't able to control it. Tension, anxiety, nerves, all these things could contribute to the tremor in her hand just as it would in a real hand.

"I…," she started to say, and I could tell she was on the verge of tears. She took a few steps back and raised her hands. "I didn't…," she tried again, but then shook her head and ran off in the direction of the central Hymag station.

Without a moment's hesitation, Riffy ran after her. I could only watch as her retreating form grew smaller and finally disappeared inside the building.

"What was that?" Reece asked, shifting his gaze from Riffy, who was still struggling to reach the building to me. I shook my head, unsure what had happened. All I wanted to do was run after her, but it even hurt to breathe, and running was out of the question.

"You want me to?" he said and pointed a thumb at the station.

"Please," I said with a wheeze in my voice.

Reece set off for the building, and I knew he would find her. If anyone could help Kelle calm down, then it would be those two, but I also knew she wouldn't talk to them. That was something I had to do myself. I took a breath and felt another shot of pain in my chest.

"You good to walk?" Maece asked while she was still holding my arm. I nodded and took a couple of tentative steps. She must not have liked what she saw in my movement because she kept a steadying hand on me while we crossed the street and headed for the station.

"Did you...," Maece said and hesitated. "Did you tell her about staying behind?"

"No," I said, shaking my head. "More or less because I expected something like this."

I stopped in the center of the steps that led up to the entrance of the building and turned to face Maece. "I've never seen her like this, not since...," I said and let out a shuddering breath as I remembered the haunted look on Kelle's face after Harp had shown up with her all those years ago. "Have you?"

Maece shook her head as she said, "No, I haven't told her." Of course she hadn't. How could she? Kelle had been with me all morning, and we had barely talked.

"What the hell was that," I muttered.

I was sitting next to Maece as I watched Reece walk down the aisle from the rear of the Hymag. One of the perks of having semi-government ties came in the form of a private Hymag platform that didn't allow for civilian travelers. There was no waiting in a queue, and as soon as we boarded, I had sunk into the first seat I could find. My chest hurt less, and I think it might have been shock that had me walking on unsteady legs.

Reece kneeled by our seats and spoke in a whisper so that the additional rebel forces cramped inside the cabin wouldn't overhear.

"She's in the last compartment, but she won't talk to us," he said with concern in his voice. "Riffy is keeping an eye on her, just in case."

I had wanted to go after Kelle, but Maece advised me to wait until we'd received word from Reece. Maece might have been right. I needed time to catch my breath and to think. *What could have been the reason for her to go off like that?*

"Thanks," I replied. Reece stood and hesitated for a moment. He stood there observing us for a while before eying the seat across from Maece. I couldn't see Maece's reaction with my eyes glued to the empty seat in front of me, but it was enough to make Reece move further up the aisle and find another place to sit.

"Aren't you going to talk to her?" Maece said. I shifted to face her.

"I don't know." The words sounded distant even to myself. Maece raised an eyebrow and waited for an explanation. "I mean maybe it's better this way, and it won't be so hard once I…" I trailed off, afraid I would choke on the words. "Once I left her behind." I couldn't voice them aloud, afraid that would make it all too real too soon.

"Was this how you felt?" I asked. Maece shifted uncomfortably in her seat and faced away from me. My decision to leave Kelle behind wasn't that much different from Maece's decision to volunteer to become an enforcer. While I wasn't about to fake my death, I could see the similarities. I was making decisions that would severely impact Kelle, and I had no right to do that, but I cared too much about her to risk her getting hurt.

"Maybe," Maece said after some deliberation. We sat in silence for a while, and I listened to the hum of the engine as the Hymag propelled at high speed through the depths of the earth. Around me, the murmurs of conversation filled the cabin.

"For you at least," Maece said out of the blue. I blinked, not sure what she meant. "You're focused on leaving her behind, but that's not what set Kelle off. She can't hurt about something she doesn't know yet."

This morning, Kelle had seemed more withdrawn than usual. I was used to her being quiet, and I hadn't paid much attention to it, but considering yesterday's emotional reaction on the Hymag platform at the rebel base, it seemed Maece was right, and something else was going on. I hadn't even known about Harp's intentions back then, so this probably had nothing to do with my plan of keeping her safe. *Maybe the death of that kid still plagued her?*

Maece shoved an elbow into my side before she said, "Go talk to her." She poked me again.

Slowly, I exhaled a long breath, and I could still feel the sting in my chest. I knew Kelle hadn't meant to hurt me, and it felt more painful to think about the reason that had caused the outburst. I hoped I'd be ready to face that pain with her.

"You're kind of bossy, you know," I said and stood.

"Yeah, well, I've learned from the best," Maece replied with a wink.

My legs shook as I walked down the aisle and grabbed hold of the seats to keep myself upright. My stomach reeled, and I tried to take long, steady breaths to keep myself from throwing up.

The last few seats were empty except for the one where I spotted Riffy. Kelle was nowhere around.

"She's in the next one," Riffy said as I approached. He indicated the door which created a barrier between the troops and the equipment we'd brought. "She won't talk to me."

Hurt reflected in his eyes, and I tried for a measuring smile, but it felt more like a grimace.

"She does that," I said and patted Riffy's knee. "Why don't you go sit with the others."

Taking a breath and not waiting to see if Riffy acted on my suggestion, I pressed the mechanism that opened the door. After I stepped through the opening, I waited until the door slid close behind me and for my eyes to adjust to the gloom.

Racks packed with weapons, ammunition, exoskeleton suits, and a whole bunch of other stuff on both sides of the space lined a path almost all the way to the back. Boxes and crates stood piled against the back wall. Evenly spaced emergency lights mounted to the ceiling were dim, but there was enough light to see. Unable to spot Kelle, I eased ahead, my eyes searching for a nook that she could have used to hide.

I found her sitting on the ground, her back against a crate with her legs pulled to her chest. She didn't look up as I approached and didn't even react as I eased down to sit beside her. My hands were shaking, and I trapped them in the folds of my knees as I pulled my legs up. I opened my mouth but couldn't think of a single thing to say and closed it again. Thoughts barreled through my mind as we sat in silence. I was wondering if I should be mad and scold the young woman sitting next to me, but after what had happened last night at the rebel base and now this, how could I? Kelle was hurting, and the last thing I wanted to do was add to that pain. All I could do was hope for an explanation.

"Did I hurt you?" The question almost took me by surprise, and I fought the urge to rub my chest. The pain had faded, but I imagined a significant bruise would remain for a while. Kelle's voice breaking on the words added a different pain, though. Instead of answering her questions I asked, "What happened?"

"I...," she said in a hoarse croak and broke herself off. Clearing her throat, she added, "It just took me by surprise."

I wanted to push her into telling me what was wrong, what had prompted her to react so strongly, mostly because I wanted to know how to comfort her, but that wouldn't work with Kelle, and I knew it. I bit my lower lip to keep myself from talking and waited.

It felt as if I'd been sitting there for over an hour when she finally said, "I was born in Two."

My stomach dropped, and I turned to face her. The soft light of an emergency light lit half of her face, and she looked paler than I had ever seen her. A tear rolled down her cheek as a muscle in her jaw flexed.

"That thing with the kid and then seeing those people and the state they were in, knowing that Subterra was going to abandon them again…it just got to me, but I didn't mean to take it out on you."

She wiped at the tears with her sleeve and shifted to face me. I waited for her downcast eyes to meet mine, and as they did, it seemed she wasn't able to keep up the I any longer. The walls she had built over the years cracked and crumbled to pieces as the tears trailed down her cheeks.

Growing up inside the plants would be hard for anyone. I should know because Maece and I had done the same until Harp pulled us out. However, Maece and I had been a lot younger, and with Harp's help, our lives had turned around.

Kelle must have been sixteen when Harp found her. He had taken her off the hands of a guy who was running a work camp for profit, but I hadn't known this had happened in Two. She'd been such a mess that first time that I saw her, and thinking about it, still broke my heart. Her clothes had looked as if they hadn't been washed in years, and her body had been covered in cuts and bruises. She refused to talk, and the slightest gesture could set off a violent response. That's why Harp hadn't been able to place her in a family and had brought her to stay with us.

I might have grown up in a different plant, but I had a pretty good idea of the kind of operation these types of guys ran. They forced kids to do all kinds of labor in exchange for scraps of food and maybe a place to sleep. It made me sick to my stomach to imagine Kelle in that situation. I couldn't even imagine what it would be like to have lived through it, but I knew it had seriously messed up Kelle.

Those first months after she had arrived I didn't even know that she could talk and thought she might be a mute until Reece said something so ridiculous that it even made Kelle laugh. The sound of laughter had been the first thing I'd heard coming from her mouth, and it had gotten me hooked.

I've known her now for five years, and in that time, we shared many intimacies, but she never shared anything about her time spent inside the plant. It was a topic that I quickly learned to avoid.

I shifted and cupped my hands around her face and swiped at the tears with my thumbs.

"Why didn't you tell me you were from Two?" I asked gently.

Kelle shook her head and opened her mouth, but no sound came out.

"No, of course, you wouldn't," I added as a faint smile formed on my lips. From the start, it had been evident that I'd be the one doing most of the talking in this relationship and I had accepted that. I kissed the top of her head and wrapped an arm around her shoulder.

"I'm gonna kick Harp's ass for sending you down there," I said in a firm tone and meant it. I hadn't known Kelle had grown up in Two, but Harp had. Returning to those plants was bad enough for us, let alone Kelle, and he should have anticipated this might be a problem.

"It's not his fault," Kelle said. Her voice was as timid as a child's. "He had offered me to sit this one out, but when we found out that Darren had jumped the gun and the process of neutralizing the regulators had begun, I figured you could use all the help you could get."

"Damnit," I said. "I really wanted to kick someone's ass."

A flicker of a smile appeared on Kelle's face but faded as soon as it had taken shape. I pulled her closer until her head rested on my shoulder.

"I'm so sorry I hurt you," she said. "So, so sorry. I didn't mean to." The pain in her voice was unmistakable.

"Don't worry about it," I said as caressed my fingers over the fine hairs on the back of her neck and soothingly stroked her. "It's fine."

NINE

MAECE

ALL GEARED up in my exoskeleton suit and weapons loaded, I walked up the steps leading to the main area of the rebel base underneath the City of Umbras. I was met by a flurry of activity on the platform and around the control center as the tension of an impending mission hung in the air. About two dozen rebels harnessed in the Subterran version of the exoskeleton suit had gathered near the bridge that led to the magnetic lift. Four at a time, a group crossed the bridge and rode up to where the transport stopped just below the surface.

The intricate tunnel system underneath the city would be our first hurdle on our way to the outer rim. As I peered into the faces of the men and women all with weapons and ready to go, I could almost feel their determination.

"You know, babe," Reece said in a low voice as he came up from behind me, "I love the look, all dark and mysterious, and the fact that this suit defines all your curves that I love so much. But it kind of defeats the purpose if you don't feel me grabbing your—"

I half turned before Reece could finish his sentence and elbowed him in the side. A smile tugged at my mouth as I watched his exaggerated reaction as if he were bending over in pain. I had barely touched him, and the Subterran version of the exoskeleton suit he wore would have absorbed most of the contact.

The slick material curved around his body and the additional hydraulics that enhanced strength and endurance made him look even broader and stronger. For a moment, I indulged in roaming my eyes over his muscled arms and chest. Reece's face, contorted in fake pain only seconds ago, screamed mischief as he noticed me checking him out, and he added a toothy grin.

Containing a smile, I refocused on the departing rebels. Reece sobered up as he followed my gaze.

"Nervous?" he asked. I closed my eyes for a moment and took a deep breath. With a slow deliberate exhale, I shook my head.

"Eager is probably a better word," I said, "although…" I paused trying to find the words of how I felt.

"Not happy with the odds," Reece suggested.

I nodded my consent and replied, "Something like that."

Across the platform, I noticed Riffy, who had joined Tyrel at her station. Two stations down from them, Harp pointed at something on a screen that

Kyran had brought up, but I couldn't locate the other members of our team.

Saera hadn't returned for the remaining duration of the trip, and I felt relieved to have seen her exit the Hymag with Kelle at her side.

I hadn't had a chance to talk to them, but except for red-rimmed eyes, Kelle had appeared as stony-faced as usual. Watching the remote way they acted, though, told me to keep my distance for a while. It seemed I wasn't the only one who had thought that. Reece had thrown them one of his wicked grins and Riffy had waved, but neither of them had dared to approach the two women.

"Have you talked to Saera or Kelle?" I asked. Reece shook his head as he started in the direction of the control center.

"I don't think I've ever seen Kelle like that," I said as I caught up with him. "Do you think that was because of the kid in Two?"

Reece gave me sideways glance that told me that he knew what I meant. He knew Kelle well enough to know that she would never talk to me about it, and he might not have seen me standing in the door of that Hymag the other night. Kelle and I had some issues over the years, although that was probably more my doing than hers. Jealousy isn't just a nasty word but also an undesirable trait to have, and it seemed that as a teenager, I had plenty.

At first, there was Reece fondling her all over, and I was too blind to see that he was just trying to help her fit in. Later, it felt as if Saera only had eyes for her, which was stupid of course. Petty things had kept me from forming a bond with one of the most important persons in my sister's life, and after I had made my choice to become an enforcer, it seemed too late. Now that I had promised to help Saera, I doubted Kelle and I would ever become close. The idea that she might hate me after me going behind her back made me appreciate the memory of Kelle showing up after the debacle in Two even more.

Reece didn't question me, though, on how I knew about the kid. "I think it might be a combination of things," he said. Reece had always been closer to Kelle than me, and sometimes I even wondered if she found it easier to talk to him than to Saera. "The kid, being back in Two, the refugees, and don't forget this wonderful excursion that we are about to undertake." He tried for a light tone and even shot me a grin, but his eyes couldn't hide his worries.

"Yeah," I replied, sounding resigned, but then added, "What do you mean, being back in Two? Did she used to live there?"

"Well, *living* is a big word when it comes to the plants," Reece said, "but yeah." I hadn't known that, and it surprised me that it hadn't come up in the pre-mission briefing.

"I guess we all know something about that," I muttered as we halted at the workstation where Harp stood.

Kyran nodded as Harp tapped on the screen. He looked thoughtful for a moment and stuck his HDA between his teeth as he started typing.

Harp stood and straightened his shoulders. He looked tired, and I figured he must have been awake most of the night planning. His gaze shifted briefly toward the bridge where the last group of four made their way across.

"We have received word from our scout team," he said. "They have secured the Hymag that will take you to the outer rim and are clearing the track."

"They did check if that old thing still works, right," Reece said.

Harp glared at him but didn't reply, although Reece's question was valid.

From the first day that Subterran society had taken their leave from the world above and chosen to live underground, they had made the inner earth their domain. In the centuries that had followed, the city, smaller communities, plants, and farms survived deep underground along with an intricate Hymag-line system. These electromagnetic Hymag lines reached far beyond the borders of Subterra and even extended to all the districts within Tenebrae.

After the war with the districts, most of these lines had either been destroyed, dismantled, or forgotten. These forgotten lines were not so much forgotten as shut down and hidden. The Combined Districts of Tenebrae might not have been aware of their existence, but for Subterra, these lines remained a tactical advantage that they never intended to relinquish. Special maintenance crews employed by the rebels and sworn to secrecy kept the lines up and running although the frequency of these checkups could have years in between. This had made Reece's question more than reasonable, although Harp would have anticipated as much.

As if someone had called his name, Harp turned, and as I followed his gaze, I saw Saera and Kelle approach.

"Let's take this to the conference table," he said. Harp gestured for the two women to follow, and so did we.

"Riffy," Reece bellowed midstride.

Glancing over my shoulder, I saw Riffy jump up. His face flushed as he gave Tyrel an apologetic look, said something, and then hurried over to us.

"Hey," I said and nudged Saera's shoulder. "You guys all right."

The weak smile she gave me didn't diminish the worry in her eyes, but she straightened her shoulders and faced me as she said, "We're good."

Kelle's eyes held a razor-sharp focus, and despite her short stature, she looked quite deadly in her black suit. Her prosthetic arm twitched as she looked up at me. She looked impassive with the mask she always wore back in place—as emotionless as ever. The apology that flashed across her eyes took me by surprise and caused a smile to tug at the corner of my mouth. She opened her mouth, but I didn't want her to voice her apology, because there was no need for it.

Before she could utter a word, I nodded and said, "We're all good, right?"

She replied with a nod, and I turned my attention

back to Harp. If he had known anything was up, it didn't show on his face.

"Are we ready?" I asked.

"There is one more thing," Harp said. "Kyran, pull up the design." His voice cut across the platform to where Kyran still sat at his station. A moment later, the screens hovering over our heads shimmered, and schematics of some device popped up.

"Oh, and Kyran," Harp added, "are the com techs still here?"

"JD has gone with the gear," Kyran said. Instead of shouting, Kyran's voice came in nice and clear over a speaker placed in the middle of the conference table. "Red is about ready. He'll join you in a minute."

"You see, Harp," Reece said in a mock tone. "That little box on the table will do wonders for your vocal cords, but then you do need to know which button to press."

From the expression on Harp's face, an accompanying growl would not have been misplaced. Unimpressed, Reece crossed his arms over his chest and grinned.

"This," Harp said in a sharp tone as he pointed up at the screen, "is a portable signal booster that we will use to tap into the Feed. Both teams will be joined by a communications technician that will plant the devices along your way until you reach your destination."

At the sound of footsteps pounding heavy on the stone floor, I shifted my gaze to see a young man running toward us. His gait appeared unsteady, and his breathing labored. The fact that he carried a pack that looked almost twice his size might have had something to do with it.

"Sir," he said between drawing in heavy gulps of air. "Reporting for duty."

"Red," Harp said.

I cocked an eyebrow as I scanned the young man again, armed with the knowledge of his name.

"That is not your name," Reece said, almost choking on a laugh. Despite the mocking, his voice held sympathy for the newcomer.

The new guy wasn't just young; he was also short, maybe a little taller than Kelle if he were lucky. In addition to his extensive pack, he also wore an exoskeleton suit that told me a bit about how heavy his load could actually be. What stood out, though, were the freckles on his round face and the neatly trimmed, bright-orange hair that covered his scalp.

Red looked up to face Reece, and he didn't look amused.

"It is, sir," he said in a clipped voice. "Is that a problem for you?" Red, shifted his pack up his back but kept his eyes locked on Reece. "Maybe too many syllables for you to remember—sir."

"Uh, no, no," Reece said in a near stutter. "It, uh…suits you." He shot me a desperate look as if he needed saving. Riffy snorted a laugh and used his elbow to shove Reece aside.

"Nice to meet you, Red," he said, still chuckling as he held out his hand. "I'm Riffy." They shook, but before anyone else had a chance to introduce themselves properly, Harp cut in.

"Save the formalities for later," he said. "Red will join Maece's team, and he'll be responsible for your communication." He turned to Saera. "JD will be on your team, but the setup for interstellar communication is a bit bigger, so we've sent it ahead."

"I thought Kyran would be coming with us?" Saera asked. Harp didn't look at her as he replied.

"Plans change."

None of the others seemed to question this as Harp turned back to the monitor. "Red has been working at the Department of Science and Technologies for the better part of three years now. With Spiro's help, he has been one of many responsible for reverse-engineering Maece's suit and building us better ones." Harp said, "Now, they have come up with this."

The device displayed on the monitor looked like nothing I had ever seen before.

"This device will ensure our communication with the freighter over long distances," Harp continued. "They'll have to be deployed at certain intervals for them to work, but JD is up to speed, so I'm not expecting any problems."

I scrutinized the screen and let the information shared by Harp sink in.

It was almost funny how he managed to avoid having to explain all of the technical bits. The initial design of the device appeared cylindrical, but as the graphic representation on the screen played out, and certain parts unfolded, it changed shape. The availability of this technology didn't sit well with me.

"Once the devices have been deployed, you'll be able to relay the information gathered from observing the station—"

"Been planning ahead, have we," I said.

Harp froze midsentence and lowered his head. Then he straightened his shoulders and laced his hands behind his back before he turned to face me. My heart rate picked up a notch as I anticipated a confrontation that I hadn't intended to elicit. Fortunately, Harp wasn't looking for a fight either.

"I like to be prepared," Harp said. He didn't say anything else, and as he stood in that statue pose of his while those dark eyes bore into me, I felt like a ten-year-old again—waiting for my scolding. Help came from an unexpected corner.

"The technology is actually rather old, ma'am," Red said. "Ever since we found out about Sulos's space station, we've unearthed it, brushed it off, and added some tidbits of our own."

"I see," I said without taking my eyes off Harp. "Thank you, Red."

"Now, if you don't mind, I would like to finish this before I die of old age," Harp said.

The constant crunch of gravel underneath boots laced with the hum of murmured voices bounced off the walls of the darkened tunnel. I hadn't been fond of my heads-up device for a while, but I started to wish that the Department of Science and Technologies had spent some time creating copies of it. If there was one positive thing to say about ArtRep, it was that they knew how to build their gadgets.

The illusion of confinement with the goggles strapped to my face often gave me a claustrophobic feeling, but I started to miss them. At least I would have been able to mute the sound around me and could have used the night-vision setting to see a whole lot better.

Scattered beams originating from wrist lights cut through the darkness ahead of me, occasionally illuminating the dark shapes walking in front of me. I had no idea how long we had walked, but my eyes were getting weary, and I feared that if I closed them, I would fall asleep midwalk.

On hindsight, maybe hitting the bar last night hadn't been one of our brightest ideas, because even though Riffy's medicine had helped, my head felt heavy. I couldn't say I regretted it. My lips curved into a smile at the memory and took in the silhouette moving by my side. His face might have been hidden in shadows, but everything about him was distinctly Reece.

At first, the trek through the pitch-black corridors reminded me of when Saera had come for me. Back then, I still thought that I was an enforcer employed by the Tenebrae Enforcer Department and feared something had gone wrong with my programming. Saera had helped me to keep an open mind even though I had remained convinced that I didn't have a mind of my own. That walk from the hospital to the rebel base had become a fond memory. This time, I didn't think this walk would end up in my memory books of things I was fond of.

All we had been doing was setting one foot in front of the other, trying not to trip over some else's feet and listen to the awful sound of rock grinding underneath the soles of boots.

"How much longer?" I asked no one in particular, although Reece walking by my side would be the most likely candidate.

"About five minutes less than the last time you asked," he said.

I didn't intend to groan, but it slipped out.

I wasn't sure how much time had passed as I first notice the crackle in my ear device, but I sighed in relief. It meant we were getting in range of the communication devices of the group that had departed ahead of us. I even picked up the pace when I noticed the light growing more evident at the end of the tunnel.

"I don't think I've ever been this glad to see a Hymag," I said as we exited out of the darkness. It wasn't as if the space we had entered had so much better lighting, but at least I could recognize the faces around me again.

The platform that stretched out along the length of the Hymag was about as broad as the tunnel we had just exited. Doors on the different Hymag compartments stood open, and the lights that radiated from inside the transport were enough to keep us from tripping on and over each other.

A hum of voices bounced off the walls as rebels worked to stock the Hymag with our supplies. Crates filled with food, guns, and other supplies were loaded onto the transport as we made our way to the first compartment.

As the last in line, I waited behind Saera at the entrance of the Hymag.

All around me rebels checked their gear and exoskeleton suits as they waited at the different entryways to get inside the Hymag. There was some murmur of voices, but it seemed conversation wasn't something that was on their minds, and the sounds of buckles snapping, hissing hydraulics, and metallic clanks filled the space.

As my eyes looked over the anxious faces, I spotted Harp standing next to a couple of boxes that hadn't yet been loaded onto the transport. His face was expressionless as he monitored the rebels' progress. He wouldn't be going with us; at least not on the same Hymag. Harp would board a different transport, one especially equipped with the latest in communications technology and monitoring equipment.

The need for answers still plagued me, and I knew that if I was going to confront Harp about them, it would have to be now.

"Hold up a sec," I said to Saera, who stopped midstride and looked down at me from the first step. "I need to talk to Harp."

A flash of worry crossed her face as she spotted Harp beyond the crowd before returning her attention to me.

"Don't worry," I said. "It's not about that." I had no intention of telling Harp about Saera's request, but even though I wanted to help her keep Kelle on Earth, I needed more information. I couldn't risk this entire operation; too many lives were at stake. Harp was the only one who could give me that information, although I'd have to figure out a way to get it from him without giving away Saera. About the question still lingering in her eyes, I said, "I'll tell you later," and handed her my pack.

Harp's expression never changed as I walked up to him and asked, "Can I talk to you?"

He inclined his head to the side before turning, and I followed him to a small structure that was once used to store maintenance equipment.

Inside, Harp leaned against a table and folded his arms over his chest. The small shack stood empty except for a couple of boxes and the table shoved against the wall.

I closed the door behind me and found myself trapped by his narrow gaze. Something was up, and I guessed it could be one of many things. He must've heard about Kelle's outburst, although I didn't think this would be about something that obvious. Harp tended to home in on the little things.

I tried not to fidget as I pondered what to say. By now I should've learned how to deal with Harp's probing gaze, and I had. I wasn't a little kid anymore, but sometimes he still got to me, and besides, he was Harp. Apparently, this was one of those times.

He did it on purpose, of course; scrutinizing us to the point of making us feel uncomfortable. I'd always compared it to an interrogation technique. When we were kids, he used the same method when he knew we had done something wrong. When we were younger, he only needed to look at us like he was doing right now to get us talking, without even having to ask a question. It didn't work on all of us; not anymore, although I don't think Riffy ever learned how to withstand it.

"I have questions," I said, and to my relief my voice stayed steady.

"I see," Harp said. I wanted to roll my eyes at his minimalistic remark, but I managed to keep my composure.

"Why the freighter?"

The corner of his mouth gave the tiniest of twitches, and I wondered if that meant that he was pleased with me. Pleased that I had seen through his diversion of not wanting to tell us. To his credit, he didn't seem to try and derail me again.

"Kelle wasn't that far off about me and wanting to go after Sulos," he said, "but not because of revenge, as she implied." I managed to keep my mouth shut and controlled my fidgeting as I waited for him to continue. "My main concerns are the neuro-regulators. Sulos could kill thousands in an instance, and I'm not just talking about plant workers and enforcers. He's been using hospitals like Icordia to implant the devices in citizens."

At the mention of the hospital's name, my stomach churned, and the taste of bile rose in my throat. I didn't think I could ever hear that name again without feeling sick—not after what they had done to me.

"But he can destroy the planet by activating the wormhole generator," I said.

"I agree," Harp replied.

"Then why go through so much trouble?"

"Because destroying the planet means no more resources," he said. "It would be much more efficient for him to control the population."

"If he can do all that, then what is the purpose of this New World of his and why the hell are we going after it?" I said and threw my hands up in despair.

Harp grimaced and shook his head as if resigned. He lowered his gaze and placed his hands on the edge of the table. I didn't think I'd ever seen him sitting in a slouched position. He had always seemed to proud to let his posture slip.

"From what Kyran has learned, the station is far from ready," he said, sounding subdued. "I have a theory, but I'm not one to act on hunches. I need to know, and that's why we need eyes on it." He watched me for a long moment in silence as if he were gauging my reaction. "I need you to trust me on this."

"Why can't you trust me and for once tell me straight what's going on?"

"Because at this point the information would do more harm than good," he said.

Closing my eyes for a second, I pinched the bridge of my nose–this situation was starting to give me a headache. I had heard those words before. Harp had used them often when we were younger and I tended to question his orders. It had taken some of us longer than others, but over the years we had come to trust his judgment and didn't even bother anymore to ask about his reasons for doing the things in the ways he did.

Facing him again, I said, "Then why not let us all go after Sulos? Why split up the team?" This time my voice did waver, but I didn't care because his decisions concerned the only family I had left.

Harp blew out a breath as if by questioning him, I had annoyed him.

"You know why," he said in a harsh tone that made me flinch. He had explained the night before that he needed to keep Darren from going after the remaining plants, and promising to go after the wormhole generator along with releasing all the intel on Sulos on the Feed had become the way to do that. Still, things didn't add up in ways that they had done on previous missions.

"Then why split us up the way you have?" I said in a raised voice. "I mean, Reece is the only one of us who's ever been on one of those ships–"

"Reece's piloting skills are not needed on that particular mission," he said.

The abrupt way in which he had cut me off

should have told me that he had no intention of continuing this discussion, but I couldn't help myself. I felt annoyed that once again Harp was keeping things from us—not that that should've surprised me.

"And you're sending Saera, who couldn't—" I started to say.

"Enough," Harp said as he stood up from the table. He straightened his shoulders while his eyes never wavered from mine.

I stood my ground because this time I wasn't going to let him get away with this so easily. It wasn't just that I needed to know what was going on to aid my decision in helping Saera or not. This was my family that he was putting in the line of fire, and I needed more of an answer from Harp than him trying to please Darren.

As if he were reading my mind, he stared at me for the longest time. The choice what to do or say next seemed to weigh heavily on him, but I didn't care.

"I think Sulos might have an insider within the government," he finally said.

Even though it shouldn't have come as a surprise, my mouth fell open, and I blinked. "Who?"

"Monroe thinks it might be Elise Henkel, but I believe it might be Luther Wear."

I let out a breath as I remembered the people sitting at a table on top of a stage after we were summoned to appear before the council. Henkel, a middle-aged woman, had worked for the Subterran government all her life and had been second alderman for as long as I could remember. Although the years started to show on her face, she always had looked the same to me with her too-long white hair trapped in a ponytail. The only thing I knew about Wear was that he sported a weird-looking comb-over that seemed unnatural and that he had looked uncomfortable with his flushed, round cheeks as we stood before him in that spacious room.

Both Henkel and Wear were part of that council and, because of it, had intricate knowledge of the rebel forces and their activities.

Fortunately, we had Monroe, who was also part of the council, to keep some things—such as our involvement at the plants—under wraps. If either of these people was associated with Sulos, then that could account for the extra amount of secrecy that seemed to hover over this mission.

"Maece, this thing is bigger than you can imagine," he said in that authoritative tone of his that I had come to know so long ago. "You of all people should know how he can use our own people against us, but I need you to let me worry about those things, and I need you to focus on your task."

With our eyes locked on each other, he leaned in. "Do you trust me?" There was no reason for me to lie, so I didn't.

"Yes."

His eyes never veered from mine as if he were attempting to read the truth from my mind. It felt a bit disconcerting as I tried not to blink. Finally, he eased off.

"Then trust me when I tell you a plan is in place,"

he said and reached out a hand to touch my upper arm.

The gesture seemed foreign to me, although it probably shouldn't. He'd never been an emotionally available parent, and I would never have asked that of him. He had been the guy that had taken us in and had kept us safe. In his own way, he had been there for us, and I was eternally grateful to him for that. Still, for the first time in my life, I actually considered breaking his trust. The promise I'd made Saera hung over me like a sledgehammer about to squash me. Saera was my sister, and I had known her long before Harp. I would do anything for her, especially after what I had put her through, but at what cost?

"Harp," I said without having given any thought to what I wanted to say. He must have heard something in my voice because his eyes softened, and he squeezed my arm with the hand still resting there.

I felt as if I needed to ask a million questions but knew I had received the answers Harp had been willing to give. I shook my head as I stared into his eyes and read the trust that lay behind them.

"Good, let's get out of here," he said as he reached around me and opened the door. "C'mon, I want you to meet Laurence Castle."

TEN

SAERA

I COULDN'T BELIEVE the tension I felt in my muscles, and it took some effort to keep myself seated. My leg kept bouncing up and down even after several attempts to stop it from doing so. Kelle seemed oblivious to my fidgeting, but Maece kept an eye on me. She pulled a face once or twice as if telling me to calm down—it didn't work.

Around me the compartment filled with nervous chatter without anyone saying anything interesting. That should have been comforting, knowing that the rebels who had joined us seemed as anxious as I felt, but then I didn't think my worries were the same as theirs.

They had a mission to focus on. A job that entailed breaching the outer rim defenses and confiscating a space freighter. After that, most of them would join me on an interstellar trip that didn't even have a follow-up plan. I probably should be worried about that, but I wasn't.

I glanced at Kelle, who sat on my left, and was surprised to meet her gaze. She'd been staring at the hands folded in her lap for most of the trip, but it seemed her attention had shifted. She moved her hand over mine and laced our fingers. Even though those fingers were artificial, her touch felt gentle. Through the glove she wore I could feel the cold metal, but I knew the sensors embedded in her hand would register it as I answered her gesture with a soft squeeze.

"Hey," she said, and my leg instantly relaxed as I turned my attention to her. "It'll be fine."

"I know," I said and tried to smile. Kelle's gaze narrowed, but I could only detect gentleness in her eyes.

"You're biting your lip," she said.

I closed my eyes for a second and stopped myself from digging my teeth into my lower lip. It wasn't a secret that being nervous had me biting my lip. Having it pointed out to me made me feel like an open book, but then I was just that to Kelle. I did not doubt that she'd figured out something was up. I just hoped I'd managed to hide it a little longer.

"I'm good," I replied with a sigh as I opened my eyes. The look in Kelle's eyes told me she wasn't convinced, but she nodded anyway. That was the only perk of being with someone who kept her own secrets; she respected me keeping mine.

At the sound of snoring, her gaze shifted to the

seats across from us, and as my eyes followed, I found Riffy sitting stretched out with his feet perched on the seat to my right—fast asleep. His lips pursed as he puffed out his breath and his mouth twitched as if surprised by the sound that followed.

Reece sat next to him with his eyes closed, but the small circles he drew with his thumb on the back of Maece's hand told me he was awake. Maece seemed entranced by watching the movement but looked up as the Hymag started to decelerate.

It wasn't long after that the transport stopped and one of the rebels who appeared to be in charge stood and started barking out orders.

"Get your gear ready, and from the moment these doors open, keep your mouths shut," he said as he moved down the aisle. "Sound travels like crazy down these tunnels, and I don't need any surprises."

I hadn't met the guy with the bald head and a noticeable limp, but I'd seen Maece talking to him before we left. He had his face set in a permanent snarl, and it seemed wise to do as he said—everyone around me did anyway. Despite the fussing around, it seemed deadly quiet inside the compartment as rebels stood to grab their gear and waited for the doors to open. Maece and the others remained seated, so I did the same. Not a word had been uttered after the bald guy had spoken, except for a tiny yelp from Riffy as the man's loud voice had jolted him out of his nap.

A soft hum indicated the doors opening, and the rebels started to file out. Reece yawned and stretched out his limbs, kicking my shins in the process.

"Sorry," he said as his joints cracked.

Riffy mimicked his friend's movements, but with a lot less flair. "So now what?" Riffy asked.

"Now we wait for the big bad-ass über-rebel to return," Reece replied.

"Who is that guy anyway?" I asked.

"That's Laurence Castle," Maece said, "Harp put him in charge of the rebel platoon." The way she said it with her eyebrows raised, I had a feeling Maece wasn't all that convinced of the man's abilities.

"How do you know?" I asked.

"Harp introduced me before we left."

Not sure how to feel about that, I lifted my head to see over the back of my chair and watched how Castle made his way back to us. *Why would Harp introduce Maece and not me?* As Castle walked, he used every seat that he passed to lean on, and I wondered if the man could actually walk without support. I figured that even Riffy would be able to outrun Castle.

A loud cough and a gurgling sound forced all our heads to turn in Castle's direction. Up close, I could see the creases that marked his face along with the scars that crisscrossed his right cheek and temple. From the way he presented himself, the experience of a seasoned soldier stood front and center, but the fact those years had long passed also was evident.

"The name's Castle," he said in a gruff voice. "I'll be your tour guide for today." The man might have been old, but he hadn't lost his intimidation factor.

Afraid to move, I shifted my eyes to see if I could catch some reactions from the others. All of them seemed to be frozen in place, not unlike me. Even Reece appeared to have been caught off guard. After the silence had stretched on for a moment too long, Maece cleared her throat.

"Then I guess, uh…show us the way," she said.

Castle's dark eyes roamed over us as if he were sizing us up one by one. I caught myself biting my lower lip again just before Castle gestured with his head and beckoned us to follow. As soon as he turned his back to us, I scanned the wide-eyed faces and raised eyebrows of our group.

"He seems nice," Reece said.

"More like scary," Riffy added.

"C'mon. Let's get moving," Maece interjected before Reece and Riffy could unleash their banter upon us.

I stood, grabbing my gear, and handed Kelle hers. She shrugged as she took it and then said, "I kind of like him."

"You like everyone who doesn't say more than five words," Reece said as he fastened his belt and checked his weapons.

"I like you," Kelle replied and added, more as an afterthought, "sometimes." A hint of mischief sparkled in her eyes, but she kept it from showing on her face.

Reece feigned being taken aback before he raised a finger.

"Don't pretend that you don't love me," he said as he shook his finger like a scolding parent. "You know damn well you can't resist my loveliness."

Kelle scoffed, but I could tell she had a hard time keeping a smile from brightening up her face. Before she could do anything else, Reece advanced, nearly stumbling over a pack that lingered on the floor, and wrapped Kelle up in his strong arms.

"Reece," Kelle muttered as he lifted her off the ground.

"Yes, and I love you, too," he said before he sat her down.

"Get off me," she said as he elbowed him in the gut. He didn't even pretend to have felt it as a grin spread across his face. The smile Kelle had been trying to hide broke out on her face, and her eyes seemed to dance as even the smallest amount of joy flashed across them.

Looking smug, Reece poked a finger into her shoulder and said, "Made you smile."

Kelle shook her head as if she wanted to deny it, but the smile was still there as our eyes met. She looked so beautiful at that moment that if I could, I would have stayed in that fraction of time forever.

Unfortunately, time wasn't on our side.

ELEVEN

MAECE

ANOTHER TREK THROUGH DARK TUNNELS. This was getting annoying. Not to mention that I had to listen to an entire platoon of boots stomping gravel into the ground. Fortunately, we didn't have to go too far. The Hymag had brought us pretty close to where we needed to be, but we hadn't dared to take it any closer to the outer rim. The engine noise might have set off an alarm.

Castle had taken the lead, and I was stunned at the steady pace the old man kept. It wasn't as if I had any problems to keep up with him, but judging by Riffy's heavy breathing behind me, Castle might have had some of us on the brink of collapse.

Our little group of five followed in Castle's wake while the rest of the platoon trailed behind us. With another of Castle's reminders to keep our mouths shut fresh in our minds, we moved in relative silence. The occasional murmur disrupted the constant pounding of boots, but that was it—until…

At first, I felt it as a distant tremor that reverberated underneath my boots. As we moved further down the darkened tunnel, the slight tremor started to resemble the effects of an earthquake, but of course, it couldn't be that. Earthquakes didn't take this long—*would they?* Questioning looks from Riffy and Saera urged me to check it out.

"What is it?" I asked as I moved closer to Castle. I almost had to shout to raise my voice over a mechanical roar that accompanied the by now constant shaking of the ground, and I had to steady myself against the wall. Castle didn't answer, and as a response, I pointed the light from my wrist device in his direction. The beam hit his face, illuminating the red lines of the scar tissue that zigzagged across his right cheek and temple.

He shifted his head to avoid the light from blinding him before he stopped and slapped my hand away. Repositioning my light a little lower so I could still see his face, I watched as he pressed a finger to his ear. His sudden stopping caused a bit of a pileup behind us, and someone bumped into me. Shifting my light, I caught Saera steadying herself with a hand on my shoulder. She mouthed a word, and I assumed it to be "Sorry," but I couldn't hear her over the noise. The beam from my wrist device trailed over the alarmed-looking faces of my friends and the rebels behind them. Then I turned my attention back to Castle.

"Red," he said with a look of concentration on his

face, "report." Before we left, Castle had sent out a group ahead of us, including Red, our new communications guy. He was supposed to set up relay devices that would make communication this far underground a bit easier.

As Castle tried to make out Red's reply, the others gathered around me while the platoon taking up the rear waited patiently. I had no doubt of the tension written across the faces of these men and women, which made me appreciate these dark tunnels a little more. The amount of tension building in my own gut felt enough to have to face at this point.

"What's going on? Is it an earthquake?" Riffy asked in a loud voice. In response Castle made an annoyed gesture with his hand that suggested for Riffy to shut up.

"Say again?" Castle shouted this time as he pressed a hand to the communications device lodged in his ear and moved away from our group.

"I have a bad feeling about this," Reece said.

"Are we too late?" Kelle asked. Her raised voice intended to reach over the rumble suddenly seemed too loud as the tremors reverberating through the ground died down. As if stunned by the silence, we remained quiet while the bright lights from our wrist devices bounced off the walls.

"I don't think so," I said as I pointed my light in Castle's direction.

He stopped and turned to us as he spoke. "That was an engine test. We need to hurry."

"How long do we have?" I called after Castle who had already started to move again.

"Depends on whether they've loaded the ship or not," he replied over his shoulder. "If not, about a day, if it's loaded, about an hour or two."

Without the need for another word, we started after him. An engine test meant that the freighter was getting ready for departure. With no indication of when another ship would arrive and the probability that it could be months, we couldn't afford to miss the opportunity to confiscate this freighter. One half of the mission depended on it.

It seemed unbelievably quiet as I sat hunkered down against the wall of the tunnel, but it wasn't as if I was alone. Saera, Reece, Kelle, and Riffy sat close by, but even though the lights from our wrist devices bounced off the walls, in the dark, I felt as if I was alone.

The up-and-coming events raged inside my head despite the fact that I had no control over them. Then there was this slight issue that Harp had asked me to trust him and Saera had basically pleaded for me to go against him by helping her get Kelle off the ship. As if that wasn't enough, all of a sudden, my brain decided to emphasize that I might lose one of the people closest to me. Harp had expressed his reasons for sending the freighter, but he kept stonewalling me when it came to what he had planned for the ship.

Was Saera right in her assumption that this was a suicide

mission? Was Harp using them as bait or as a distraction? Could it be that he had set up this entire mission just to figure out who Sulos's insider within the Subterran government might be?

I glanced at Saera, who sat by my side, and the anxiety wreaking havoc inside her was apparent. She kept fidgeting as she alternated between checking her weapon and her suit.

The eerie staccato of a single pair of boots echoed inside the narrow space as Castle paced up and down the tunnel. He'd been doing that ever since we had stopped while he waited for a word from the scouts he had sent out ahead.

To successfully execute our plan, we needed three exit points. Castle's group would create a distraction while Saera's group would seize the ship. I would lead the third group, and it was our job to retract the shield, so the space freighter could take off. The scouts Castle had sent out were looking for ways to access the landing platform that would help us in carrying out that plan.

"How's this JD person doing?" I asked in a hushed voice. Saera turned to me, and she seemed a bit surprised by my question as if she was unsure why I'd asked. "You know, do you think she can handle it?" I asked, probing her for a reply. Trying to get Saera to talk was the only thing I could think of to keep her nerves in check. Besides, listening to her voice had a calming effect on me.

"She seems all right," Saera answered with some hesitation. She checked to see if the seasoned rebel were anywhere near, but I knew JD had stayed at the back of the platoon to stay close to her gear. "I've talked to her a bit on our walk over. Apparently she comes from a line of military folk. Her grandfather fought in the war. Her family wasn't too happy when she decided on a career in technology. They don't know she's with the rebels. She knows her stuff, though, and she seems nice, but I don't know her yet, and going on big missions, you need to depend on people, so I'm not sure."

"But you think she's up to it?" I asked.

"I guess...she should be up for the task...," Saera said and hesitated again. The light from my wrist device caught her face, and it bounced off her sharp-edged jaw. Her fair skin tone seemed even paler than usual as she bit her lower lip and shot me a knowing smile when she realized what I was doing.

"Is this because I'm nervous or because you're nervous?" she asked.

"I think it might be a little of both."

She nodded as she reached for my hand and squeezed it in appreciation. We had done this ever since we were kids—this little tension breaker. Saera always seemed to relax when I got her to talk, and to get her to talk, I needed to ask the questions. As a reverse bonus, hearing Saera talk relaxed me.

Castle moved toward us again; his limp seemed worse after the walking we had done. There hadn't been much time to rest for me or the rest of us, so this short intermission had come as a blessing. I had a feeling there wouldn't be much rest in the time to come. It didn't seem to slow Castle down, though.

Castle stopped pacing, with his hand pressed to his ear, and I noticed the others watching him expectantly. My stomach churned as the anticipation grew that this had to be it. One look at Saera told me she felt the same, as a muscle in her jaw flexed.

"Copy that," Castle said to the person on the other end of the line before he turned to face us. In a moment of unnerving silence, he let his light flicker over the anxious faces staring up at him. He cleared his throat before he spoke with an authority that reminded me of Harp.

"Attention!" With that one word every member of the platoon, including the five of us, climbed to their feet. Except for the five of us, all of them stood at attention in one long line of men and women eager to carry out their mission.

"We have come a long way together," he said, "but this is where we go our separate ways. Some of us may meet again, and some of us won't. Know that I have faith in all of you. Remember your training, listen to your group leaders, and victory will be ours."

I might have expected applause or a loud cheer, but then remembered Castle's order to remain quiet. Apparently, authority was the only resemblance between Harp and Castle. When it came to Harp, I didn't think he had ever issued an order with more than five words. From the approving faces, I figured these men and women didn't just appreciate Castle's approach—they needed it.

"Let's move out!"

There was no need for him to explain the plan

again because we had gone through it several times. All that was left to do was to get into position and actually do what was expected of us.

Our primary objective was to get the members of Saera's group to the space freighter. Boarding the freighter was our first priority, and although we hadn't expected a lot of crewmembers aboard ship during the planning phase, things might have changed. The engine test had proven that the maintenance work had all but finished. Loading crews could already be hard at work stocking the ship together with the ship's crew to get the freighter ready for departure. This could mean more resistance.

Castle had chosen a few loyal rebels to accompany him in setting up a distraction. He hadn't disclosed much of his plan, and that didn't sit well with me, but I had it on good authority that Castle was a man that I could trust.

After our talk inside the small storage shed, Harp had walked me over to meet Castle, and I had learned a thing or two about him. Harp had asked me then to trust him. It turned out that they had been friends for years and that Castle had once saved Harp's life. Harp being Harp, he hadn't gone into any details, and he had kept his emotions from showing on his face. I hadn't told Harp that for me it was easy to read the truth behind his eyes. He wouldn't have liked that. It was enough for me to trust Castle, though—even if it meant we had to put our lives into his hands.

The last and smallest group would be my own. Only Reece, Riffy, and Red, our new communications guy, would join me in an attempt to seize control of the shield. Similar in construct to the shields protecting the main cities, a generator would be used to create a protective dome.

Fortunately for us, where the cities would need several generators, the smaller shield, used to protect the outer rim, only needed one. Circuit breakers with the ability to add or reduce power were used to control the size of the shield. For a space freighter to take off, it would have to be unrestricted. If it weren't, it wouldn't be able to take off and the output of the freighter's massive engines would heat up the inside of the dome until everything inside it melted—including us.

I didn't expect much of a challenge in overtaking the building that held the shield-generator controls. That wasn't the problem, and it wasn't what I felt nervous about. After all, I had managed to take out five freaks. A shiver ran up my spine at the memory of trying to get to that last freak as it had its artificial fingers wrapped around Saera's throat and had attempted to choke the life out of her. The how and what of what had happened next seemed to elude me. It felt more like a dreamlike blur of motions, but even though the lingering memories of that event didn't make it feel as if they were real, it did, however, make me feel confident enough to know that I'd be able to do this.

Another problem lay in getting the shield down without having any of our troops caught outside the shield. With the dying sun hovering over our heads, radiation and the heat would be unbearable. Our frail human bodies would boil from the inside out if caught outside the shield. The freighter was built to withstand the harsh environment, so to prevent certain death, the rebels should either get themselves on board or retreat underground as soon as the shield started to retract. The thing that really me nervous, though, was the promise I had made to Saera.

We stood with our backs pressed against the wall as the rebels headed out. As they moved past us in a single file, wearing their exoskeleton suits and armed to the teeth, it would have been easy to have mistaken them for enforcers. As if these men and women were some mindless automatons made for battle. A quick look at the passing faces told me they weren't. Even though eagerness showed on several of the faces, it was a combination of anxiety and fear that was revealed on most.

Beyond the faces, I caught a glimpse of Kelle, who had moved to stand on the other side of the tunnel to let the rebels pass. Like the rest of us, she, too, stood with her back against the wall. Every so often her face was illuminated by one of the wrist devices of the passersby and revealed her stoic features. Her dark, focused eyes did not move even one second from the person standing beside me.

I looked at Saera. She held that gaze, and for an instance, I wondered how that must feel until I found Reece's eyes fixed on me. Those same lights from the passing rebels illuminated Reece's face, and my breath caught as I drowned myself in those blue depths, causing me to feel a sense of relief. Relief that, no matter what was about to be thrown at us, we'd be together. The sensation quickly evaporated as I remembered that Saera wouldn't have that, and neither would Kelle if I did as Saera had asked. The last of the rebels strode by before I could linger on the consequences of my promise to Saera.

"Maece, Saera, a moment please." Castle's voice rose above the footsteps of the marching rebels, capturing my attention. I gestured for the others to stay before Saera and I moved further down the tunnel to where Castle stood. We kept our lights down, and Castle's face remained hidden in shadows as he spoke.

"The advance teams have cleared our exit points. These tunnels are like a maze. Keep going down this main one, and someone from your team will be waiting for you to direct you to where you need to go. Harp told me to give you guys a moment before show time—you have five minutes."

Castle paused a moment and even though I couldn't see much of his face, I knew his eyes had ventured over my shoulder toward the others.

"You are a strange bunch," he said with a chuckle. As he spoke again, his voice held something somber. "Harp has the utmost faith in you, and therefore, so have I. Make us proud."

I shifted the light on my wrist, so I could see his face. Despite the faint smile, Castle looked resigned, and it seemed to me as if he were trying to hide something. Something that he didn't want us to know.

A strange feeling that Castle might already know part of the outcome fell over me, and I fought the urge to voice it. Considering Castle was friends with Harp, I didn't expect the subject to be open for discussion.

Without another word he turned and started his way down the tunnel. It wasn't long before his form became engulfed by the surrounding darkness and I faced Saera. She looked anxious, and it wasn't hard to imagine why.

Moving my mouth closer to her ear, I said so the others wouldn't hear, "You still sure about this?" I didn't have to explain that I meant the promise she had asked me to make.

She shifted her hand, so her wrist device gave us ample light to see each other. There was a determination in her eyes as she replied.

"You're the strongest and fastest of all of us. You'll keep her safe, because…," she started to say, but her voice wavered. As she cleared her throat, she briefly glanced back at the others, and as our eyes reconnected, there was a smile on her face. "Because that's what you do. That's what you've always done."

"But what about you?" I hadn't meant to ask the question, and I hadn't intended for the desperation I felt to resonate in my voice. I would never question Saera's ability to take care of herself because she had done that along with taking care of me for years and still did, but I couldn't hide the helplessness I felt. That sensation was brought on because I still felt conflicted about going through with this. I had promised Saera, and I could never imagine breaking that promise—not after having abandoned her for years, but what about Harp? I could still hear the urgency in his voice as he reminded me that there was more at stake here. *Why couldn't he have just told me what he had planned for the ship?*

Maybe then I'd been able to convince Saera that her situation wasn't as dire as she thought it was. The fact that Harp hadn't explained caused me to share Saera's concerns, and thinking about it made me feel sick to my stomach—I wasn't ready to lose her. Nausea threatened to overtake me as the horror I had put her through dawned on me.

At the sound of footsteps drawing closer, she threw her arms around me and pulled me close.

"Don't worry about me," she said near my ear. "You keep your promise, please, that's all I need."

I nodded against her shoulder as I returned the hug. I clung to her as I had done years ago just before I had left to become an enforcer. She hadn't known what I had planned, but for me, it had been one of the hardest things I had ever had to do. For some reason that seemed to pale compared to this. Even though Harp had tried to reassure me that he had a plan, I couldn't get past this sinking feeling in the pit of my stomach that this could be the last time that I saw her. *Was she thinking the same thing? Was that the reason she didn't want Kelle to come?*

As I held on to her one thing became clear. If this was the last time we'd be together, I was going to make damn sure that she'd end up resenting me for breaking my promise. I had to keep Kelle from taking off on that ship.

Drawing in a deep breath, I noticed Kelle standing several feet behind Saera, and I cleared my throat as a way of telling Saera that it was time.

"You got this," I said as I released Saera from my grip. The confidence in my voice surprised me even though the feeling didn't resonate inside.

"Thank you," she said before she kissed me on the cheek. "And be safe." She released me and took a step back.

"Be safe," I managed to say, and she gave me a final reassuring nod before she turned to Kelle.

Maybe I had hoped she'd change her mind. My conversation with Harp might have had something to do with it. He knew things I didn't, and I feared that keeping Kelle from going with Saera might turn out to be a big mistake—she might be needed up there. I wasn't willing to lose Kelle just as much as I didn't want to lose Saera, but I also didn't wish for Saera to have to do this on her own.

My legs felt as if they were about to give out, and I didn't even think the exoskeleton suit would have kept me upright if it hadn't been for the supporting arm that wrapped around my waist.

"You okay?" Reece asked in a gentle tone.

He led me further down the tunnel to create a bit of a distance between us and the others. Our bodies appeared merged as one as our shadows created by the combined lights of our wrist devices graced the walls where he pulled me to a stop. Not sure if my voice would hold up, I nodded my reply and slid my arm that held the wrist devise behind Reece's back.

He did the same, effectively bathing our faces in darkness. My other hand rose to cup his face. Underneath my hand, I felt a smile form on his face, but as his lips closed in on mine, I failed to see it. All I could do was feel the warmth of his mouth and the strength of his body pressed against mine.

"Better now?" he asked as he pulled back.

Unable to contain a smile, I replied, "Almost."

He took that as his cue to kiss me again. As if moving on their own, my arms snaked over his shoulders, and I let my fingers trail through his hair. It was at times like these that I regretted the need to breathe. My chest heaved as Reece pulled away again and pressed his forehead against mine.

"This'll be over before you know it," he said a little breathy, "and then we'll stay in my room for a week."

"A week?"

"We might have to come out for food," he said and kissed me again. As an afterthought, he added, "Maybe I can get Riffy to bring us some. Don't worry. I'll figure it out."

"Are you sure?" I asked seriously, unable to keep the joke going. Needing to see his reaction, I shifted my arm with the wrist light, so it would illuminate his face.

"Babe," he said as he shot me a cheeky grin, "I'm always sure, and you should know that by now."

Strangely enough, his words felt reassuring, and I wished we could've stayed in that moment a bit longer.

As if he sensed that I was about to ask he added,

"And don't worry about Kelle, I have a plan." Before I could ask what he had come up with, Reece presses his lips to mine. A hesitant voice pulled us back into reality, though.

"Guys, five minutes are almost up," Riffy said as he trailed his wrist light over us. His timid voice forced my lips away from Reece's, and I turned my head to look at him. Riffy looked lost as he stood in the dark with one hand in his pocket. He shifted to look over his shoulder to where Saera and Kelle had retreated into their own little dark corner. The sight of him standing there alone felt a bit heartbreaking.

After one last kiss, I said to Reece, "It's time."

Despite his bold words, Reece seemed reluctant to release me from his hold. Riffy was right, though: Castle and his rebels counted on us, and we couldn't let them down. He looked a bit embarrassed as I walked up to him and pulled him into a hug.

"Sorry about that, Riff," I said as I kissed the top of his head. "Be safe."

He looked up at me with a grateful smile and nodded. "You, too."

Saera and Kelle joined us, and I hesitated. Seeing Kelle set my nerves on edge again, and I feared she might sense my oncoming betrayal. Because that was what it would be. That's how she would see it once I kept her from going with Saera. Of course, she had no way of knowing of what we had planned. Reece wouldn't have told her and certainly not Saera.

Setting the thought aside, I moved toward Kelle

and slid a hand over the stubble of her shaven scalp. Without a hint of hesitation, she gave me a swift hug.

"Be safe," she said and quickly pulled away. This wasn't usually Kelle's routine. She wasn't that fond of the hugging part and it took me a little by surprise. As I looked down to face her, she had her stoic mask back in place and seemed ready to go.

"Be safe," I said.

With our sort of standard routine out of the way, it was time to get our heads into the game. I made eye contact with everyone standing around me in a circle. Saera nodded as my gaze lingered.

"Let's do this," I said and headed down the dark tunnel.

TWELVE
SAERA

THE INITIAL TENSION started in the pit of my stomach as we walked through the dark tunnel to find our exit point. Maece's groups had already split off, and at this point, it was only Kelle and me following a bunch of strangers. Anxiety seemed to spread from my gut to engulf the rest of my body and started to reveal itself through trembling hands. To keep my nerves from showing, I clamped one hand around the handle of my weapon and kept the other balled into a fist.

Focused on the sensation caused the unnerving feeling inside me to grow, and I hadn't even noticed our companions walking ahead of us had stopped until I slammed into the rebel standing in front of me.

The man, whose face was hidden in shadows and who was wearing his exoskeleton suit, didn't even flinch as our bodies collided. I apologized, but he didn't pay me any attention. He was probably feeling the same tension I was, although he didn't show it. As the line started to move again, Kelle stepped closer, and I shifted my light in her direction. She placed a hand on my arm and looked up at me. Biting my lower lip, I shot her a smile, but I seemed unable to hide my nerves.

As we started walking again and came upon Castle, I noticed a few of the men and women ahead of us taking a right-hand turn while the bulk of rebels ventured into a different section of the tunnel.

Castle gestured for us to stop and waited until the rebel last in line had moved far enough out of earshot before he spoke.

"This is where we say our goodbyes," he said in his gruff voice.

Further down the darkened tunnel, lights bounced off the walls as the last of rebels disappeared around a corner. The experienced soldier must've read something in my face that didn't have him convinced that I knew what was going on.

"You'll be exiting closer to the freighter," he said as if he was explaining the plan to me for the first time. "The rest of us will head down here and set off a distraction. Wait till you hear it and then head for the ship."

"Yeah, I know," I said, hoping to sound certain. "I got it the first time." I didn't know if he read it off my face or noticed the tremor in my voice, but Castle raised a hand and placed it on my shoulder.

"We have a lot riding on this," he said, "but Harp trusts you, which means that I trust you." He had said it before, and even though we had gotten used to the vote of confidence to be unspoken, it was nice to hear it said aloud.

"Thanks, I guess," I replied.

Castle patted my shoulder and then gestured toward the tunnel that was ours to take.

"Good luck," Kelle said.

Castle nodded before he turned on his heels and limped down his section of the tunnel. My eyes stayed on him until he was swallowed up by the darkness.

"Harp has been talking about us," Kelle said as she raised an eyebrow. "Odd, don't you think?"

I looked at her, not sure what to make of her comment, or perhaps it was a question. Kelle wasn't the type to start a conversation just for the sake of conversation. It didn't come naturally to her, and I wondered if she were trying to emulate Maece, knowing that asking questions would help me calm my nerves.

The notion made me smile as I replied, "Well, let's hope he doesn't make a habit of it."

A moment of silence fell as we started after our group down the tunnel.

The light from my wrist device bounced off the rebels walking in front of me, and I shifted it a little, so I could catch a glimpse of Kelle. She seemed deep in thought, but she kept glancing up at me as if she wanted to say something.

"Riffy really seems to be into Tyrel," she finally said.

I looked down at her, a bit dumbfounded, not sure what had caused the subject to come up.

Kelle seemed uncertain as she added, "They seem like a good fit." Her gaze kept shifting from me to ground and the light that illuminated our path down the tunnel.

In the distance, I could hear voices, and I figured we were closing in on the others. Kelle cleared her throat as if she were about to say something else, and it confirmed to me what she was trying to do. She was trying to be my tension breaker. With Maece off on her own mission, Kelle must have figured I needed someone else to ask the questions so I could babble on about them. Before she could open her mouth, I pulled her to a stop.

"Yes," I said, "I think Riffy and Tyrel would be perfect for each other." I raised my hands to her face and placed my palms on her cheeks before giving her a gentle kiss on the lips. "And thank you."

Kelle shot me a look that reminded me of earlier conversations back when we were younger and still testing out the beginnings of a fragile relationship. Kelle was never much of a talker, and after all this time together she still kept things to herself. It took me some time to figure out that she needed longer to wrap her head around things; she preferred working things out on her own before she could talk about them. I knew now that she would confide in me when she was ready, and it had eventually stopped bothering me, besides her actions spoke louder than words.

That had become clear to me years ago when she'd pulled me out of harm's way and lost her right arm in the process. We had been supposed to disable a

Hymag line delivering goods to a hospital called Icordia. Harp had wanted to know what cargo they'd been carrying, but our intel about the Hymag's arrival hadn't been accurate. The transport had turned up early and would have run me over if it hadn't been for Kelle.

The electromagnetic energy that had surged through the spirals, keeping the pod and its cargo secure as it propelled the transport at high velocity, had all but disintegrated her arm. The shock of seeing Kelle in so much agony had driven me to confront her about the stupidity of her action after the doctors had managed to get her back to her feet. Her only response had been to kiss me right then and there in the infirmary at the rebel base and it had become the first of many.

"I'm sorry," she said as we started to walk again. "I'm just not good at this." Not quite ready to let her go, I had kept my hand on the back of her neck and let my fingers weave through her short hair.

"I think you're perfect at it," I replied and leaned in to kiss the top of her head.

Once we had caught up with the group, I took a moment to watch the activities. While most of the rebels sat crouched down the length of the tunnel, others had gotten to work. They had built a metal contraption of stairs that reached as far as the roof of the tunnel. A stepladder lowered down from a hole in the ceiling wide enough for one person to climb up.

I was about to ask for a status update when JD approached us. I hadn't seen much of our new communications expert, and within the confines of these dark tunnels it had been hard to get a good look at her. With about two dozen rebels cramped into the narrow space, most of them pointing their lights up to aid the men working, there was enough light to see that the woman approaching was older than most of the rebels. She looked closer to Harp's age.

Although her primary purpose was to make sure that the modified relay stations with built-in boosters would be launched at the appropriate intervals once we were traveling to Sulos's New World, she exuded the experience of a seasoned rebel.

"Won't be long now," JD said as she stopped at my side. A red ponytail stuck out from underneath her helmet, and I noticed that she was about my height. With her arms crossed over her chest, she stared at me with her focused green eyes, and I found her entire posture to be a bit intimidating. "We have one man keeping an eye out. He'll signal when it's time. The first five heading out will go straight for the freighter to secure it—then we follow."

Her short matter-of-fact sentences made her sound like someone in command, which seemed odd for a person assigned the role of communications tech. Harp must have had his reasons to send her along, but he had also made this part of the mission my responsibility, and if there was something that I had learned over the years, then it was that everyone needed to know their positions within the team.

"And?" I said in a firm tone that surprised even me.

Kelle raised an eyebrow, and I had to look away from her to keep a straight face. JD narrowed her gaze, revealing creases around her eyes. I wondered if she was assessing me, but then she just turned and gestured behind her.

Four large packs stood propped against the wall. Even from a distance those things looked heavy, and I hoped we wouldn't be the ones who had to carry them up.

"Eight men are assigned to get the communications gear on board. One will carry while the other will protect," she said. "It is essential that we get all of these on board because if we don't—"

"Yes, I know," I said, sounding as annoyed as I felt. *Why did everyone think they needed to explain everything to me twice?* "Those things are our only chance for communications with rebel command once we're farther out there. We need those things to bounce the signal back and forth. I get it." Before I could add anything else, a voice announced itself over the coms device stuck in my ear.

"This is group two. Be advised we are in position," Castle said in a voice that, over the coms, sounded as if he had swallowed gravel.

"This is group one. Copy that. Awaiting your signal," I replied before I turned my attention back to JD. "Are you ready for this?"

With a grin and a slight nod, she turned to the rebels behind her. One hand signal from JD and they were on their feet, grabbing for the large packs. Facing me again, she said, "Always, you?"

I didn't detect any challenge in her voice and felt glad for it. It wouldn't be in the best interest of the mission if we started bickering over who was in charge. I looked up past the improvised stairs and blew out a breath.

"I guess we'll find out," I said and let my eyes fall on Kelle. Her jaw was set in a tight line, and her face per usual lacked any expression, but her eyes spoke to me. A sudden rush of nausea hit me as I realized that this meant goodbye. I had no idea how Maece would manage it, but I knew she'd come through for me. Before the end of this day, I'd be on a space freighter, and she'd be down here. It was all I could do to keep myself from throwing my arms around her and hold her tight.

Kelle narrowed her eyes, and I read the concern behind them. Swallowing around the lump in my throat, I forced the thought from my mind. I needed to focus.

"Let's get up there," I said in the firmest voice I could muster and started for the stairs.

The signal turned out to be a loud explosion that rocked the makeshift stairs underneath my feet. I grabbed the first rung of the stepladder that hovered just above my head to keep me from falling. An arm took a firm hold of me, and I looked down into Kelle's intense gaze.

Above me, shouts erupted and JD's boots, that had

been placed a few steps higher up, started to move. No more than two or three rebels would have been able to exit the long-abandoned drainage pipe to reach the surface in the short amount of time that had passed, but I could already hear shots being fired.

Knowing that holding up the line could mean the loss of life, I pulled myself up and began to climb. The narrow conduit felt claustrophobic as I climbed the steps leading up to the landing platform. There was barely enough room to bend my knees, and I felt glad I wasn't built like some of the broad-shouldered rebels in our group.

I rushed up the ladder, and as soon as I poked my head out of the hole in the ground, I felt the hot trail of a magnetic blast rush over my head. I ducked and instantly felt Kelle jerk my belt to pull me back down for cover.

"I'm okay!" I yelled at her over the noise of constant weapons fire.

Someone below us yelled, "Go, go, go." The urgency in the stranger's voice caused me to climb again, but this time I eased my head out of the drainage pipe with a bit more care to check my surroundings.

The massive bulk of the space freighter stood to my right. The ship was so big that I couldn't see the entirety of it—just its rear end. Its loading bay sat open, and a ramp that could probably fit a Hymag sat lowered to the ground. Across from me, I could see the outline of a building. I noticed several figures weaving their way between shipping containers as a second explosion coming from my left rocked the ground.

My weapon drawn, I hurried after JD who had gone ahead of me, and I didn't have to look back to know Kelle would be right behind me. Except for a bunch of crates that I figured were supposed to be loaded onto the freighter, our immediate surroundings were nothing more than an open field. There was nothing to provide us with cover besides those few crates, and most of them were being used as cover by the rebels who had gone out ahead of me.

JD noticed our approach, and she nudged the rebel by her side on the shoulder. The wearer's helmet bobbed up and down in acknowledgment. He or she tapped the next person on the shoulder, and before long, three rebels rose, firing their weapons as they hurried toward the freighter. JD had already made room for us as I dropped to the ground beside her, my back pressed against the crate.

Even from that short run, I was breathing hard. My heart hammered in my chest as I felt another body collide into me. Before I knew it, Kelle was already crouching by my side firing her weapon. Overwhelmed by the massive explosions, I hadn't been able to gather my bearings yet, and I hadn't figured out from where exactly our enemy was shooting at us.

Not wanting to appear wholly out of place, I mimicked Kelle's position and peered over the crate. The scene unfolding before my eyes stopped the breath from reaching my lungs. The earlier explosion had left a building in flames. Black clouds of smoke billowed up into the sky until dispersed by the shield. It wasn't the apparent destruction, though, that had my heart racing. About half a dozen enforcers had descended upon the group led by Castle, and even though the small number of rebels maintained steady weapons fire, it wouldn't be enough to stop the unrelenting attack.

"They're pinned down," I said, more to myself, but Kelle picked up on it.

"I have a feeling Castle knew about this from the start," she said. The pained expression on her face told me that those men and women who had followed Castle would not be likely to leave this place alive. The sight of the enforcers shouldn't have come as a surprise, but somehow, I had pictured us fighting a bunch of workers as we interrupted them loading the freighter. Perhaps it had just been the hope for a simple resolution that had kept me from picturing the enforcers.

Another round of weapons fire made me flinch and duck at the same time. Hiding behind the crate wouldn't have done us any good if those shots had been aimed at us because they came from behind us.

Some of the rebels had managed to make it to the freighter and were running up the ramp as they engaged in overtaking the ship. Someone returned fire from inside the transport, but I couldn't determine who. They might have been part of the ship's crew. The thought of them being enforcers made my stomach churn. The enforcers' exoskeleton suits were made of far better quality than ours, and we would have a hard time in taking them down. On the other hand, it could also be the workers loading the ship because shipping crates were scattered all over the place.

The remaining rebels climbed out of our exit point, and while some of them hurried in the direction of the ship, most of them hid behind the abandoned materials and equipment.

"Cargo bay secure," someone shouted over the coms.

Among the chaos, I searched the open area in the hope of seeing Maece, but all I could see was the rectangular building that stood along the length of the space freighter. There was no time, though, to contemplate how she would help me keep Kelle from joining me on the mission to come. The resistance provided by Castle's group had become nearly nonexistent, and enforcers were about to converge on us.

"Let's go." JD shouted for us to move, and after firing several more rounds, I grabbed Kelle's collar and urged her to follow. As fast as we could, we ran after JD, who moved from one shipping crate to another as she tried to use them for cover. Weapons at the ready, we finally made it to the ship and ran up the ramp.

A group of rebels had positioned themselves along the incline. They were careful not to fire upon friendlies, but as soon as we passed them, the sound of endless magnetic blasts resumed. At the top of the ramp, we were met by a rebel with his helmet sitting low on his head. I couldn't even see his eyes.

"Ma'am," he said, but I wasn't sure if he was talking to me or JD. It probably didn't matter. "Not much resistance from within the craft as of yet, but there is still a lot of ground to cover." Even though a helmet covered his head, which told me that he was still a rookie because most senior rebels refused to wear the damn things, I felt a tinge of relief as he finished. Finally, something that we had anticipated that seemed correct. Even though this was a significant ship that could hold tons of freight, it usually carried the minimum amount of crew. I guessed the fewer passengers, the more cargo it could take.

I turned to find Kelle sitting crouched at the edge of the ramp.

"Kelle!" I shouted and shot her a questioning look. She shook her head as she got to her feet and jogged over to us.

"They're moving in fast. We have to hurry," she said, "and—" A voice shouting over the coms broke her off.

"We've got freaks!" A loud scream that could only have been out of terror nearly punctured my eardrums.

"And that," Kelle said to finish what she was saying before.

"Damn," I muttered under my breath. We had to ward off those freaks and enforcers until we could close the ramp and we couldn't do that until we had control of the ship and everyone on board. I fixed my eyes on the rebel's helmet. "Hold the line! Don't let any of them aboard." Turning to Kelle and JD, I added, "You two on me."

I had no other choice. It was my responsibility to get this ship ready for takeoff, and that meant clearing it of all enemy combatants. I couldn't do that on my own, and while other rebels had already ventured deeper inside the bowels of this vessel, it wouldn't be wise to wander around alone. Kelle and JD would have to come with me. Besides, as long as Kelle was here, I wasn't going to let her out of my sight. I would just have to trust that Maece would find a way to get Kelle off this thing.

Without any explanation, I ventured further inside the cargo bay. The first part of the area looked like an empty warehouse surrounded by metal walls. They must have only barely started stocking the ship. All sorts of shipping containers and crates were strewn haphazardly around the enormous space.

The empty husk of a load-carrier suit, similar to what I had seen Cyril move around in back at Power Plant Two, stood abandoned in the middle of the floor. To my right, a hangar-sized door stood open to reveal a room used for stocking equipment. Three more of the heavy load carriers had remained there without being secured into their travel positions. I had a feeling the workers must have fled as soon as they had noticed something was up.

We zigzagged past them as we ventured deeper inside the belly of the ship. I could hear the residual sound of weapons fire as it echoed off the walls. The magnetic blast originated from inside the vessel, and I picked up my pace. The rear part of the bay contained large racks that reached the ceiling of the ship. Each shelf would fit about two dozen standard shipping crates that would lock into place so they wouldn't shift during flight.

Cautiously, I shifted my weapon from left to right as I ran past the massive racks. Some rebel might have declared this area clear, but I didn't want to be taken off guard if it turned out he'd been wrong. Every so often, I checked behind me to reassure myself that Kelle was still on my heels. I hadn't heard back from Maece or Reece, and I wondered what was going on out there. *Was Maece backing out of her promise?* I banished the thought from my mind. She wouldn't do that to me—*would she?*

The sound of panicked voices that reached me over the coms seemed endless. I wished I could turn the device off and with it the words that radiated fear and the occasional agonizing scream. Freaks were out there, and our rebel forces would be no match for them. The only person that could deal with them was Maece, but she was on the other side of the clearing trying to gain access to the shield controls. That shield needed to be down if we wanted any chance of getting this thing off the ground.

I reached the stairs at the end of the bay that would lead us up to the next level. If I remembered the layout correctly, we would find the crew quarters first. The flight deck should be one level up while the engines resided within the depths of the ship.

At the top of the stairs, a walkway ran along the width of the ship, and I grabbed the railing as I turned back to see down the way we had come. Some of the rebels had retreated away from the ramp, and the fighting had ventured inside the cargo bay itself. I gripped the railing tightly, needing it to keep my balance. This mission was heading down the drain fast. Kelle, who had reached the top of the stairs behind me, took hold of my upper arm.

"It's not over yet," she said through gritted teeth. She was right, and I knew that. Even though she held me with her artificial limb, I placed my hand on top of hers, knowing she'd register the sensation. JD had made it halfway up the steps and seemed to have a little trouble keeping up the pace.

"Let's go," I shouted. "We're running out of time." JD looked up to face me and then turned to where my finger pointed at a hatch. She muttered something I couldn't decipher and started up again.

Kelle and I didn't wait for her, and entered the hatch that led to the front of the ship. We found ourselves in a narrow corridor that only allowed for one person to move comfortably, and I had to force myself to ignore the feeling of claustrophobia that started to creep up on me again.

The sound of our boots echoed loud as it bounced off the walls and reverberated down the length of the hall. Two doors stood open across from each other halfway down the corridor. Instantly wary, I raised my weapon and checked over my shoulder. Kelle stood at my back with her weapon pointed at the ground.

"Right behind you," she said.

"And me," JD said as she stepped through the hatch.

Not wanting to take my eyes off the two doors, I nodded and edged forward.

Every step we took announced our presence, and we wouldn't be able to hide our approach, but that didn't keep me from going at a steady pace. Despite the narrowness of the space, I moved closer to the wall as we came upon the open doors. Even though the chatter over the coms had become a constant companion, I tried to tune it out. I couldn't be sure if this area had been cleared and needed to focus.

I gestured with my hand to let Kelle know that I was going to take the door on the right and that she should take the left one. From the corner of my eye, I caught a confirming nod, and she pressed her body against the opposite wall. JD hung back a little, and I couldn't see her, but I had a feeling she would know what to do. I felt my heart race and bit my lower lip as I readied myself to enter the room.

The sound of a sharp whistle nearly made me jump out of my skin, but with enough training ingrained into my brain, my weapon automatically pointed in the direction of the sound. One of the rebels poked his head around the corner at the end of the narrow corridor and gestured for us to join him.

"We cleared them," he said as he waved us over again. My muscles relaxed, and I lowered my weapon. I couldn't help checking the open doors as I passed, and saw glimpses of empty bunk beds.

"The name's Tanner, ma'am," he said and raised his voice as he used the title. I raised an eyebrow at him, not sure if I appreciated the designation he offered, but I noticed the flicker of a grin on Kelle's face as I checked the intersecting corridors. Instead of the usual rebel haircut, Tanner had only shaven the sides of his head, and a strip of black hair stood up straight, giving him an ancient warrior-like appearance. His golden brown skin wasn't nearly as dark as Maece's, but they had the same dark eyes. "The flight deck is clear. Serino and Cammy are already busy with the pre-flight checks."

Tanner pointed at the corridor straight ahead before gesturing with a thumb over his shoulder. "We did not have enough manpower to take both at once, so we've decided to clear the starboard engine room first."

I scanned the opposite direction from where he was pointing his thumb.

"And no one has cleared the, uh…other engine room," I said as my eyes roamed down the corridor on my left.

"No, ma'am," Tanner said. I rolled my eyes but made sure Tanner wouldn't see.

"Right," I said and turned to JD. "You head up to the flight deck and see if those guys need a hand."

"On it," JD said and, without further notice, wiggled her body past us in the narrow space.

"We'll take the——" I started to say to Tanner.

"Port," Kelle interjected.

Without any reason to doubt her, I echoed, "The

port engine room. See if you can go around and provide backup."

"Yes, ma'am," he replied as my gaze shifted to Kelle. The total look of trust that I found in her gaze felt undeserved, but I took it as I turned and headed down the corridor to my left.

A staircase led us down into the darkened insides of the ship. I felt a sense of foreboding as I poked my head around a corner. The only lights came from the machinery cramped into every available spot. Hoses, electrical wires, and pipes ran over our heads and along the walls.

Even with the hum of engines and the noise of turbines, I cringed at the sound of my footsteps as I stepped onto the walkway wedged between the equipment. With my weapon raised, I peered down the poorly illuminated passage and gestured for Kelle to take the opposite direction. She didn't hesitate as she eased her small frame between the machinery.

I moved forward, mindful of my steps, and debated using the light from my wrist device as I caught a flicker of movement. The nozzle of my weapon trailed over the area where I had noticed the occurrence, and I narrowed my eyes. Nothing seemed amiss, but I waited a beat to give my eyes a chance to adjust before I took another step. As I blinked, a figure appeared not far ahead of me. It was impossible to identify the black silhouette, and it occurred to me that it could be one of the rebels that had ventured in here from the starboard engine room. The two compartments might easily be connected, and that notion kept me from firing my weapon.

"Identify yourself," I shouted. The silhouette moved, and all hesitation on my part vanished as I caught a glimpse of reflective metal. I fired several times. The flash from my weapons fire that struck the unknown figure would not have been enough to show me a clear picture of the situation, but the repetitive impacts gave enough light for me to determine that the silhouette slumping to the ground had not been a rebel. Weapon held out in front of me, I moved toward the downed body.

"Saera, you all right!" I heard Kelle shout over the coms. The shots would have reverberated through the entire compartment and triggered Kelle's frightened response, but I couldn't let myself answer—not just yet. Where there was one, there could be more, and talking would undoubtedly reveal my position.

The thought had barely crossed my mind when I felt something impact my right side. Pain coursed through my upper arm and caused my weapon to fall to the ground. My suit could withstand some weapons fire, but the sudden shock that accompanied the impact dropped me to a knee. Something with the ability to hurt me through the layers of my protective suit would probably have the potential to kill me if it were to strike me in the head.

It turned out to be a good choice, as I heard the sound of metal clank above me. Propping myself up on my uninjured arm, I shifted and kicked out a leg. My boot connected with my assailant, but I already knew the impact wasn't powerful enough as I saw someone loom over me. It was too dark to see his face, but the massive-looking pipe he held over his head appeared quite clear.

On the ground, I scrambled backward, and my hands swept the floor as I searched for my weapon.

"Die, you rebel scum," the man said in a ruff voice. I did not doubt that he meant that. I tried to think of something to do besides cowering away from the man as all around us lights flickered on. I had to shield my eyes from the sudden brightness and could only hear the verbal interjection although it wasn't as if I wouldn't recognize that voice out of every person still left on this planet.

"Hey, you with the pipe," Kelle said. "You die first."

The man didn't even have time to turn before his body jerked as Kelle shot him in the back. I had just enough time to scramble backward as he sagged to the ground, and the pipe he had held clattered to the ground.

"Talk to me, Saera," Kelle said as she swung her weapon from left to right to check the walkway for any other resistance. With the lights on, it was a lot easier to spot my weapon lying on the ground, and I reached for it, groaning as pain shot through the muscles of my upper arm.

"Saera?" At her question, I lifted my gaze and met

Kelle's concern-filled eyes. I rolled my shoulder and stretched my arm.

"I'm still here," I said as I got to my feet and held my weapon with my uninjured arm. "He just caught me off guard."

Kelle seemed to accept that and gestured in the direction I had been heading in the first place.

"The other end was a dead end, and I didn't encounter anyone else," she said. Kelle had barely uttered the words before the sound of footsteps drew our attention. Simultaneously we raised our weapons in the direction of the sound and within seconds saw a figure edge around the corner. Before I could identify the person, he or she pulled back to stay hidden.

"Ma'am, is that you?" Tanner's voice called out. I lowered my weapon and felt my muscles relax.

"You found us," I called back. "Are we secure?" Tanner stepped into view and waited for us to move closer before he said, "Forward is secure, but we're having trouble at the cargo bay."

"Then I guess we should go and see if we can help them out," I said. "Lead the way."

I LEANED against the wall of a large container. Walls constructed out of the twenty-feet-long boxes comprised the entire area. At eight feet high and stacked on top of each other, the long rows of shipping units provided excellent cover.

As soon as we had heard the explosion and felt the residual tremors reverberate through the ground, we had climbed up a drainage pipe. Instead of the chaos that came along with a battle, the red light of the sun hovering over us provided the only discomfort as I had followed Riffy up the steps. The surrounding containers hid us from view and provided cover as we maneuvered closer to our target.

"From the sound of it," Reece said as he edged closer to me, "it seems we've gotten the easy job."

Reece might have been right, but I didn't want to acknowledge it as I peered around the corner of a container. I would have imagined that these units were supposed to be loaded onto the ship, but it seemed the workers hadn't gotten around to that yet. The thought made me wish that we had waited longer before initiating the strike. The supplies stored in these vessels might have been of use for the team boarding the freighter.

From my position, I had a clear view of the open clearing that had the enormous bulk of metal in the form of a space freighter parked in the middle. The rear loading dock stood open, and I could see rebels as they fought their way inside. My stomach clenched at the lack of cover that protected their assault. Except for some haphazardly placed shipping crates and a couple of loading vehicles, there was nothing to aid the men and women in their fight. There was nowhere to hide or take cover behind on the massive field of concrete.

"Red," I said as I waved him over. "Do you have a fix on what's going on?" Red raised an eyebrow at my question.

"I wasn't aware I was supposed to do that," he said, sounding confused.

"Well…do it," I said. I knew I sounded snarky and that was probably uncalled for because I wasn't supposed to interfere with the other groups unless the request came from Harp. At this point, I didn't really care about protocol, not as long Saera and Kelle were amidst the chaos that was unfolding before my eyes.

It looked as if most of the workers had cleared out at the first sign of trouble, but the number of enforcers who seemed to rain down on the rebels had my gut twisted in knots. I strained to see if I could spot Saera or Kelle, but all the figures moving around the open area looked the same.

"I never should have agreed to this," I muttered under my breath.

"Hey," Reece said as he notched my shoulder, "they know how to take care of themselves." I turned my head to face his reassuring blue eyes. "Let's focus on our bit and make sure Saera can get that thing off the ground."

He said Saera without mentioning Kelle. That was the other part I probably shouldn't have agreed to. Reece was right, though; I needed to focus.

"You're right," I said so only Reece could hear and then added in a louder voice. "Let's go." With one more check of our surroundings, I crossed the gap between two containers and kept moving until I spotted our destination.

My earpiece crackled, and I heard Harp's voice coming over the device.

"Maece, you there?" Harp said. I gazed at Reece by my side, and he tapped his ear to indicate that he had heard as well.

"I hear you," I replied.

"Rebels have boarded the ship, but we've encountered more resistance than anticipated," Harp said in a voice interrupted by static over the coms. "Be ready to retract that shield."

Across the field, I noticed most rebels held a line too far from the ship. Inside the building we'd be safe, but if we were to retract the shield right now, those rebels would be caught outside. The way the enforcers had them engaged, they would never make it to the ship in time to reach safety.

"Oh no," I exclaimed before my breath got stuck in my throat. My eyes landed on a pair of freaks that had somehow had made it past the line and were engaging the rebels defending the ship. "Where the hell did they come from?"

"Harp, we have freaks closing in on the ship," Reece said. At least one of us was clear enough of mind to relay the information back to Harp. All I wanted to do was to charge across that field and help those men and women before the freaks slaughtered them.

"Our forces will need a miracle to reach that ship," I said. "How are you—"

"Castle has a plan," Harp interjected. "He managed to circle around the incoming troops."

I raised an eyebrow at Reece's frowning face. He must have been thinking the same thing as me. It seemed Castle's first distraction hadn't worked as well as we hoped. Instead of luring enemy forces away from the ship, it turned out those forces had anticipated our ruse and launched an attack on the vessel. I just hoped this next plan would have a better outcome.

"What's the plan?" I asked.

"You'll find out," Harp said in a clipped tone. The frown on Reece's face deepened before he added to the conversation.

"So…is that like code for 'I have no idea what Castle's gonna do'?"

"You have your orders." Static filled my ear before the line fell silent. I guessed we had our answer.

"Well, that's just sweet," Reece said, sounding all but amused.

At my side stood Riffy and Red who had their backs pressed against the container. Tension radiated from their faces as their eyes flickered from Reece and me back to surveying our surroundings. They had heard Harp's orders just as Reece and I had. It seemed the stakes had been raised that much higher, and it revealed itself on the faces around me.

"Let's go," I said again and turned in the direction of our target. Trying not to think about the lives that would be at risk if we retracted the shield too soon, I moved along the stacks of containers and headed toward the building. We had to get to the control room first, and who knew what we would encounter inside? I needed to focus on that.

Reece stayed close to my heels, and I heard Riffy running behind him, already panting like crazy. Other than Red, we were on our own, and with him being a communications expert, I doubted that I'd be able to rely on him in a tight spot.

Ducking low, I left the relative safety of the wall of containers behind and hurried across the clearing that stood between us and the long rectangular building. The structure stretched the entire length of the space freighter. Massive cargo doors sat centered at the width of the building while the rest of the wall seemed to be covered by a black, almost liquid-looking material.

I found cover behind a couple of shipping crates and an abandoned load-carrier suit. Reece and the others followed my lead, cramming their bodies beside me and out of sight. While I peered over a metal box, a smaller door at the side of the building caught my attention just as an ear-piercing alarm sounded. It seemed odd that the warning signal only sounded now, long after the battle had commenced.

The large cargo doors slid open, and a pang of dread washed over me as I saw the two freaks step through and out into the clearing. They stood unmoving as the doors closed behind them. A pair of security doors slid in place over the first doors and locked with a loud clank. There was no way we'd be able to pass those heavily armored doors, but fortunately, I hadn't planned on taking the front entrance.

After the doors had locked into place, the two freaks headed in the direction of the fight. I slumped behind the crate and gestured for the others to be quiet. We were far enough away from them that I didn't think they'd detect us, but I could still hear the hydraulic and mechanical parts hiss and grind as they moved their limbs.

I scanned the area but couldn't detect any movement as more weapon fire erupted from the other side of the clearing. From this angle, I couldn't see much of what was going on, but if the shouts and magnetic blasts were any indications, I feared the outcome—especially with those additional freaks joining the fight.

"That door might become a problem," Reece said as he poked his head above the crate next to me. I shot him a sideways glance, and as he winked at me, I felt pretty sure what he was aiming at.

We hadn't talked specifics about how we were going to get Kelle off that ship. The reason for that was probably because I had been avoided addressing the issue. It felt as if I was forced to make a choice between Saera and Harp, and that didn't sit right with me. Back in the tunnel, Reece had mentioned that he had a plan, and I figured this must be it.

"It looks solid enough," I replied. "Do you think we have the time?" I shifted my gaze in the direction of the freighter. The promise I had made to Saera seemed to be a constant at the forefront of my mind, and I wanted to keep that promise, but at what cost?

"What looks solid?" Riffy asked. He and Red had also risked a peek over the rim of the crate.

"I don't think we should risk it with that door," Reece said. "We should get Kelle."

"What do you mean?" Riffy said as his eyes grew wide. "I can do it." I could tell Reece had trouble not to cringe. Riffy would be perfectly capable of opening that door even though Kelle would surely be much faster; openly challenging it undoubtedly hurt his best friend's feelings, and Reece knew it.

Riffy shook his head, unable to understand. We hadn't told him about our plan. In part because we had no idea what that plan would be. In discussing it, last night, Reece and I had come to the conclusion that we would have to figure it out along the way. A mission like this held too many variables, and I had figured that we would just have to wing it. Fortunately, Reece seemed to have come up with something on his own.

"What's the holdup?" Red asked as Reece pulled Riffy down behind the crate as he tried to explain while Red eyed us suspiciously.

"We need help opening that door," Reece started to explain.

"But we don't have time for that. Let me try, Reece," Riffy sounded desperate and with good reason. We were wasting time, and I knew it.

"Damn it," I muttered as I started to doubt if I should keep my promise.

Reece met my gaze, and I searched his eyes. I found determination in those blue depths and something else. Something that I wasn't sure that I could admit to, let alone commit to, but still. He was creating a ruse that would help me get Kelle off the ship and keep my promise to Saera.

"Are you sure?" I mouthed, so the others wouldn't be able to hear. He shot me one of his wicked smiles, and combined with the mischievous twinkle in his eyes, I knew he had already made up his mind.

"I got this," he said.

There was no way for me to articulate how grateful I felt to have him here with me and to have him on my side, but I wanted to try. I opened my mouth, but before I could utter a word, Reece grabbed my hand and squeezed it as he held my gaze. His gaze held all the reply I needed, causing me to feel warm inside. I just hoped I'd be able to convey the same without the exchange of words because a moment later he had turned his attention to Riffy.

Knowing that Reece would be better at handling something like this, I took a breath and tuned out the conversation to keep an eye out.

Although I could hear the weapon fire and explosions from where the main fight was taking place at this angle, I could only see the ship with its ramp lowered and several rebels defending the entryway. I wondered how Saera and Kelle were doing as a voice over the coms filled my ear. The chatter varied from Castle shouting orders at his troops and someone who seemed to be on the flight deck of the ship asking for an update.

"Maece," Harp all but shouted into my ear, "are you in position?" I froze at the harsh tone of Harp's voice. It wasn't as if I had never heard it before, but the overwhelming sensation of having been caught doing something I wasn't supposed to settled in my stomach.

"We're having a little trouble with the door," Reece replied in my stead. I shifted my gaze across the clearing for one last pass before I lowered myself and settled down beside Reece and the others.

"What do you mean, trouble with the door?" At Harp's question, I placed a hand on Reece's arm. Our eyes met, and I knew I didn't have to utter the

question for him to understand my meaning. I needed
his reassurance that we were doing the right thing.

.   He shot me one of his all-or-nothing smiles and
placed his hand on top of mine as he said, "We're
going to need Kelle."

"Follow me," I said and avoided Riffy's accusing gaze
as I hurried toward the side door. We had called for
Kelle without him even having touched the door. It
seemed Reece and I would have some explaining to
do, and it wasn't just to Kelle. Even Red had seemed
baffled, and I felt glad he hadn't felt the urge to
question our request during our conversation with
Harp over the coms.

Harp had voiced his own doubts, and Reece and I
had had trouble enough convincing him to order Kelle
to join us. I wasn't sure if Red's reluctance to relay his
concerns had come out of a fear of addressing Harp
or from extended knowledge on how this team
worked. Our shenanigans were well known among
rebel ranks, but they knew that we would get the
job done.

A sudden sense of dread stopped me in my tracks.
Half turning, I found Reece right behind me, running
at full speed. I read the shock in his gaze as he braced
himself for an unavoidable collision. I managed to
keep a full-on clash at bay with my outstretched arms,
and over his shoulder, I saw what had caused me to
stop in the first place.

A freak stood on one of the towers made out of containers, looming over us like some ancient predator. Metal parts gleamed in the red haze that emanated from the sun. A black-matted coating not unlike the materials that made up our exoskeleton suits covered the rest of its body. Without warning, the freak fired its weapon, and Riffy shrieked as the magnetic rounds impacted the ground near his feet.

Red looked as shocked as Reece as he turned to search the area around him. It did not occur to him to look up. I grabbed Reece by the shoulders and shoved him in the direction of the building.

"Get to the door," I said as I elbowed past him and sprinted toward Red. I didn't check whether Reece did as I asked but focused on the newest member of our team. As I neared him, Red stood with his weapon at the ready scanning the area. I grabbed him by the shoulder, and he whirled around as I spun him. Fortunately, I had enough sense to grab the nozzle of his weapon and force it up before he managed to pull the trigger. The shot whizzed past my head and into the sky as the freak leaped down from its position upon the containers.

Red's pale face turned a shade of pink as our eyes met.

"I'm so…," he started to say, but before he could finish his sentence, I pushed him behind me. The freak landed with a loud clank as its artificial legs flexed.

"Head for the building," I said as I hurried to get to Riffy.

My young friend never did have the stamina to

keep a rigorous pace, and his heavy breathing confirmed it. His face was flushed, but it was the wild look in his eyes that had me more concerned. His gazed shifted from the freak raising its weapon behind him to me as he kept running.

"Get down!" I shouted at him as a magnetic blast tore from the freak's weapon. I stepped into the weapon's trajectory and raised my arm to protect my face. The magnetic blast slammed into my side, and I hissed in pain as heat trailed down my leg through the material of my suit.

Fortunately, the integrity of my suit could withstand the standard rounds fired from the freak's weapon, although only up to a point. The freak kept shooting, and I swirled around to avoid another hit. As I did, I grabbed the weapon from my holster.

From my peripheral vision, I could see Riffy go down, but I had no idea if he'd heeded my warning or if one of the blasts had struck him. Without time to think, I launched myself at the abomination.

Most of the freak's body was either covered in black material or added parts constructed in a bioprinter. The added bone and muscle matter made them hard to defeat, but before I slammed into it with force, I had already spotted its weak point. The freak's face looked mostly human, although the additions made by the bioprinter bulged underneath its skin. The suit it wore had left its neck exposed.

I pressed my weapon to a spot just below its jaw and fired. As I pulled the trigger, I could feel its claw-like hands grab at my upper arms in an attempt the ward me off, but I wouldn't let it. I kept firing.

Its skin melted under the onslaught of my weapon, and the metal underneath turned red hot. Sparks flew, and the freak's grip on my shoulders relented. It twitched several times before its body slumped to the ground.

As I turned, I noticed Reece had ignored my previous order. Instead of hunkering down by the door, he had made it back to Riffy. He had swung one of Riffy's arms over his shoulder and was dragging him along.

"Oh no," I muttered to myself as I hurried toward them.

Riffy wasn't the easiest to carry, but between Reece and me, we managed it. Red waited for us at the door where he sat in a crouch. We deposited Riffy beside him. He was still breathing, and as far as I could tell, Riffy's suit was intact. Except for a burn mark below his left ear, I couldn't detect any serious injuries.

Still, Reece took his time to check Riffy as I scanned the area again. There weren't any signs of other freaks, and the one that had attacked us remained where it lay in a heap.

My heart hammered in my throat as I waited for word from Reece to confirm Riffy would be all right. It nearly drowned out the chatter that reached me over the com device. It took me a moment to realize I heard Saera's voice and that she was talking to Kelle. The conversation paused, and I strained to hear beyond the static.

"You need to go!" Saera shouted and nearly blew out my eardrum. Kelle responded with a negative, and someone in the background said something about enforcers breaching the cargo-bay area.

Reece shot me a look that told me he, too, had overheard the conversation and shook his head. Doubt was written all over his face. We hadn't anticipated this much resistance. Although I should've known Sulos would have heightened security around anything that would have to do with this New World and his plans for survival.

Besides, if Harp and Monroe were right, then he had an insider among our ranks. I was pretty sure the council had not been informed about this mission, but that wouldn't mean that they didn't have the means to find out and inform Sulos.

"You need me here," Kelle shouted. "Riffy can deal with the door." As expected, Saera seemed adamant in her reply. She wanted Kelle to leave the freighter before it took off, even though her argument probably sounded flawed by any means.

Saera knew Riffy's skills, and he should've been able to open the door with ease. He probably would've had the door open already if Reece and I hadn't wasted so much time. In doing so, we had managed to get Riffy shot, and our need for Kelle had become real.

"Kelle, Riffy is out of commission for a while," Reece said over the com as he sat in a crouch at his friend's side. "We need you to get your ass over here." He shot me a sideways glance before he shifted and moved closer to me. He kept his voice low as he spoke again. "I think you'll be able to keep your promise to Saera."

"This isn't what I wanted," I said sharply.

"Maece, freaks are making their way to the ship. We need that shield down!" Harp's voice had an urgency in it as he spoke over the coms. Reece relayed our situation and informed Harp about Riffy being incapacitated for the moment. I did not register Harp's reply as I looked at Riffy's unconscious form.

"This isn't what I wanted," I repeated under my breath.

"It'll be okay," Reece said as he placed a hand on my face. His blue eyes held something I couldn't read or if I were honest, something I didn't want to read. "See you soon."

"Wait, what…," I asked as he kissed the top of my head. Before I could do anything, Reece got up and jumped over the crate. Confusion took over my brain as our eyes met. I wanted to shout at him, wanted to know what the hell he was doing, but within seconds, he had his back turned to me and was running across the open clearing.

My throat felt as if one of those freaks had a hand clamped around it and was squeezing the air from my lungs. I shouted Reece's name, but he didn't react. At full speed, he ran in the direction of the freighter in a zigzag pattern as he attempted to dodge weapon fire. Reece had always been a good runner, and anyone taking a shot at him would have a hard time. Still, as he ran up the ramp at the back of the freighter his body jerked, and he stumbled before he disappeared inside.

"What's going on?" Riffy asked from behind me. He sounded groggy and confused. I couldn't tear my eyes away from the freighter even though I knew I should check my friend.

"They're sending in Kelle," Red answered in my place, "and Reece has been ordered to take her spot on the freighter."

My hands balled into fists, and I squeezed them hard as I started at the freighter. I wanted to scream. I wanted to find Harp and tell him exactly what I thought of him and his stupid plan. Instead, I flinched at the heat that whizzed over my head and ducked as the magnetic blast impacted the wall behind me.

I checked to see how Riffy and Red were doing before my eyes shifted to the freak running toward us at full speed.

FOURTEEN
SAERA

I HAD ASKED JD to find us a way off this ship that wouldn't entail running down the ramp. With the loading area under attack, it would be too dangerous an exit for Kelle. JD had taken a position on the flight deck and had access to all of the ship's databases.

"Damn it, Saera. You can't do this," Kelle said as she stomped after me down a short corridor. Ignoring Kelle, I followed JD's directions to the bow of the ship, at least that was what JD had called it over the coms. I didn't have a choice, I had to ignore her or at least try, too. If I didn't, I felt sure that this terrible feeling that had settled in the pit of my stomach would consume me and I wouldn't be able to go through with it.

They had told us Riffy was out, and I had no way of knowing if this was for real or part of a ploy to get Kelle off the ship. I wasn't sure how far Maece would go, but considering the request to get Kelle off this freighter had come from me, I had a feeling she'd go a long way. Still, if Riffy was out for real, then this mission was in danger of getting a lot of people killed, and I couldn't let Kelle's pleas interfere with what had to be done.

"You should be getting close," JD said over the com. "There should be a door to your left."

"Got it," I replied and stopped at the heavily fortified hatch.

"You'll find an emergency exit behind it that'll give you access to the underside of the ship," JD said. "You're pretty much at the front of the ship, so I don't expect you to encounter any immediate resistance as you exit."

"Thanks," I managed to say. JD added something that sounded like good luck, but I didn't think I could have replied if I wanted to. My throat had closed up as soon as my hand touched the lever that kept the door sealed shut.

"Saera, please," Kelle said as she gripped my arm. Her hold tightened as I pulled the lever and the door opened with a hiss.

I pushed it open and wanted to step inside, but Kelle held me back. Without looking at her, I said, "They need you."

"That's just stupid," she said, "Riffy can open any door." The anger in Kelle's voice was evident, and it made me wonder whether she suspected something was off. I'd never been able to lie to her, and I wasn't even sure if I was lying to her. I would definitely be lying if this was all a part of Maece's plan to honor my request and I had no reason to think it wasn't.

"Not if he's hurt," I said, hoping to sound convincing, and pulled my arm loose from Kelle's grasp. The cramped space had barely enough room to maneuver as I stepped around the hatch that appeared bolted to the floor. I knelt beside it and flipped open a cover to reveal a button and pressed it. A light above the button switched from red to green, and with a clank, I heard the lock disengage. My hand reached for the lever that would release the manual lock, to open the hatch as Kelle spoke.

"Why won't you look at me?" The anger had dissipated from her voice and sounded as small as I had ever heard it.

Tears stung at my eyes, and I squeezed my lids shut to force them back. Determined, I tilted my head, but at the sight of Kelle's boots, I couldn't make myself face her. I feared that she would see the lie.

Instead, I pulled the lever and opened the hatch. The outside air rushed in along with the sound of weapons fire. With the hatch closed, the magnetic blasts impacting the hull resembled an annoying thumping, as if someone was beating it with an iron rod. With the hatch open, the sounds of a battle raging outside could not be ignored.

"What are you doing?" Kelle asked as she stepped and knelt beside me.

I shook my head, keeping my eyes downcast and stared down the hole at the ground underneath the ship. Kelle cupped my face with her good hand and forced me to look at her.

"They'll overrun the ship if we can't retract the shield," I said. My voice broke as soon as our eyes met.

"What aren't you telling me?" she asked. The first tear rolled down my cheek at the sound of hurt in her voice. In an act of desperation, I grabbed on to her and pulled her close.

"I'm sorry," I said near her ear, "but you have to go." I felt Kelle struggle against me as she shook her head in protest.

"No," she started to say, but JD's voice entering our ears over the coms broke her off.

"What's your status?" JD said in an urgent tone. "We've got freaks coming in and no movement on the shield."

"What about Riffy?" Kelle asked. Her voice sounded muffled with her face pressed against my neck.

"Took a shot," JD replied matter-of-factly. "Still out, but should be fine."

"You have to go," I whispered into Kelle's ear before easing away from her.

"If I go now, I won't be able to get back!" Her eyes glistened with tears, and her voice sounded hoarse.

"I know," I said as I caressed the short hair on her head. "It'll be okay."

I knew she could read that lie without a doubt, and before she could reply, I pressed my lips to Kelle's. I placed everything I had in that kiss because I wanted her to know how I felt. It seemed stupid. Kelle knew damn well what we meant to each other, but I couldn't help the feeling that I wouldn't be able to tell her ever again.

I lingered on her lips before I pressed my forehead to hers. For a moment I breathed in her essence.

"You have to go," I said again. I had said it so often by now that I wondered if the words were meant for Kelle or me.

With more force than necessary, I grabbed her arm and guided her toward the hole in the floor. She placed a foot on the first step that would lead her down but then hesitated. She shot me a look that nearly shattered my heart.

Those dark piercing eyes held mine as she lowered a few more steps. A tear ran down her cheek as she said, "I love you."

Those three words left my heart in shards on the floor. I bent down and kissed her hard on the mouth. My chest heaved as I pulled back and held her gaze.

"I love you," I said before pulling back and grabbing the hatch.

"Saera," Kelle said. I stared into her questioning eyes as I started to close the hatch and forced Kelle to lower herself faster. I had to ignore the plea in her voice or else I'd never be able to close that hatch.

As soon as Kelle cleared the opening, I slammed the hatch closed. A soft pounding echoed through the metal as I locked the lever back in place and pressed the button to seal the hatch.

As the light switched to red, it seemed as if all the strength left my body and I slumped back against the wall.

I had no idea how much time had passed as I listened to the thuds impacting the hull. At first, I had thought Kelle was standing on the ladder just below the hatch banging her fist against the metal, and I had to keep myself from releasing the lock. It took a while for me to register that the sound had come from magnetic blasts as they abused the ship.

The constant hammering was a clear reminder that I had to get a grip on myself. The ship was under attack, and the rebel forces defending the loading bay might need my help. Soon, if we were lucky, the shield would retract, and the ship would take off. That was the thought that kept me rooted in place. The idea of never seeing Kelle again stirred something inside me that even surpassed the pain that I had felt after Maece had disappeared. The fact that I had chosen this only intensified the ache I felt in my chest.

Radio chatter over the coms pushed through the fog in my mind. I shook my head as if that would clear the haziness, and wiped at the tears on my cheeks. I checked the time on my wrist device and noticed barely an hour had passed since we had first assaulted the vessel. It seemed odd because I didn't think all the events that had occurred would fit within an hour, but apparently, they did.

After taking a few deep breaths, I pushed myself to my feet. We hadn't anticipated this much resistance, but at this point, I had a feeling there might be more to come. I just hoped that this wasn't because Sulos had somehow anticipated our plan. Feeling unsteady on my legs, I held on to the door as I stepped out into the corridor and closed it behind me. The lock hissed as I shifted the lever back into place.

As I stood there in that empty corridor, a cold shiver ran down my spine. I was alone. For as long as I could remember, I had never been on my own. First, there had been my parents, and after they'd died, Maece had stood by my side. Ever since our group of misfits had grown, I never had to worry about being alone. Now they were all gone, and I was on my own.

"Stupid," I muttered under my breath. I was always the one to rely on others; how the hell had Harp figured that I could lead this mission? The thought made my stomach heave, and I braced myself against the wall. Taking deep breaths, I forced the bile from my throat.

"Get a grip, Saera," I said to myself. There was only one way to ease the hurt that tried to overwhelm me. I had to take control. I had to make sure this ship took off, find Sulos, and kick his sorry ass off his own station, and then come back home. If I summed it up like that, it didn't sound that bad.

Forcing my legs to move, I headed down the corridor. My boots clanked loud as I ran back the way I had come. The way I had come with Kelle. I shook my head to push the thought from my mind. *Take off, find Sulos, kick his ass, and come home.* Those were the four things I had to focus on now, and I repeated them in my head like some kind of mantra.

With my mind distracted, I nearly ran into JD as she came around a corner.

"Well, that was close," she said while panting. She paused a moment to look at me before she asked, "Are you all right?"

I nodded, unable to use my voice as if some invisible force squeezed at my throat.

"Did she get out okay?" she asked.

I shrugged and pushed past her around the corner. After a while, I found myself at the intersection that would lead me back to the loading area.

A hand on my shoulder made me jump until I realized it was JD. She must have followed me back here, but I hadn't even noticed her.

"Are you even listening to me? I've been trying to reach you," she said and paused as I stared at her. "Guess not," she added and then muttered, "This is going to be a long day."

"Sorry," I said. "I was...never mind, what is it?" JD narrowed her gaze as if she were checking that I was paying attention.

"I just received a message from Harp," she said. "Maece's group is getting ready to retract the shield. We have to lift the ramp."

"Why haven't we?" I asked.

JD rolled her eyes before she said, "Well, listen to it."

The screams and weapons fire that echoed down the hall reminded me of the fact that I was still screwing this up.

"Damn it," I muttered as I started down the

corridor and cursed myself as I ran until I came upon the steps leading down into the loading bay. We needed to get those rebels onboard.

I bolted down the steps and ran past the giant racks until I made it to the open area. Just beyond the ramp, I could see enforcers rapidly fire in multiple directions. Castle's group attacked them from the rear as the enforcers tried to make their way up the ramp while the rebels fought hard to keep them from entering the ship.

From my position, it was hard to take a clear shot. Too many rebels stood in my way. Keeping my head down, I edged closer while using shipping crates for cover. I tried not to let my eyes linger on the bodies that littered the ground.

A magnetic blast too close for comfort whizzed over my head, and I threw myself behind a crate for cover. The shouts and desperate cries of men and women disappeared into the background as I found myself staring into the vacant eyes of a young rebel. He couldn't have reached adulthood that long ago, and it seemed that was all the life awarded to him. My hand shook as I eased my fingers over his lids and closed his eyes.

Anger surged inside me as I lifted my weapon over the top of the crate and fired. The enforcer slightly jerked at the impact, but it didn't keep him from returning fire. I could only imagine him searching the information given to him by his heads-up display as the barrel of his weapon trailed in my direction. Ducking, I could feel the crate shift as the magnetic blast impacted the small container.

I drew in a deep breath as I readied myself to return fire and pushed to my feet. My finger rested on the trigger, but there was no need to pull it. A rebel strapped inside a load-carrier-suit had a firm grip on the enforcer. I recognized Tanner as he used the large clamps attached to the mechanical arms of his suit to squeeze the life out of the enforcer.

JD fired her weapon as she ran past me and sought cover behind another crate at the edge of the ramp from where it descended to the ground. I followed her and plopped down by her side.

"Having fun?" I asked as I noticed the grin on her face.

"Could be worse," she said as she raised her weapon. "We could be one of them." She fired several times at an enforcer and managed to hit his head.

Finding my own target, I pulled the trigger several times until I heard a familiar voice shout.

"Incoming," Reece shouted as he clambered up the side of the ramp half stumbling. He fired his weapon at one of the freaks trailing behind them. The thing seemed to absorb the energy, and it did nothing to slow the freak down.

"What the hell are you doing here?" I shouted as Reece ran past my hideout.

He quickly turned before he threw himself to the ground and found a spot by my side. Shock ran through me at the sight of him. *What was he doing here?* He was supposed to be with Maece, helping them retract the shield. My mouth opened and closed as I conjured up some appropriate way to berate him, but nothing came to mind, except that he shouldn't be here.

"Hey, Saera," he said in what sounded like a way too chirpy voice. I always felt suspicious of that tone of voice as if he was hiding something. I just glared at him as I sat there at a loss for words.

"Hey, Reece," JD shouted from beside me.

"Hey, yourself," he said. "I thought you might need a hand." In the same instant, he rose from behind the crate and fired his weapon.

I followed his lead and noticed the enforcer had gone down—someone must have taken him out. It didn't take me long to find a different target and kept firing at a freak where it stood at the foot of the ramp.

"Castle," Reece shouted over the coms, "what's your status?"

I monitored my own communications device but could only hear static reverberated back to me.

"Why is it so damn hard to get a solid feed in this day and age?" I said and sounded agitated, even to myself. I glared at JD sitting by my side. She shrugged as if she wasn't the one assigned to that job.

"The line is open," she said. "He's just not answering."

"Is there any way to check?" Reece asked. "We can't let those freaks aboard because we'll have a hell of a time getting them off, and we can't lift the ramp until everyone out there is inside."

"I doubt it's the line," JD replied as she got to her feet, "but I'll go check." She was already running toward the front of the ship and kept her head down as she shouted the last few words back to us.

I noticed Reece's eyes on me as I pulled my gaze away from JD's running figure.

"What?" I said in a harsh tone. He didn't flinch or react in any way as he held my gaze. I wanted to punch him, but I knew that wouldn't erase the pain I saw in his eyes, which felt like my own. It was as if looking in a mirror.

He placed a hand on my shoulder and squeezed it gently.

"They'll be okay," he said and sounded convinced by his own words.

I couldn't deal with this now, and the fact that we found ourselves in the middle of a gunfight meant we probably shouldn't deal with it right now. I nodded and hoped the gesture would be enough as I tightened my grip on my weapon.

"How are we going to buy ourselves some more time?" I asked.

"That's the million-dollar question," he replied as he raised his head to see over the crate. He must have been working on a plan already, because before I could add anything else to the conversation, Reece shouted and pointed at two figures taking cover behind some machinery bolted to the inner hull.

"You two, get your asses in those suits." He

pointed at the storage room that I had noticed before. The doors had remained open, and I could see the load-carrier suits stocked inside. I didn't recognize the rebels as they seemingly took in the storage room. In their exoskeleton suits and helmets, most rebels looked the same except for maybe some difference in height. One of them had a ponytail, and dark hair trailed down her back. I figured her to be a woman because most of the men usually had their heads shaven close to their skulls.

"Go," Reece shouted as he noticed the rebels' hesitation. As if they needed that final incentive, the two of them hurried toward the storage room.

If those two rebels managed to get their butts seated inside those load-carrier suits, and if they had any skills operating the things, then that could help hold those freaks at bay. It wouldn't hold them off for long though, and I wanted to know how much time we needed.

I got to my feet but stayed in a crouch so my head wouldn't stick out above the crate and become a target.

"What are you doing?" Reece asked as he grasped my arm.

"More of us should be on board by now. I need to know what's going on," I said as I peeked over the crate.

About a handful of rebels had made it up the ramp. They provided a steady barrage of magnetic blast directed down the ramp from where they hid in various places. I didn't understand why there were only so few of them. The bulk of the rebels were still outside, and we needed them to get on board. "I'll be right back."

I didn't wait for Reece's reply. I kept my head low as I headed for the ramp.

FIFTEEN
MAECE

I HELD my eyes fixed on the freak running toward us from across the field as I registered the sharp tone of an angry young woman.

"What the hell, Maece," Kelle shouted as she jumped over the crate and landed beside me. "What is taking so long?" Kelle shot Riffy a look that demanded an explanation and the poor kid nearly shrunk on the spot.

Riffy looked confused as his gaze shifted from Kelle to me. He had no idea of what Reece and I had planned for Kelle; he only knew that we had faltered and that had gotten him shot.

"Later," I said in a clipped tone. "Get the door." I pointed at the armor-plated door. On the right side, there was a panel that would be used to identify people trying to enter. With some skilled tweaking, the security measures could be avoided, and with a little training, Riffy had become quite proficient at it.

"This thing should've been open already," Kelle said in protest. She turned to Riffy, but at the sight of the nasty burn on his neck, her expression softened.

"Are you okay?" she asked. Riffy nodded in confirmation although considering the grimace he showed on his face, I figured that the medicine Reece had undoubtedly given him wasn't working to its full effect yet.

"Just get it open," I shouted as the freak nearing us opened fire. I pulled Kelle down, and the blast impacted the wall.

"Damn persistent, these things," I muttered and got to my feet. Back at the power plant, I had taken out five of those freaks, so I felt pretty confident as I charged the half-man, half-machine running toward us.

I fired my weapon. As expected, the freak's armor absorbed the energy, but the impact did cause the freak to stumble and gave me time to execute my next move. Holstering my magnetic blaster, I reached for the knife sheathed at my belt. The thing was on me before I could grasp the blade. Even digging my heels into the ground didn't keep it from pushing me backward as if I was just some toy to play with.

It wasn't until my back hit the wall that I realized how much strength the freak had. Kelle yelped in surprise as she found me standing beside her again and watched me trying to break free from the freak's hold.

From the corner of my eye, I could see Kelle's prosthetic arm entangled by electrical wires. She had removed the panel on the wall along with her glove and had stuck her hand inside the rectangular opening.

Bile rose in my throat as I watched nasty yellow-tinted drool run from the freak's mouth down its chin.

"I've had just about enough of this," I said and released the knife from my sheath. For a second, I reminded myself that I wasn't wearing my heads-up display and couldn't spot the freak's weak points, but then I hadn't been wearing my heads-up the last time I had to fight these things. Holding on to that thought, I took a deep breath and tried to open my mind; I just needed to react.

Knife in one hand, I pushed at the freak's chest. I needed to get some space between us so I could assess the best place to strike. Below my hands, I could feel the mechanics underneath the freak's skin.

The freak twitched, and I could feel rather than see the magnetic blast as its heat coursed through the metal parts. I couldn't tell who had fired the shot, but the action hadn't gone unnoticed by the disfigured creature. Artificial eyes shifted to my right before the freak lashed out. The thing's weight pinning me against the wall disappeared as it eased off and found someone else to focus on. I wasn't about the let the opportunity pass, and I lashed out with the knife.

The blade sank into the back of the freak's neck, and I twisted it sharply. Some sparks flew as the sharp edge of the knife severed electrical wires. The partially manufactured body bucked and jerked. Somewhere in the back of my mind, I recognized the sound of a bone snapping. My body didn't register any pain, and I was too absorbed in getting rid of this thing that I didn't pause to look up. I pulled the knife from the back of its neck and jammed a foot into the back of its knee. The freak stumbled, but before it could fall to its knees, I grabbed its head and slid the knife along its throat. At first, the surface underneath the blade hit something solid, and I feared I had chosen the wrong spot to strike, but then I felt the knife dig into the freak's flesh.

The creature's body froze as gurgling sounds rose from its throat before it fell to the ground. Only then I realized my mistake as I stared into lifeless green eyes.

"Oh, God," I exclaimed as I fell to my knees beside Red and searched for a sign of life. His body lay pinned underneath the freak's body with robotic fingers clutched around the young man's throat.

"There, I've got it," Kelle shouted. "You're on your…" Her voice died in her throat before she finished her sentence. I turned to her and shook my head.

Red had been the one firing his weapon at the freak and had distracted it enough so I could take it out. The sound I had heard had been the freak snapping his neck. Red must have died instantly, and although I was glad that he hadn't suffered, the thought didn't give me much comfort.

"Incoming," Riffy shouted as he scrambled for the door. I had just enough time to clear away from the two bodies before magnetic blasts slammed into them.

Lying on my stomach, I peered across the field and noticed an enforcer heading our way.

Kelle had ducked behind the crate but was already trying to get to her feet. Anticipating her move, I grabbed her before she could jump up the crate, and onto the only thing that stood between that enforcer and us, and pulled her down again. She struggled against my grip, but I managed to hold on to her just as another blast hit the crate this time. Bits of metal and other junk exploded into the air before it came raining down on us.

"Is that thing supposed to make that noise?" Riffy said, crouching next to the open door. I followed his gaze and noticed the sound he mentioned coming from the freak lying on top of Red. The high-pitched noise became louder, and it stirred a foreboding feeling in my gut. Riffy inched closer to inspect the freak's mutilated body, and his eyes widened.

"I think it's rigged," he exclaimed.

"Go," I shouted as I grabbed Kelle by the arm and pulled her up.

"No, I have to get back to the ship," she called and lashed out with her prosthetic arm. I managed to avoid the jab and grabbed her around the waist. Pushing Kelle inside with a bit more force than probably necessary, I grabbed Riffy's collar in the same move and pulled him inside after us. I slammed the door shut just as the high-pitched sound ceased and was replaced by a loud explosion that made the metal of the door tremble underneath my fingertips.

For a moment, it seemed as if time had stopped

and the world had gone silent. We stood in an abandoned hallway, and although I could still hear the sound of weapon fire, it had faded into the background. Riffy said something about checking Red's communications gear that was still outside. Red had carried it around in his backpack, and I had spotted it wedged underneath the freak. I didn't bother to reply that it had probably been blown to pieces because all I registered was the anger in Kelle's gaze. That was until I heard voices behind me.

"Get behind me," I told Riffy and Kelle as I heard footsteps coming along with the voices further down the hall. Without even thinking about it, I rushed in that direction at full speed without knowing what lay ahead of me.

A young man dressed in a gray guard's uniform stepped out of the first door I reached, and I slammed into him. The shock of seeing me was evident on his face as he hit the ground hard. Bending over his form, I grabbed his collar and jabbed a fist into his face. Before his body could go limp and his eyes closed, I was already running for the next guard. I tackled him without even looking at his face and spun around to kick another in the chest. These weren't freaks or enforcers, and with the added strength rendered through my suit, it seemed most stayed down after one kick or a well-placed punch.

Without having to check, I knew Riffy and Kelle

would be right behind me, and they followed me into the control room. With Harp's help, we had gathered enough information to know the layout of the building, and it hadn't been difficult to find the area that we needed to reach.

The shocked faces of people dressed in guard uniforms stared back at me as I took in the space. The control room had one large window that looked out over the clearing, and it wasn't hard to miss the enormous space freighter parked outside. Lights from magnetic weapon fire flashed beyond the window as the battle raged outside. Energy bursts slammed into the large vessel, but unless our opponents started to use high-powered explosive rounds, I knew the low-energy caliber weapons wouldn't make a dent in the ship.

The communications device in my ear crackled as I stood in the doorway, and I heard Castle's voice.

"We are bogged down and won't make it to the ship. Retract the shield now." The calmness in his voice reminded me of the impression he had given me before—back in the tunnels—as if he had known something we hadn't. It reaffirmed the sense that he had known that this scenario would be waiting for him. I had seen him talking to Harp before we left, and even then, he had looked resigned. I didn't know the extent of their friendship, but I had a feeling Harp had a hard time saying goodbye. Perhaps because he already knew this would be their last.

"Is the ship secure?" I asked in return. I was willing to retract a shield, knowing that the men and women fighting alongside Castle would perish as soon as the outside atmosphere touched their unprotected skin. What I wasn't willing to do was risk the mission; if the ship wouldn't be able to take off, everything had been for nothing.

I had to tell myself that it was all about the mission because the thought of Saera being inside that ship along with Reece was too much to bear. I needed them to be safe, even though being on board that ship would mean an entirely different kind of jeopardy, but then they would be safe for now.

It was probably better that I hadn't heard the radio transmission telling Reece what to do because I knew I would have argued. I had a feeling; I'd know precisely how Kelle would feel after all this played out. For now, I couldn't allow myself to think about it.

Shocked faces stared at me as I stood in the doorway of the control room. Two rows of consoles with blinking lights flashing among monitors and buttons stood in a row along the length of the window manned by people dressed in guard uniforms.

It seemed all movement had stopped, and it reminded me of wearing my heads-up device with its advanced warning systems counting down the milliseconds in the corner of my screen. As if I was the only one on regular time and everyone else inside the room was moving in slow motion. Mouths opened, and I didn't know if they intended to scream, shout orders, or whatever, but I didn't think I would've registered what they were saying if I had tried.

I moved between the two rows of consoles with an iron fist until every last one of the guards lay knocked out on the floor. Two of them had managed to pull out their weapons, and I had taken a hit to my left arm, but my suit had protected me against the magnetic blast. Riffy and Kelle had filed inside the room right behind me, but I doubted I had left them much to do.

"Riffy, lock the door," I said in a tone that could not be mistaken for anything else but a command. He did as I asked without hesitation. It was Kelle who started to argue.

"I need to get back out there," she said in a voice that seemed filled with fear and anger at the same instant. She knew what was about to happen and she knew she wasn't in any position to do anything about it.

She didn't flinch as I turned to her with a hard look. Instead, she gave me one of her own. I hadn't expected her to back down. Kelle had always been one of the few who could withstand Harp's demanding scrutiny.

"You have your orders," I said and moved to one of the consoles. Kelle didn't reply, and even if she had, I would have ignored her. Peering at a monitor, I started typing, but the system didn't react as I had hoped it would.

"Riffy, get over here. I can't get this system to respond," I said. Riffy took my place behind the monitor and shook his head as his eyes roamed the information displayed on the screen.

"This thing has better security than the ArtRep towers," Riffy muttered as he pressed a couple of keys.

When nothing happened, I spoke over the coms, "Harp, can Kyran help out here?" Kyran and Tyrel had played a great part in retrieving the intel on Sulos from the ArtRep building. Without their tech-savvy brains, we would never have found the information. Unlike last time, we didn't have a heads-up that could help tap into systems from a distance. It made me wonder why Harp hadn't assigned either of them to any of our team, but knowing Harp, he must have had his reasons.

"I have no way of tapping into their system," Kyran replied instead of Harp. "Not without a direct link. It is off the grid."

I swallowed the curses that lay on the tip of my tongue. This breaking into systems bit had been so much easier with a heads-up device. With it, Kyran would have had no problem hacking the system. After we had broken into Sulos's office, Saera and I only had to sit back and relax while Kyran did all the work from a distance—well, at least until Sulos and his enforcer had shown up.

Shaking my head, I shot another look in Kelle's direction, but this time without the hard glare. She must have read the concern on my face, because without a word, she moved to the console and took a position at Riffy's side. Her hands moved over the console in sync with Riffy's as she sought a way to override security parameters that had been obviously set into place to stop whatever we were trying to do. Castle's voice came over to coms again.

"Maece, what is taking so long?" he called out. Explosions and weapons fire almost drowned out his voice, but I didn't need to hear his words to know what he had asked.

"We're working on it," I replied and turned to Kelle.

At the same time, Kelle ripped a panel from the console and stuck her prosthetic hand inside. From the part that stuck out, I could see some hydraulics shift and heard mechanical sounds before something clicked.

"I have a connection," Kelle said. She fiddled her hand from left to right then it was another click. "You see it?"

Riffy shot her an appreciative nod and then turned his focus back to the monitor as his fingers slid over the glass surface activating virtual keys, and it reminded me of Tyrel and Kyran sitting behind their workstations inside the rebel base underneath the City of Umbras. It made me wonder if Tyrel had any idea how tech savvy Riffy could be.

The kid had a limited focus so in a conversation with multiple people he might seem little dense because he couldn't decide which discussion to follow. If you did manage to get him to focus on something like patching up someone hurt or hacking a highly sophisticated console, then a person would be amazed at what he could do. Reece had been the one to have figured this out a long time ago, and he knew just how to direct Riffy in these kinds of situations. Fortunately, it seemed Riffy was in his element even without Reece's aid. He grunted a little without saying anything as his gray eyes focused on the screen.

"Well?" Kelle asked impatiently.

Undeterred, Riffy continued tapping his fingers without answering Kelle's question.

Unable to do anything, I stared through the window outside and watched two freaks standing on the ramp of the ship. From one of the monitors, I could tell that most of the ship's interior had been locked down, and according to the vessel's internal systems, it appeared ready for takeoff. The freighter's engines hadn't yet engaged while the ramp at the back of the ship still stood open. If they didn't hurry, they were about to be boarded by freaks.

Through the window, I could see that some of Castle's rebels had engaged freaks from the rear, but they didn't even turn around to face them as they stood on that ramp. It was apparent that these freaks had only one mission, and that was to stop the ship from leaving.

It made me wonder if Sulos had an inkling of what was going on down here. I didn't even know if the old man was hiding on his New World or had come back here to deal with the impending situation.

He had talked to me over the coms when we were down in the power plant, and although he had used my own heads-up to boost the signal, I didn't think there'd be enough relay stations along the route to communicate directly from his New World with this planet. The one time we had actually met, Saera had shot him, but Sulos had used an artificial representation to carry his consciousness so I wouldn't put that past him either. With all the technologies the ArtRep corporation provided and perhaps even concealed for the general population, it would've been easy for him to construct a vessel that he could control from a distance. A construct like that would surely help him in his day-to-day dealings without putting himself at risk.

I caught a glimpse of Reece standing halfway down the ramp as he fired his weapon, and my heart stopped. Saera stepped in slightly behind him in a similar position, shooting at the freaks. My throat worked hard in an attempt to swallow, but my mouth had gone dry. All I could do was watch them from a distance, and it was killing me on the inside. And on top of that, we were running out of time.

"We need to retract that shield now," I said. When Riffy didn't react, I added, "Damn it, Riffy. They're about to be overrun."

"Got it," he said, and for a second his face beamed with pride, but it soon faded as his eyes veered to the window.

"Ready or not, moving in," Castle shouted over the comps. "Lift the ramp."

A loud explosion sounded, but I couldn't see it from where I stood. The ramp Saera and Reece occupied started to lift. It seemed as if the movement had awoken the freaks, and they made their move.

My hands itched to get out there and force those

freaks off the ramp, but I knew that wasn't possible. Even in my suit, if I were caught outside the shield, I would die instantly.

"Retract the shield," I said, but my remark wasn't necessary. The shield already started to retreat. The dome was getting smaller, and as I watched, the men and women still outside desperately scrambled toward the ship. I felt sick to my stomach.

On the ramp, Reece shot one of the freaks full in the face, and the thing stumbled. A moment later, someone wearing a load-carrier suit charged down the ramp. Seated within the metal frame, the rebel operating the load carrier stood taller than the freaks, and with its large clamps extended, it looked as if it might have a chance.

Saera and Reece kept firing their weapons as a second load carrier appeared on the ramp. While the first rebel used the heavy clamps to trap the freak, this second one took a different approach. Within the suit, the rebel crashed into the freak's body, and they both tumbled to the ground.

The first rebel, seemingly with ease, pushed the freak backward until it fell over the edge of the ramp. The second rebel had a bit more trouble, and the freak had gotten the upper hand. On the ground, it was hard to maneuver those load carriers, and the freak was quick to get to its feet. Fortunately, the rebel in the second suit came to his or her aid as they continued their struggle right on the edge of the ramp.

Keeping their distance, Saera and Reece had ceased fire as they tried to help other rebels to climb up on the lifting ramp. My heart sunk as a rebel failed to hold on to Saera's hand. Lying on her stomach, she gazed down at the person whose life as of then had been forfeited. I could imagine how something like that would affect Saera.

As if through some weird form of communication, Saera looked in the direction of the building and seemingly right at me, although I knew she couldn't see me. She didn't seem aware that behind her one of the load carriers tumbled over the edge of the ramp along with the last remaining freak. She just kept staring in our direction.

A moment later, Reece grasped her arm and pulled Saera to her feet. All that remained in view were their legs as they ran up the ramp. From the corner of my eyes, I could tell Kelle had watched the same scene. She let out a groan as she muttered under her breath, "No, no, no."

I refocused on the ship to see one of the freaks dangling from the back of the ship as the ramp was about to close. My breath caught in my throat as I watched the half-man/half-machine struggle to get aboard. As the ramp locked into place, I remembered to breathe again. The lower half of the freak's body fell to the ground just before the shield started to retract across the rear of the ship's hull and exposed it to the deadly atmosphere.

Everyone out there became affected by the harsh environment as soon as they were exposed, even the enforcers and freaks. I couldn't watch anymore as Castle's rebels perished one by one, and I closed my eyes. I couldn't watch them, but it didn't stop me from hearing their screams over the coms.

As soon as the shield had retreated past the rear of the ship, the enormous engines of the space freighter came to life. Within the control room, lights flashed on the consoles, and Riffy read something aloud that was showing on one of the screens.

"Engines are in the green. You're good to go," he said. The sound of the roaring engines outside increased, and it became hard to decipher Riffy's words as he shouted over the coms. The building started to shake, and I held on to the console in front of me for balance as I forced a hesitant glance in Kelle's direction.

In profile, her expression held her usual stony-faced demeanor as if she had closed herself off to all that was happening. I figured it would be easier to face her with her mask in place. Still, I promised myself not to overanalyze her reaction. Kelle would be mad and rightfully so, and I just had to deal with that.

She must have noticed me staring, because she looked up to meet my gaze. I was wrong; it was her eyes that told the story I would have wanted to refuse to face. Both of them were gone. Saera and Reece were gone, and I had no idea if I was ever going to see them again.

SIXTEEN

SAERA

"YO, BRIDGE, SOMEONE UP THERE?" Reece shouted over the coms. "It would be nice if someone closed the hatch now." The ramp had lifted, making it impossible for anyone else to get aboard, but it hadn't fully closed.

"We're working on it," a disembodied voice sounded over the communications device lodged in my ear. I had lost track of the freaks after Reece had forcefully grabbed me and dragged me deeper into the cargo bay. The ground underneath my feet shook, and I fought to keep my balance.

"Damn it," I muttered as I stumbled and grasped Reece's arm in support. The ship groaned as if it was a living entity while the engines made it hard to make out any other noises. Warm gushes of wind whipped at the hair on my head, adding to the rough ride. I hoped this wasn't how the entire trip was going to be like because I didn't think my stomach could bear it.

My eyes strayed toward the ramp that at first

glance looked closed, but that wind had to come from somewhere. The heat radiating from the whirlwind that raged inside the loading area burned my skin where my suit couldn't protect it.

"C'mon!" Reece shouted near my ear. "Let's get out of here before we catch an irreversible sunburn." He tugged at my arm, and I followed.

Reece was right. Even though the ship's makeup protected us from direct exposure to the radiation, the tiny particles would still flood the cargo bay. The effects wouldn't be as bad as being outside, and we had medicine to counteract the effect. These days if something didn't kill you in an instant, then there would probably be some substance to remedy physical complaints or near-mortal injury, but it was better not to risk it.

The track across the loading bay seemed endless, but it gave me time to think about what had happened. It took me until we reached the top of the stairs at the end of the massive space before everything clicked into place.

Reece waited for me just beyond the hatch, and I stared at him as I took the last step. I wasn't sure what to say, knowing what he had done, and I wondered if he even realized how much of a sacrifice he had made, and he had made it for me.

"What did you do?" I asked. I wasn't sure if the question was for Reece or me.

Reece tilted his head and shook it slightly as he motioned to his ears. He grabbed my arm and pulled me over the threshold before he closed the hatch behind us.

Unable to look at him, I stared at my feet before I repeated my words.

"What did you do?" The words came out a mere whisper that was barely audible to me. Feeling the urge to explain myself better, I looked up at him. "I mean…I didn't want to…" My voice vanished as I couldn't find the words to describe how I felt. His blue eyes met mine with kindness although he couldn't hide the hurt behind them.

Reece being Reece stepped closer and pulled me into a hug.

"We'll sort this out later," he said. "Let's just get out of here." I nodded against his shoulder, at a loss for words as he released me. Guilt gnawed at my consciousness as Reece took my hand to guide us to the bridge of the ship.

"Ms. Lux," one of the rebels said as I entered the bridge trailing behind Reece.

We had passed JD on our way to the bridge, and she had informed us about wanting to get back to the cargo area to check on her equipment, but Reece had advised against it and told her to find a safe place to sit out the bumpy ride.

Reece and I wanted to assess the situation. Besides that, I wondered who Harp had found to fly this boat. I wanted to meet the people who had the potential to get me killed if they weren't good at their job. Knowing Harp, though, I didn't doubt that he had found excellent pilots. It just seemed weird that he hadn't picked Reece for this mission. He was the only person I knew who had experience with space travel, but I guessed Harp had a different idea. Whatever that idea had been, it wasn't going to work anymore.

The ship tilted a little, and I grabbed on to the doorpost before I could fully enter the bridge. I had never been on a spaceship before, so I didn't know what to expect. The sun hovering over us appeared as big as I had ever seen it. The fact that I was able to look up at it without squinting my eyes told me that something similar to the domed shields protecting the remaining cities on Earth must keep the blazing light from blinding me. The window nearly expanded the entire width of the bridge and even dropped below my eyesight.

A walkway constructed in a half circle ran from one side of the window to the other side. A handful of seats stood in front of consoles that held screens, blinking lights, and all kinds of bells and whistles.

I crossed the walkway and leaned against the railing next to a set of steps that led down to a cramped area with two seats. Two rebels sat wedged in those seats surrounded by all sorts of equipment. From the immense shaking of the ship, I would have suspected we had taken off and would have been halfway into outer space, but through the window, I could still see the ground and the long rectangular building with the control room to our left. A few small buildings stood in the distance, and I noticed several vehicles heading our way. Someone must've called for reinforcements.

The dimmed glow of the dying sun hovering over us seemed to shine brighter with every second that passed. The shield hadn't fully retracted yet, and its edge slowly crawled across the ground and over the ship. As soon as the shield had started to retract, I had turned off the communication's device lodged in my ear. It had been too hard to listen to the tormented voices screaming in agony. I had no idea how many rebels had remained out there, but even one would have been too many.

The vehicles I had seen earlier came to a sudden stop. Several of them made sharp turns, and two even collided with each other. The occupants of the transports must have noticed too late that the shield had started to retract. Most vehicles could withstand the heat and the toxic atmosphere for a while, but I'd bet no driver wanted to be caught beyond the energy field that protected us from outside radiation.

Maece had done it; the shield had retracted, and nothing would stop us from taking off. The thought of Maece made me consider switching the coms back on. I wasn't eager to hear the despair in the voices of the rebels still on the ground—if they were still alive out there. I didn't want to think about their deaths and how futile they seemed to be. All I wanted was for one last chance to talk to Kelle or Maece, or even Riffy. I felt sure that it would be a long time before I would hear from any of them and perhaps not even ever again.

"Ma'am." The rebel spoke again. I looked down at where he sat wedged in his seat. His hands were poised on the controls in front of him as he looked at me over his shoulder. I figured his position wouldn't allow him to move, even if he wanted to.

Like most rebels, he had a shaved head, and barely a millimeter of hair covered his scalp. His freckle-covered face gazed up at me with eyes wide and his mouth slightly ajar. "Your orders, ma'am." As if this weren't some dire situation he waited with patience for me to speak.

"Whoa, whoa, let's take a step back here," Reece said as he shook his head. He leaned against the railing on the other side of the steps as he waved a hand in the air. "I'd say things have changed since I'm here now."

I couldn't help feeling dazed. The task looming before us was enormous, and the thought of having to do it without Kelle, even though it had come at my own request, didn't mean all of this didn't scare the hell out of me. Still, Harp had tasked me with a job, and I wasn't about to let Reece walk all over me.

"Excuse me?"

Reece rolled his eyes as the young rebel shifted his gaze between us.

Before Reece could intervene, I turned to the young man and said, "What's your name, pilot?"

"The name is Serino," he replied.

"You're not serious?" Reece said as he stepped

closer to me. "I think it would be better if I took command."

I glared at him before shaking my head. "Shut up, Reece." I turned my attention back to the pilot with his gaze still shifting between Reece and me as I asked, "Serino, who's your copilot?"

"The name's Cammy, ma'am," the copilot said as she turned to me. A handsome face with the regular rebel haircut and a strong jaw that reminded me of Kelle stared up at me. To my surprise, I recognized the face as one of the rebels I had met in Two, just outside the power plant perimeter. As she had been dressed in an exoskeleton suit and had a shaved head, I hadn't been sure if the young rebel had been male or female. Looking at her now the thought seemed futile.

"Call me Saera," I said to both of them before I addressed Serino. "Can you get us out of here?"

"Already trying, ma'am," he said.

I rolled my eyes at his courtesy, but I doubted Serino had noticed as he was already pressing buttons on the console in front of him.

The tremor that had massaged my feet worsened, and I gripped the railing tighter. The roar of the engines increased, and lights flickered all around us.

As my gaze drifted toward the long, rectangular building to my left, I had to fight the urge to run back to that airlock and make my way down that same ladder Kelle had used. Every nerve inside me screamed, "Abandon ship!" The thought was stupid enough because I'd never survive the harsh atmosphere outside now that the shield had retracted.

Reece seemed to have relinquished his position on the command issue, but I knew that wouldn't be the case for long. His gaze had drifted in the same direction I had been looking only a moment ago. Concern radiated from his face, and I recognized sadness as our eyes met. He tried to hide it with one of his charming smiles, but it didn't work—I knew better. I knew where his mind had strayed, and I knew I wouldn't be any help to ease the pain.

The engines made more noise than I would have imagined as the freighter started its ascend. The vessel shook and groaned, and it seemed that holding on to the railing wasn't going to be enough. Scanning the space, I spotted the chairs bolted to the walkway. I wished I would have thought of them sooner because the way the ship shook, I didn't think I'd make it to one of those seats in one piece if I'd let go of the railing.

"Is it supposed to be this bumpy," I shouted over the roar.

Serino shot me a worried look over his shoulder, and the expression on his face was enough to tell me that this was not normal.

"Something is wrong," Cammy shouted.

Reece stood close by with his hands clamped tightly around the railing, and he yelled back, "What do you mean, something is wrong. How can something be wrong?"

A light started flashing on the console in front of Serino, and he pressed a couple of buttons. An image of the ship appeared on the screen, and he shared a look with Cammy before he glanced over his shoulder.

"We have a breach in the rear loading area," he said. "It looks like the ramp hasn't properly closed."

"Well, close it," I yelled as it became harder to stay on my feet. If this continued, we would never be able to exit the atmosphere. Serino flipped another couple of switches and then punched a fist on to the console. That did not seem to be a good sign.

"It's not moving. It'll have to be done manually," he said.

I shot Reece a look, and the expression on his face expressed the panic I felt in my gut.

There were only four of us on the bridge, and although I had seen JD, I had no idea where the rest of the rebels had gone or how many had even made it aboard the ship. An inventory would have to wait, though, because this would be a short trip if Serino and Cammy couldn't get the vessel to reach outer space.

"Is anyone back there? Can you reach anyone?" I asked. Cammy was already calling out over the coms but didn't receive any replies. Reece reached for my arm.

"I guess it's up to us."

I was afraid he was going to say that. Internally cursing the shitty start of a shitty mission, I nodded.

"Let's do it then."

Holding on to the railing, Reece shifted sideways

until he was closer to the door. Then he awkwardly balanced his way toward the opening until he reached the doorframe. He stuck out a hand as it was my turn to breach the gap. I grabbed his hand gratefully and let him pull me into the narrow hallway.

"We're on our way," I shouted in the hope that one or both of the pilots would hear.

"You better hurry." I had no idea who had replied and didn't wait for anything else either of them might have to say as I followed Reece.

I mimicked Reece's movements as I followed him. He held his arms spread to keep himself steady against the opposite walls. Our progress slowed as the shaking of the ship increased, but we made it to the loading area without falling on our asses. I flung myself from the exit across the narrow walkway and held on to the railing before maneuvering down the steps. As we entered the cargo bay, the fact that we had a breach was evident.

Feeling stupid, I swiped at the blond curls that whipped at my face. The same hot air that had tormented my skin before still whirled inside the open space, and my eyes started to tear up from the strong wind.

Within the cargo-bay area, it became harder to move because there was less to hold on to. I tried to grab hold of a shipping crate but missed and tumbled to the floor. Reece grabbed my arm and held me up as we all but crawled closer to the area from where the wind was coming.

Once there, it was easy enough to recognize the

problem we faced. The mechanical torso from one of the freaks that had attacked the ship sat wedged between one of the hinges and kept the door from locking.

"You want the winch or the deformed man-chest?"

I gaped at Reece as I tried to determine the meaning behind his words. He nodded toward a manual override that looked similar to the airlock mechanism I had used to get Kelle off the ship. A sturdy-looking wheel sat bolted to the wall, and it had to be turned to lift or lower the ramp.

It seemed ridiculous that a wheel like that, relatively small in size, would be able to move the massive ramp up and down, but I didn't want to deliberate the mechanics behind it. The thing looked firm enough, though, that I doubted I'd be able to move it on my own, and I turned back to Reece.

"I have a feeling it might need both of us."

Reece nodded before he grabbed my arm and we shimmied across the floor to the hull of the ship. He held on to the wheel as he shot me a worried look.

"Which way do we turn?"

I looked at him dumbfounded, not sure if he was kidding. I maneuvered to stand across from him.

"My way," I replied.

"Of course," he said as he shot me a mischievous grin.

Ignoring him, I gripped the wheel tightly and threw my weight back. Reece pushed from his side, and after several tries, the wheel started to turn. I had barely felt the relief of seeing the ramp lower as the wheel locked into place.

"This must be why it hasn't worked from the bridge," Reece shouted. "I think the thing is hooked on something and it must be stopping it somehow." I held on to the wheel and frowned at the torso stuck in the opening. We would have to break it free. Looking around, I searched for something that would help pry the lodged piece of metal and spotted the crates.

On hands and feet, I crawled over to the metal box standing closest and felt grateful for its sturdy build. The crate was substantial enough to withstand the ship's tremors, and I felt hopeful it contained something hefty enough to use.

Inside the crate, I found a piece of equipment that looked like a pipe. It would have to do, and I made my way down the ramp.

"Let me do it," Reece shouted as he reached out a hand. Ignoring him again, I maintained my course.

The ship tilted and took me off balance. Tears ran from my eyes but seemed to evaporate as soon as they hit my cheeks. The heat rushing inside was becoming unbearable, and it was all I could do to ignore it. Lying on my stomach, I used my arms to pull myself ahead.

As I closed in on the wedged piece of freak, space around me to maneuver became more and more cramped with every inch. Finally, I managed to jam the pipe between the hinge locked in place and the remaining torso. I tugged at the makeshift crowbar, but the damn thing didn't move. Maybe I should have let Reece do this. Our Subterran version of the exoskeleton suit did add some additional strength, although it wouldn't be much.

Then there was that horrendous smell as if someone had set fire to rotting garbage. I retched as the rod punched through something squishy and an organic matter that looked suspiciously like organs slid from the hole I had poked.

I shifted the piece of metal in my hands from left to right and groaned out of frustration. The metal rod was starting to feel warm to the touch, and I didn't even want to think about my sensitive skin.

"Come on, you stupid piece of—" Something snapped and with renewed vigor I jabbed at the remaining body part with the rod before wedging it in there again until finally, it broke free.

Instantly the ramp started to close, and I had to pull the pipe away from the gap before a different piece of metal got the ramp stuck. It didn't take me long to realize that the space I occupied was getting even more cramped by the second.

"Saera!" Reece shouted. I probably would have commented on the concern in his voice to reassure him, if I hadn't been so busy getting myself out of the awkward position that had the potential to turn lethal. Rolling clear from the closing ramp, I scrambled to get back to Reece.

I was shaking all over, and it took a moment to realize that it was just me this time. The constant tremor that had rocked the ship before had ceased.

Sweat trickled down my face and bit into my burned skin.

Reece ran to me and dropped to his knees at my side.

"Nice one," he said. "You okay?"

I ignored his question as I shouted over the coms, "Are we clear?"

It took a while for either of the pilots to answer. I sensed that we were moving, but somehow closing the ramp and sealing off the ship had significantly smoothed our ride. The final word came back to me.

A relieved voice sounded in my ear. "Serino here. We are at a steady climb." I felt a similar relief as I turned to Reece and nodded that I was okay.

He shook his head.

"I don't know about you, but I'm not staying here." He gestured at the front of the ship as he took my arm and helped me to my feet. He grabbed an abandoned pack that most have been left behind by one of the rebels and said, "C'mon. Let's find someplace for you to cool down."

With the help of my suit my body temperature returned to normal fairly quickly, but my hands and face still felt as if they were on fire. I climbed the steps out of the cargo area, trailing after Reece and followed him into the narrow corridor. Before long the ship started to shake again, and I guessed we were nearing the edge of the atmosphere.

Reece opened one of the hatches and peered inside. It must've looked fine because he waited for me to catch up and then gestured to go inside. I stepped into one of the crew quarters with bunk beds lining one side of the wall and narrow benches on the other. I sat down on one of the beds and held on to the railing at the foot of the bed.

After fiddling with the pack he'd retrieved, Reece joined me on the bunk. I noticed a cylindrical vial that he placed in a dispenser, and cringed at the needle as he held it out. I didn't think our exposure to the outside atmosphere had been extensive and wouldn't require direct medical attention, but it was better to avoid the risk, and besides, I didn't feel like arguing with Reece.

Without comment I offered my neck and felt Reece slip in the needle. The small dispenser shaped like a gun hissed as Reece pumped the medication into my veins. I sighed in relief as the burning sensation on my skin instantly faded. Reece repeated the process and injected himself before he dropped the dispenser on the bed and took hold of the edge of the bed.

Even though the ship shook and the hull moaned, it felt as if this was the first quiet moment I'd had in a long time. Reece let out a long breath before he turned to face me.

"So," he said.

I looked at him and felt my throat close.

"So," I echoed. I didn't know what, but it felt as if I needed to say something. "You shouldn't have come." I instantly regretted the harsh tone in my voice.

Reece flinched and then just stared at me.

"What do you mean, you shouldn't have come?" he said. "The ship was getting shot at and attacked by freaks, you were missing Kelle on your team—"

"We could've handled them; you didn't have to come aboard. You were just supposed to keep Kelle from coming." I knew I must have come across as an ungrateful brat, but Reece being here meant he wasn't with Maece. It was enough to deal with the fact that my actions had angered Kelle to the point that she'd probably never forgive me. I didn't think I could deal with that and having to worry about Maece too—or about Reece for that matter.

"Yes, as if that was such an easy task, to begin with," he said. "I think we did rather well, and you might want to consider saying thank you."

"You want me to thank you," I said under my breath as I got to my feet. My legs were unsteady, and it wasn't all because of the ship's turbulence. Shaking my head, I added in a louder voice, "Thank you for making me responsible for your death."

"We're not going to die." The firmness in his raised voice sounded reassuring, but I wouldn't be fooled by it. I knew how this was going to play out. Harp had no idea how to take out Sulos's space station. He might have pretended to have a plan. To send JD along for the ride as if the ability to communicate with Earth would make any difference. This vessel wasn't equipped with any weapons, which meant only one thing—the freighter itself was the weapon.

"We are as soon as I have to give the order to ram this ship into Sulos's station," I said.

"You don't even know Harp's plan?" Reece said as he looked up at me.

"There is no plan!"

"He wouldn't do that," Reece replied, sounding almost offended. "He wouldn't send us out on a suicide mission."

"Oh, like he did with Maece." Anger surged through my veins, and I didn't think I could listen to anyone defending Harp at this point. Maece might have betrayed my trust by faking her own death, but only at Harp's request and because she didn't think she'd be coming back. I knew Harp's cause to be just and all that, and I knew someone would have to pay the price, but it wasn't going to be Kelle, and it shouldn't have been Reece.

The floor underneath my feet shook, and I had to grab the railing of the top bunk to keep myself upright. Reece's knuckles turned white from gripping the edge on his side of the bed. The hull groaned, and the shaking became so violent that all I could do was hang on. Time passed, and I watched Reece as he scrutinized the room as if that would stop it from shaking—strangely enough, it did.

The tremble underneath my feet dissipated before fading completely. A soft hum was all I could hear, and I figured it to be the sound of the engines. The muscles in my legs ached from all the strained standing, and I sat down on the bunk bed beside Reece. I took a deep breath before I turned to look at him and said, "You shouldn't be here."

Reece threw a hand in the air and let out a groan.

"The two of you are just alike, you know that." He stood, grabbed the bunk above mine and leaned in. "Listen to me…"

Before he could finish, I opened my mouth, but at the stern look he shot me, I closed it again.

"I get the intentions, and I get that for some reason you both feel the need to carry the whole world on your shoulders and keep everyone safe."

"It's not like—"

Reece pressed a hand over my mouth and shook his head.

"Naha, I'm not finished yet," he said and glared at me with raised eyebrows.

I nodded that I understood, and he removed his hand.

"Now, where was I?" he said with an exaggerated look of contemplation on his face. His eyes held mischief, and I couldn't even fathom how he could manage that in a situation like this.

"Right, keep everyone safe," he continued. "The way this works is that the five of us, let me repeat that: the five of us, along with our grumpy uncle, Harp, are all in this together—a family if you will." He inched his face closer and squinted a little as he stared into my eyes. "Nod if you understand."

I wasn't sure if I was to take this serious or not, but I did as he asked.

"That's a start," he said as he eased off. "This means that we have each other's backs, but this does not mean that you decide what's best for us, and as soon as you and your sister get that sorted inside those thick skulls of yours, then I think we'll be fine."

Reece paused as if he wanted to give me time to let his words sink in. His tone might have been a playful chastise, but as I stared into his eyes, I knew him to be as sincere as he had ever been. My eyes stung with tears and I averted them, unable to look at him anymore.

"I didn't want her to die," I said and nearly choked on the words. Reece sighed as he released the bunk above me and sat down beside me. He wrapped an arm around my shoulder and pulled me close.

"I know you don't, but who's said anything about dying? I was thinking more in the line of kicking butt."

I gave a small chuckle at his remark, and it reminded me of the words I'd recited like a mantra just after Kelle had left the ship.

"Take off, find Sulos, kick his ass, and come home," I said. The words were meant as a reminder to myself, but Reece picked up on them.

"See, that's more like it," he said with a smirk, "and we've already taken care of one of those, only three left."

I couldn't help but smile at the contented look on his face. Maybe he was right. Maybe I had jumped the gun on deciding what was best for Kelle, just as Maece had done all those years ago when she had decided that it would be too painful for us to know her plans of becoming an enforcer. She had thought she was going to die anyway, just as I had—but she hadn't. Maybe we had a chance after all.

As the communications device in my ear beeped, Reece patted me on the head as if he was comforting a child. He had heard the signal just as I had and beat me in replying first.

"Bridge," he said over the coms, "this is Reece. Give me a status update."

I could only glare at the smug look he gave me. I might've breached protocol by forcing Kelle off the mission, but this was still my command.

"This is Serino. All is in the green. With any luck, it will be smooth sailing from here," came the reply. "Solar panels are recharging the ship's systems, and we should be able to activate the interstellar drive engines within a couple of hours."

Before Reece could reply I piped in. "Serino, this is Saera," I said. "I need all senior rebels to assemble within the cargo-bay area within thirty minutes. Please let them know."

"Yes, ma'am," Serino replied.

I looked at Reece and said, "We need to work on our command structure."

He shook his head and grinned from ear to ear.

"Yes, ma'am."

SEVENTEEN

MAECE

I WOULD HAVE THOUGHT that I could handle silence. It shouldn't be hard to maintain, let alone endure. Instead, this silence was starting to become unbearable. It had started soon after the ship had departed and Riffy had returned the shield back in place.

It had been silence that had greeted us as we stepped out into the clearing—a deadly silence. I tried to keep focused as we made our way along the stack of containers and down the hole to find the Hymag, focused on getting the hell out of there, away from the smell of engine fumes laced with a tinge of burning flesh and that dreadful sun hovering over our heads. I wanted to get underground as soon as possible as if the surrounding darkness could help forget the day's events and prevent me from feeling sick in my stomach.

Despite my efforts to ignore it, I couldn't avoid the

heavy silence and hadn't kept my eyes from trailing along the clearing. The ship was gone, and all that remained were the bodies of the dead and a coldness that resided inside my chest.

None of us spoke as we had taken the short trip on the Hymag. The transport had brought us relatively close to the City of Nebula, but we couldn't risk it being detected and had to walk the rest of the way.

What felt like hours later, the silence remained. Even Riffy seemed to have lost his ability to speak. Kelle was never one to say much, so there wasn't a surprise there. It wasn't as if I was the most prominent talker, but walking down dark tunnels surrounded by an uncomfortable silence wasn't my idea of having a good time. Not that I had expected to have a good time, but then I hadn't expected this feeling of loss to be so overwhelming.

Riffy and Kelle trailed behind me as we walked in a line and their wrist lights caused my shadow to reflect on the walls of the narrow tunnel as we headed in the direction of the City of Nebula. I wished we could've traveled here by Hymag. Within the well-lit compartment of the transport, this silence would have been easier to bear than these dark tunnels.

Harp, who had set up his command on a different Hymag, had informed us that after an unsteady lift, the ship had resumed an easy climb and would soon reach outer space. He hadn't mentioned anything about the mission having gone askew, but I knew I'd get an earful once we got home—if we got home. Unfortunately, with Red dead and his equipment destroyed, we wouldn't have any way to contact Harp again now that we've ventured out of communications range.

Relief washed over me as I felt the incline of the ground underneath my feet. The tunnel started to ascend again, and it might have been my imagination, but I thought I noticed a light shimmering at the end of the long, dark corridor.

It turned out it had been my imagination because it took us at least an hour to finally reach the top.

"Wow," Riffy said with a gasp as we exited the tunnel. I looked at him in surprise. The short phrase reminded me that I hadn't lost my hearing. He shielded his eyes as he squinted against the orange haze that was quite a contrast to the darkened tunnels that we had just vacated. The time it took to adjust to the light didn't diminish the wonder displayed on Riffy's face as his gaze drifted in the direction of the city.

The tunnel had guided it us out to the side of a cliff. The rock surface arched to our left in a half circle to the point where it evened out, sloped down, and seemed to transform into the City of Nebula. With the massive stone wall on one side, the remaining surroundings contained the flat planes of what once would've been a vast ocean.

At this distance, the city looked beautiful with all its bright lights and its buildings nearly engulfed by a fog that shone purple in the remaining halo produced by the sun and filtered by the dome shield. Except the fog wasn't just a fog. The thick cloud that hovered just above the ground was made up of gases that rose to the surface from beneath the ground.

The temperatures within the dome caused residual substances in the ground, probably left behind by the ocean to react with each other. This created a mix of fumes to settle on top of the surface that looked beautiful to the eye but wouldn't be very good for your skin.

The substance wasn't poisonous or anything, and it wouldn't kill you, but it wasn't comfortable if it came in contact with your skin, and the people living in the city dressed to accommodate. We would have to do the same. Our suits would protect most of our bodies, but our faces were vulnerable; besides, we needed to blend in.

"Here," I said as I shifted my pack down my shoulder. Leaving the Hymag behind, we hadn't been able to take many supplies—just the bare essentials. The shapeless fabric that I pulled from my pack wouldn't be very fashionable, but it would work for what we needed.

"Thanks," Riffy replied as I handed him the cloth. I held on to a piece of the material and Riffy looked up when I didn't let go. His eyes didn't hold the playful brightness that I was used to, although I didn't sense any anger. What I did detect were sadness and concern.

"How are you doing?" I asked as I reached out a hand to lift his chin. The burn still looked nasty, although it appeared to be healing rapidly, and I was glad we had medicine available to treat these kinds of injury so efficiently. He shot me a thin smile and nodded.

"Fantastic!"

He wanted to put on a brave face, and it felt as if he was trying to channel Reece with his response. I would have laughed if the thought hadn't reminded me of why Riffy would attempt it in the first place. I appreciated Riffy's efforts, consciously or not, but only Reece displaying his nervous bravado would have been able to make me feel better at this point.

"You did good back there," I said and was unable to stop a smile at the way his eyes grew wide.

"Really?" he asked, and I nodded in confirmation.

"Really." Riffy beamed as I added, "That freighter wouldn't have gotten off the ground if it hadn't been for you."

As his face flushed red, I turned to Kelle and handed her the fabric. The vibe that radiated from her would have made me shiver if it hadn't been so damn hot underneath the dome shield. Her face held her usual stoic expression, and I would've thought it had been carved from stone if a muscle in her jaw hadn't flexed.

She snatched the cloth from my grasp, and before I could say anything, she walked away from me. Her anger was evident, although I wouldn't have needed heightened senses to determine that. Riffy would've figured that one out. What I couldn't figure out was who her anger was directed at, but I had to assume it was me.

I couldn't blame her if it was. Not that things had

gone according to plan. Reece and I had delayed our mission too long and had managed to get Riffy shot. After that, things had played out in a way that I couldn't have imagined. My intentions had remained the same, though: to keep Kelle stuck on this planet while Saera took off in a space freighter. Now we all paid the price. I shivered at the thought while I watched Kelle kick at a rock as she walked away.

Draped around my body to hide my suit, the fabric looked more like a robe than actual clothing. The garment looked well-worn and smelled even worse. Someone had packed the disguise for us, and apparently, Harp had found it necessary for us to blend in, smell and all. That fact made the prospect of wrapping the material around my face to protect my skin not that inviting, and I pushed the thought from my mind. I'd deal with that later.

The sun hadn't fully set. Not that the shining disk would ever fully set behind the horizon, but I thought it best to head for the city with the least amount of light possible. Newcomers always drew attention, and this place wasn't as big as the City of Umbras, where a person could hide among the crowds. Someone was bound to spot our approach, tracking us across the desert-like landscape.

I found myself a corner to sit with my back against the rock and let my gaze drift over the city. Nothing much was said after we had left the outer rim, and perhaps there wasn't anything to say, even though questions nagged at the forefront of my brain. The strange urge to search for answers did not seem to let me go.

While Kelle had wandered off somewhere, Riffy lay on his back a little way away from me with his arms perched underneath his head and his belly rising and falling to a smooth rhythm. From my two companions, he was probably the better choice to talk to, but he was fast asleep. Besides, I didn't think he was up to it. His mind had seemed elsewhere from the moment we had left the outer rim. He hadn't had much time to adjust to this new situation.

Reece was Riffy's best friend and his go-to guy for everything, and now that guy was gone. It had been Reece who had become Riffy's tension killer by distracting him with his silly banter and helping him focus by telling him what to do.

The thought of Reece and his brilliant smile made me feel as if someone had sucked the life out of me. I hadn't even come to terms with the fact that going on this mission meant doing it without Saera, and now both of them were gone. Thinking about it made me feel empty inside, and I needed to find a distraction.

I looked up at the dome shield as the sun made its descent behind the rock surface of the landscape. Never having been here before, I didn't know if the hill would be able to block out the light that usually curved over the planet's surface to stop the darkness from wrapping around us. I hoped that the night would prevail. I felt a need for a bit of darkness at this point.

The sound of gravel and rocks crunching pulled me away from the purplish glare caused by the sun penetrating the shield as it hovered over the city that, with its lights, added to the mysterious glow. I turned my head, expecting to see Riffy woken up, but his body lay still, and he looked fast asleep. Instead, it was Kelle who stood a few feet away from me. Her eyes fixed on mine, and as usual, she placed great effort in keeping her feelings hidden behind a stony expression.

She had built a wall that perhaps Reece had managed to crack, but only Saera had managed to breach. She knew how to hide her feelings, and for some reason, that made it easy for me to be around her. As she stood there with her eyes locked on mine, it seemed as if some of that had changed.

It felt as if she could spear me with her intense dark gaze. Her eyes spoke more loudly than I had witnessed before, and they screamed with pain, anguish, and concern.

Without a word, she moved closer to sit down next to me. As if she knew that she wasn't able to hide her feelings from me, she kept her eyes averted, looking at the city at the foot of the hill, but I could sense the tension that radiated from her body.

I felt an urge to ask her how she was doing but managed to keep my mouth shut. It would have been a stupid thing to ask because I knew how she was doing. Our loss had been the same, and the empty feeling that resonated inside my chest would surely reside in hers. The silence stretched on as the sun disappeared behind the rock ledge. It was only when a soft glow shimmering over the ridge remained that Kelle spoke.

"What the hell happened out there?" she said without looking at me.

My body tensed at her words. I had no idea how to respond to that, even though I knew that the question would eventually have come up. Calling her away from the ship might have turned out to be a necessity, but that didn't negate my intentions. I wanted to keep my promise to Saera, which lead me to fumble up the mission and getting Riffy shot.

I shot her a sideways look and inclined my head. I couldn't lie to her, but it wasn't my place to explain, and I had trouble forming the words. It had cost Saera to do what she'd done. She had wanted to keep Kelle safe. She wanted to do the right thing and now had to live with the fear that Kelle would be mad at her and, even worse, that they would never see each other again.

I had lived with that fear after I had decided that knowing Sulos's plan and finding out what had happened to our parents was important enough to betray my family and fake my death, but I didn't want that for Saera.

I didn't sense the anger that I would've expected coming from Kelle. Somehow, she managed to keep it hidden.

"I screwed up," I said and knew it to be true. *Wasn't that what it had come down to?* The struggle to choose between the mission and aiding Saera had kept me from thinking this thing through. If only I had talked our plan over in more detail with Reece and perhaps had included Riffy, then the latter might not have gotten shot.

"I...," I started to say, wanting to give her a better explanation as an image of Red lying dead underneath that freak flashed before my eyes. The memory brought tears to my eyes and whatever I wanted to say strayed from my mind. There wasn't anything I could say to make this sound right.

"You don't screw up," Kelle said as she turned to face me. "In all the years that we worked together, you never—" The words seemed to die in her throat as our eyes met. She looked at me for a long moment, and as if she could read the thoughts from my mind, her eyes grew wide.

"She asked you, didn't she?" she said. The accusation in her voice was unmistakable, and I had to swallow past the lump in my throat before I could answer.

"Yeah," I said in an uncertain voice, "she did."

Kelle kept silent for a moment as if she needed to absorb the information. After a while, she said, "And you asked Reece?"

I wasn't sure if I could make my voice work, but I forced myself to answer.

"I did." A tinge of guilt shimmered in the forefront of my mind. We'd all been keeping secrets from one another. Something we would never have done a while back.

"I guess you hadn't expected this outcome?" she said. I shook my head. This time I really didn't trust my voice to answer. She turned back to face the city.

"I thought so," she said. After a moment she added, "I guess we both got screwed." I took a moment to let that sink in, unsure of how to reply. I didn't care if she was angry with me, I just didn't want her to resent Saera.

"Did she tell you why?" Kelle asked.

I hesitated; Saera had told me why, but I wasn't sure she had told me the entire truth. Yes, she wanted me to keep Kelle safe, but I had a feeling that Saera had experienced that same ominous feeling I had after Harp had explained his intentions. Saera didn't think she was coming back and I had seen it in her eyes. I had just been too much of a coward to face it.

"Look…," I said and hesitated again. My throat felt dry, and my heart hammered in my chest as if I had just climbed a building or something. "She just wanted you safe—"

"Just stop it," Kelle said, sounding agitated. She got to her feet and tugged at the rope draped around her small frame. "Do you two ever stop to think about the rest of us, what your actions do to us?"

Her words felt like a knife digging into my chest as I watched her turn and walk away. I scrambled to my feet just in time to grab her arm. She jerked it from my grasp before lashing out. A glove-covered fist hovered before my eyes, only inches away from connecting with my face. I blinked and wondered if I would have survived a full blow to the head with that prosthetic arm of hers.

Shock flashed across Kelle's face as she pulled her arm back and clutched it to her chest. She muttered a curse under her breath before she shook her head.

Stunned, I watched as she turned and walked away. Her accusation racked my brain as I turned her words over in my head. She hadn't just referred to Saera, but to me as well.

"Kelle?" I shouted after her. Without turning, she threw a hand up in the air.

"Go away."

Kelle disappeared into the tunnel as I stared after her. The urge to make this right almost had me running after her, but at this point, I knew Kelle would want to be alone.

My gaze shifted to the city as I wondered how on earth we were ever going to do what we came here to do with this tension hovering over our heads. Sulos had significantly strengthened the freighter's security. Something that made me think that he might have been made aware of our intentions beforehand. *What would that mean for the wormhole generator?* The three of us were in no way capable of taking out an army of freaks and enforcers. The thought made my blood run cold and I pushed it from my mind.

From the corner of my eye, I noticed Riffy had woken up and was watching me. He fidgeted with the rag draped tightly around his body and looked utterly uncomfortable, but it was the question in his eyes that had me pause.

"Hey, Riff," I said and hoped to sound casual. I had no idea if he had heard my conversation with Kelle and braced myself for having to explain what had transpired.

"Hey," he replied as he got to his feet. With clumsy hands, he patted at the fabric and tugged at it in several places.

"Are you all right?" His gaze shifted toward the city as if he needed time to think about his answer.

"They're not gone, you know," he said, turning back to me. "Just far away." His simple reasoning brought a smile to my face, however faint. I took a deep breath as I walked over to him and placed an arm around his shoulder.

"You're right," I said, "It's just…" My voice faded, and I didn't seem to find it again.

"It'll be okay. You'll see." Not a hint of doubt resonated from Riffy's voice, and I felt oddly comforted by it. He looked up at me with his big gray eyes as he added, "I just wished Red's gear hadn't been destroyed. Then we might have been able to contact them."

Riffy's words reminded me of the part of Saera and Reece's mission that I had nearly forgotten. Along the way, JD would release the modified relay stations with built-in boosters that would enable Harp to contact them. They would apprise him of the situation and plan the next stage of the mission.

During our conversation in that shed, Harp had promised me that he had a plan. That this was bigger than I thought. It wouldn't be the first time that Harp would have left out some intricate detail of a mission just so we wouldn't linger on it too long and focused on the problem at hand. *What if JD releasing those modified relay stations with built-in boosters was part of that intricate detail?*

Harp wouldn't have lied to me, and there was no way he'd send Saera on a suicide mission, however dire the situation might seem. The sooner we finished our part of the mission, the sooner we could get back and find out the rest of Harp's plan. A plan that might help us get Reece and Saera back.

Riffy could have been reading my mind as he said, "We should probably get going."

I wasn't sure if it was foolish hope that had me feeling wired all of a sudden. The urge to get out there and get this over with seemed to overrule everything. I figured hope was hope, however foolish it might be, and turned toward the tunnel.

"I'll get Kelle."

AFTERWORD

Thank you for picking up this book and I hope you've enjoyed it.

As an independent author, getting a review or rating on any site is a pretty big deal. It helps us to keep the story going. So, if you had fun with this book, I would really appreciate it if you left a review on Amazon or Goodreads

Thanks again.

If you would like to find out more,

visit mvanauthor.com and join the mailing list.

Don't worry I won't fill up your mailbox, just

keep you updated on new releases.

ABOUT THE AUTHOR

It feels a bit awkward writing this page. I guess I prefer writing about characters having extraordinary adventures over telling you about little old me. Well, here goes nothing.

I live in the Netherlands, and most of the time, I'm a reader, writer, a sometimes slacker and a music junkie who is weirdly obsessed with Dr. Pepper and Vanilla. Unfortunately, I have no sane explanation for the latter two.

My love for stories originates from watching too many movies and TV series with the word Star in the title. From Wars to Trek, to Gate, I love them all, and one day I hope to reach for those stars.

And for a certain someone in the US and you know who you are,

"Not Amsterdam!"

SOCIAL MEDIA

You can find me on most of the social media platforms although it doesn't come naturally to me. On those places, I'm not that great at creating content, but notifications are on, and if you'd like to reach out, I'd love to hear from you.

facebook.com/mvanauthor

twitter.com/mvanauthor

instagram.com/mvanauthor

ALSO BY M. VAN

The Wheels and Zombies series

Ash: A novella in the Wheels and Zombies series

Brooklyn, Wheels and Zombies

Aground: Book III in the Wheels and Zombies series

Wheels' End: Book IV in the Wheels and Zombies series

Stand-alone novel

Behind the Glass

Recall series

Recall

Resist

Coming soon in the Recall series!

Revolt